Virtually
Now

OTHER PERSEA ANTHOLOGIES

SHOW ME A HERO: GREAT CONTEMPORARY STORIES ABOUT SPORTS
Edited by Jeanne Schinto

FIRST SIGHTINGS: CONTEMPORARY STORIES OF AMERICAN YOUTH
Edited by John Loughery

INTO THE WIDENING WORLD:
INTERNATIONAL COMING-OF-AGE STORIES
Edited by John Loughery

AMERICA STREET: A MULTICULTURAL ANTHOLOGY OF STORIES
Edited by Anne Mazer

GOING WHERE I'M COMING FROM: MEMOIRS OF AMERICAN YOUTH
Edited by Anne Mazer

IMAGINING AMERICA: STORIES FROM THE PROMISED LAND
Edited by Wesley Brown and Amy Ling

VISIONS OF AMERICA:
PERSONAL NARRATIVES FROM THE PROMISED LAND
Edited by Wesley Brown and Amy Ling

Virtually Now

STORIES OF SCIENCE, TECHNOLOGY, AND THE FUTURE

Edited by
Jeanne Schinto

PERSEA BOOKS
NEW YORK

PERSEA BOOKS, INC.
171 Madison Avenue
New York, NY 10016

Library of Congress Cataloging-in-Publication Data
Virtually Now : stories of science, technology, and the future
edited by Jeanne Schinto.
p.   cm.
ISBN 0-89255-220-4 (trade pb : alk. paper)
1. Science fiction, American. 2. Science fiction, English.
I. Schinto, Jeanne, 1951–   .
PS648.S3H48   1996
813'.0876208—dc20   96-14745
                                                              CIP

Designed by REM Studio, Inc.
Typeset in Cochin by Keystrokes, Lenox, Massachusetts
Printed and bound by Haddon Craftsmen, Scranton, Pennsylvania

First Edition

I wish to thank all the writers, publishers, and agents who gave me permission to use the stories in this book; as well as my editor, Karen Braziller, and her assistant, Tracy Marx; the staff of Memorial Hall Library, in Andover, Massachusetts; and my students at Brooks School.

J. S.

For
Ruth and Dan Frishman,
who love both science and art

Contents

x

■

Introduction

This anthology was designed for people who don't ordinarily read science fiction. But mainstream stories with themes of science, technology, and the future have been cropping up lately, and some science fiction writers have crossed over into the mainstream literary world, where their work has taken on a new importance and power in our burgeoning cyberworld.

I should admit that I used to be someone who avoided anything that smacked of science fiction; as a result, I had many misconceptions about it. When I was in graduate school, a professor assigned Italo Calvino's *Cosmicomics*, and I groaned. I had never heard of the great Italian fabulist, and the title of his slim volume of stories, published in the United States in the late 1960s, sounded suspiciously interplanetary. In fact, it was. Yet, I found myself captivated by it and by Calvino's charming narrator, old *Qwfwq*, who tells of a pair of young lovers who climb a ladder to the moon and what happens when one of them can't climb back down; of the days before the universe started to expand, when everyone lived all on one mathematical point; of a poor guilt-ridden soul who is beamed a message from a hundred million light-years away by someone who says simply, accusingly: I SAW YOU.

Still, though *Cosmicomics* delighted me, I remained skeptical of science fiction. My father-in-law, a chemist, suggested I read the Polish writer Stanislav Lem, but secure in my prejudices, I ignored him. Nor did I heed my brother-in-law, a neurophysiologist, who urged upon me a novel by Ursula K. Le Guin. I now know that Lem and Le Guin are among the most highly regarded "literary" science-fiction writers in the world. But when my relatives mentioned their names, I could only ask myself: What did scientists know about art? At the time I had never heard the words of British writer Brian Aldiss, who said that science fiction is no more written for scientists than ghost stories are written for ghosts.

What made me change my mind—or, rather, what made me open it? A first step was the realization that many books I've long admired do, in fact, have traditional science-fiction themes. *The Handmaid's Tale* by Margaret Atwood, for example, is quintessentially futuristic, depicting a society where a dwindling number of fertile women are effectively enslaved. So is *A Clockwork Orange* by Anthony Burgess, inventor of a postrevolutionary jargon for his teenage thugs. *Cat's Cradle* by Kurt Vonnegut and Ray Bradbury's *Fahrenheit 451* are two more. And what about George Orwell's *Nineteen Eighty-Four*, Aldous Huxley's *Brave New World*, and Edward Bellamy's *Looking Backward*? Likewise, many of my childhood preferences—Madeleine L'Engle's *A Wrinkle in Time* and Edward Eager's *Half Magic*, among them—often treaded the borderland between science fiction and its cousin, fantasy.

My "conversion" was also the result of an education. I have been humbled by a new understanding of science fiction's literary lineage, which, some convincingly argue, stretches all the way back to Homer and his Amazons and Lotus-Eaters. Dante's *Inferno* is considered by some other aficionados to be an early work of science fiction. Works by H. G. Wells and Jules Verne are certainly prime nineteenth-century examples. Mary Shelley's classic, *Frankenstein*, is another. Like Wells and Verne, Shelley published her novel during the turmoil created by the massive social changes spawned by the new technologies of the Industrial Revolution. It's no wonder she wrote about a man who manufactures a monster!

Finally, I realized that as today's society struggles to adjust to changes engendered by computers, stories of science, technology, and the future might be exactly what we should be reading. I'd even go so far as to suggest that students might do well to read science fiction at school. Any literary form follows certain traditions and repeats various devices and themes, but those conventions don't automatically make it inferior—*or* superior. As Le Guin herself has pointed out, modern poetry is a genre too, since it shares a common stock of concepts, icons, images, and patterns. Le Guin does give a warning, however: "The artist is not expected to reinvent the wheel—only to use it well."

While putting this volume of contemporary pieces together, I must admit, I read a lot of troubling material: dystopian views of the future abound these days. Yet, I was pleasantly surprised to find so many hopeful visions and so much humor. Margaret Atwood's "Homelanding" and Terry Bisson's "They're Made Out of Meat" are two of the funniest pieces collected here, and both treat a very common science-fiction theme—the alien-earthling encounter. In fact, the more familiar you are with the cliché that they are toying with, the more enjoyable you may find their fresh approaches.

"The Hole" by Stephen Dixon is one of my darker selections; but the master story writer gives us more than a Kafkaesque account of a series of explosions and rescue attempts in an unnamed American metropolis of the future. Written more than twenty years before the bombings of the World Trade Center in New York and the federal building in Oklahoma City, it is disturbingly prophetic.

Fittingly, loss of language—any language—is the subject of "Speech Sounds" by Octavia E. Butler. One of the few African Americans publishing science fiction today, Butler has set her story in a postcataclysmic Los Angeles, where frustrated people struggle to communicate with gestures only—a situation that often leads to outbursts of deadly violence. How will they ever relearn what they have lost? This visionary writer is able to convince us that it will be possible.

Butler used to be known to few readers outside science-fiction circles; then, in 1995, she won what is popularly called a "genius grant," awarded annually by the MacArthur Foundation, and the mainstream literary community abruptly took notice. At least two other contributors to this volume—Karen Joy Fowler and Michael Bishop—have written for both science-fiction and mainstream audiences. And, like Lem and Calvino and Le Guin, both of them are considered to be "literary" science-fiction writers. What sets these writers apart from others isn't simply their superior writerliness, however. What makes their work so engaging is its ability to do what all first-rate fiction does: reveal human truth.

Fowler's "The Poplar Street Study," for example, is as powerful a statement about collective human behavior as Shirley Jackson's classic, "The Lottery," though it isn't the least bit chilling or bleak. Inspired by an old *Twilight Zone* episode that took itself much too seriously, Fowler's piece is, in fact, quite funny. Like Atwood's and Bisson's, it is a parody of an alien-human encounter, but it is also a send-up of suburbia. How it manages to be a spiritually cheering piece too is one of the mysteries of art.

The mystery of creation, on the other hand, is Michael Bishop's subject in "The Ommatidium Miniatures." A meditation on dust mites, cat-flea eggs, and other microscopic phenomena, it is an amazingly vivid account of a virtual experience of that infinitesimal world. Bishop's theme—alteration of scale—is as old as *Gulliver's Travels* (and as recent as the movie *Honey, I Shrunk the Kids*). What makes it special is Bishop's talent, which combines an infectious love of science (both real and imagined) with a virtuosic demonstration of the writer's craft.

While making my choices for this anthology, I relied on indexes of previously published fiction, but I advertised in a national writers' magazine, too, hoping to make some discoveries of my own. I asked for "fiction about science, the future, space/time travel, technology, and/or new ethical and social issues that these advancements raise—of highest literary quality only." My mail carrier brought me pounds of stories for weeks.

One gem of a story that came to me that way is Richard Goldstein's "The Logical Legend of Heliopause and Cyberfiddle," in which a "datajock" of the future "with a hardwired hacker's hook" attempts to make a violin, though he has never seen or heard one. What I admire most about the piece, beyond its technical brilliance, is Goldstein's ability to enlist our hearts to resist the very coldness that his story portrays.

Another "discovery" is Audrey Ferber's "Drapes and Folds," which describes a future society where a high-tech dress code is strictly enforced ("Utility or Futility" is its slogan) and where an epidemic has left most women either "slants" (one breast surgically removed) or "flats" (both missing). And you might think you'd be against any leadership that outlaws nonconformist clothing, but what if one of the acceptable fabrics prevents cancer?

Advances and experimentation in medicine are a popular choice of many science-fiction writers today and always. (Think of Robert Louis Stevenson's *Dr. Jekyll and Mr. Hyde*.) Much to my own surprise, I could not resist one of the most distressing of the medical stories I read, "Tissue Ablation and Variant Regeneration: A Case Report." Written in stock case-study language by Michael Blumlein, a physician as well as an author, it is a political satire every bit as effective as Jonathan Swift's "A Modest Proposal."

A sex-change operation is the subject of Alison Baker's "Better Be Ready 'Bout Half Past Eight," which begins with this memorable exchange:

> *"I'm changing sex," Zach said.*
> *Byron looked up from his lab notebook. "For the better, I hope."*

Baker is a mainstream writer who has written in a more or less realistic vein about what has been another major science-fiction theme for decades: gender. Her tale of technology and strained friendship between partners in a lab makes the point that for some of us, tomorrow has indeed already arrived.

Two writers here treat directly the subject of relationships in our tomorrowland. Thomas Fox Averill's charming "The Onion and I" is the story of an early cyberspace couple who live with their son, the narrator, in the virtual town of Bidwell; a piece that pays homage to Sherwood Anderson, it is also an affecting comment on the nature of reality itself.

Ralph Lombreglia's irresistible, word-playful "Somebody Up There Likes Me" is the story of a long-distance marriage, which is carried on, for better or worse, via e-mail. Some things never change.

For unity's sake, I decided not to include translations in this anthology; hence, no Calvino or Lem or any of the other fine science-fiction writers from the international community. At least initially, since they are so often difficult to read out of context, I also decided against novel excerpts, but in the end I made an exception for Doris Lessing. A novelist of the first rank, whose range and depth are sometimes alarming and who has produced a science-fiction quintet in addition to her mainstream (though ultimately unclassifiable) literary novels, she once published a series of lectures, *Prisons We Choose to Live Inside*, in which she gives some pertinent advice. She says we should all try to see ourselves as might either visitors from another planet or people living on our own planet in the future. She frequently does, she says, noting that it is "a deliberate attempt to strengthen the power of that 'other eye,' which we can use to judge ourselves." Lessing also says that she thinks writers are among the best equipped for this seeing task and that literature is "one of the most useful ways we have of achieving this 'other eye,' this detached manner of seeing ourselves."

In the excerpt I chose from her novel *Shikasta*, included here, Lessing perfectly follows her own advice. (Incidentally, she herself excerpted this portion of the novel in *The Doris Lessing Reader*.) Written by a fictional historian of the future, it is a treatise on our "viciously inappropriate technologies," especially the ones that have made possible our world wars.

Though it may sound preachy, it isn't. In fact, it is hopeful, even inspirational.

"Men on the Moon," by Simon Ortiz, which ends this volume, displays that enviable "other eye" that Lessing hopes we all strive to acquire. Ortiz tells his story from the point of view of an old Native American who is watching a moon-landing on TV. It's his first television set and he's just as bewildered by it as he is by the astronauts. When his grandson tries to explain that they have gone there to look for knowledge, the old man is more than ever convinced that the place he goes looking for the same—his dreams—is where it will be found.

Doubtless, today's high-resolution television screens, computer monitors, and telescopic lenses would not impress Ortiz's old man, either; what he's after is a clearer *inner* vision.

That's exactly what the authors of the fifteen fine stories in *Virtually Now* are offering.

"It's always best to know the truth about yourself," chirps the frighteningly cheery narrator of Le Guin's gem of a story, "SQ," in which the world of the future is run by a man determined to raise the Sanity Quotient. (By trying to do so, however, he himself is driven insane.) Will scientific and technological advances increase our SQ, our capacity to love, our ability to set worthwhile goals for ourselves, to assign values? Or will these same advances diminish the very qualities that make us human? Reading—and valuing—stories like these may tip the odds in humanity's favor.

—JEANNE SCHINTO

Virtually
Now

Homelanding

1.

Where should I begin? After all, you have never been there; or if you have, you may not have understood the significance of what you saw, or thought you saw. A window is a window, but there is looking out and looking in. The native you glimpsed, disappearing behind the curtain, or into the bushes, or down the manhole in the main street — my people are shy — may have been only your reflection in the glass. My country specializes in such illusions.

2.

Let me propose myself as typical. I walk upright on two legs, and have in addition two arms, with ten appendages, that is to say, five at the end of each. On the top of my head, but not on the front, there is an odd growth, like a species of seaweed. Some think this is a kind of fur, others consider it modified feathers, evolved perhaps from scales like those of lizards. It serves no functional purpose and is probably decorative.

■

My eyes are situated in my head, which also possesses two small holes for the entrance and exit of air, the invisible fluid we swim in, and one larger hole, equipped with bony protuberances called teeth, by means of which I destroy and assimilate certain parts of my surroundings and change them into my self. This is called eating. The things I eat include roots, berries, nuts, fruits, leaves, and the muscle tissue of various animals and fish. Sometimes I eat their brains and glands as well. I do not as a rule eat insects, grubs, eyeballs, or the snouts of pigs, though these are eaten with relish in other countries.

3.

Some of my people have a pointed but boneless external appendage, in the front, below the navel or midpoint. Others do not. Debate about whether the possession of such a thing is an advantage or a disadvantage is still going on. If this item is lacking, and in its place there is a pocket or inner cavern in which fresh members of our community are grown, it is considered impolite to mention it openly to strangers. I tell you this because it is the breach of etiquette most commonly made by tourists.

In some of our more private gatherings, the absence of cavern or prong is politely overlooked, like club feet or blindness. But sometimes a prong and a cavern will collaborate in a dance, or illusion, using mirrors and water, which is always absorbing for the performers but frequently grotesque for the observers. I notice that you have similar customs.

Whole conventions and a great deal of time have recently been devoted to discussions of this state of affairs. The prong people tell the cavern people that the latter are not people at all and are in reality more akin to dogs or pota-

toes, and the cavern people abuse the prong people for
their obsession with images of poking, thrusting, probing,
and stabbing. Any long object with a hole at the end, out
of which various projectiles can be shot, delights them.

I myself—I am a cavern person—find it a relief not to have
to worry about climbing over barbed wire fences or getting caught in zippers.

But that is enough about our bodily form.

4.

As for the country itself, let me begin with the sunsets,
which are long and red, resonant, splendid and melancholy, symphonic you might almost say; as opposed to the
short boring sunsets of other countries, no more interesting than a light switch. We pride ourselves on our sunsets.
"Come and see the sunset," we say to one another. This
causes everyone to rush outdoors or over to the window.

Our country is large in extent, small in population, which
accounts for our fear of empty spaces, and also our need
for them. Much of it is covered in water, which accounts
for our interest in reflections, sudden vanishings, the dissolution of one thing into another. Much of it, however, is
rock, which accounts for our belief in Fate.

In summer we lie about in the blazing sun, almost naked,
covering our skins with fat and attempting to turn red. But
when the sun is low in the sky and faint, even at noon, the
water we are so fond of changes to something hard and
white and cold and covers up the ground. Then we cocoon
ourselves, become lethargic, and spend much of our time
hiding in crevices. Our mouths shrink and we say little.

Before this happens, the leaves on many of our trees turn

blood red or lurid yellow, much brighter and more exotic than the interminable green of jungles. We find this change beautiful. "Come and see the leaves," we say, and jump into our moving vehicles and drive up and down past the forests of sanguinary trees, pressing our eyes to the glass.

We are a nation of metamorphs.

Anything red compels us.

5.

Sometimes we lie still and do not move. If air is still going in and out of our breathing holes, this is called sleep. If not, it is called death. When a person has achieved death, a kind of picnic is held, with music, flowers, and food. The person so honored, if in one piece, and not, for instance, in shreds or falling apart, as they do if exploded or a long time drowned, is dressed in becoming clothes and lowered into a hole in the ground, or else burned up.

These customs are among the most difficult to explain to strangers. Some of our visitors, especially the young ones, have never heard of death and are bewildered. They think that death is simply one more of our illusions, our mirror tricks; they cannot understand why, with so much food and music, the people are sad.

But you will understand. You too must have death among you. I can see it in your eyes.

6.

I can see it in your eyes. If it weren't for this I would have stopped trying long ago, to communicate with you in this halfway language which is so difficult for both of us, which exhausts the throat and fills the mouth with sand; if it

weren't for this I would have gone away, gone back. It's
this knowledge of death, which we share, where we over-
lap. Death is our common ground. Together, on it, we can
walk forward.

By now you must have guessed: I come from another planet. But I will never say to you, take me to your leaders.
Even I—unused to your ways though I am—would never
make that mistake. We ourselves have such beings among
us, made of cogs, pieces of paper, small disks of shiny
metal, scraps of colored cloth. I do not need to encounter
more of them.

Instead I will say, take me to your trees. Take me to your
breakfasts, your sunsets, your bad dreams, your shoes,
your nouns. Take me to your fingers; take me to your
deaths.

These are worth it. These are what I have come for.

THOMAS FOX AVERILL

The Onion and I

My father was, I am sure, intended by nature to be a cheerful, kindly man. He had been raised, the son of farm people, in the state of Kansas. He rose early each morning, as though some irregular but insistent rooster still sounded in his head, as though restless stock waited for hay and oats, as though it might be best to get into the garden before the heat of a summer day peeled his skin again. He might have spent all his life happily bent to the rhythms of agricultural life, the hard work by day, the sound sleep by night, the sun in its seasons, the moon in its cycles, except that first his mother, and then mine, had ambitions for him: Grandmother matched his intelligence to a future at the university; there, he met Mother.

At university, he found himself happiest doing simple things. He earned his tuition money each year selling onions, and nothing made him happier than watching onions grow: the limp slips of green he pinched into the earth stiffened into substantial, firm scallions, then began to swell at the roots, pushing at the soil—which my father kept pliant with his hoe. They added layer upon layer, pound upon pound of sweet flesh—white, yellow, red—until the green tops withered to gray and brown and my father knew that under the soil lay his wealth, happy to stay in the earth until whenever he might want to dig it up and deliver it to a local produce market.

"My hands," he told me, "would smell of onion juice for weeks. People looked at me oddly in Calculus."

All but my mother. She admired this quiet man, who smelled of earth and produce. She had been raised in a suburb, and smelled of French lilac. She was an ambitious young woman, enlivened by whatever was in the air, whatever forced the barometer of opportunity up or down. Not even spring weather could keep up with her shifting studies at university: from psychology and its use in the corporate business world; to biology, and how certain fungi might feed a growing world population; to physics, so that she might someday design rounded, energy-efficient dwellings; and on to computer science. Where she stayed. In the computer she found all the rest of the world.

My parents had a Home Page before they had a home. I believe history will support me when I say they were the first couple to be married in Cyberspace. My mother had written a Home Page for herself, then one for my father. Then she joined them. She and my father were married in a chat room, one of Mother's various chat groups as witnesses. An Internet minister of no particular faith sat at his keyboard and typed in the "Do you take this . . . ?" and my parents took turns typing "I do." My mother had downloaded graphics for the rings and the final kiss, and her chat group keyed in cheers, congratulations and best wishes—everything but their tears.

The first venture into which the two people went turned out badly. My mother wanted to provide a wedding service for others on the Internet. Now, understand that these were the very early days of the system. The government—along with all the television networks and cable

companies, and the huge telecommunications corporations, and the software giants, and the computer programmers, and the hardware companies, and even all of the
visionary people like my mother—did not quite understand what the Internet, what the Virtual World, what
Cyberspace would really become. Early life on the
Internet was chaotic, sporadic, risky. There were all kinds
of opportunities, but no coordination. Perhaps an analogy
will do: it was as though my father, growing onions, might
have thousands of seed onions, yet have to plant them in
fields miles apart, and then walk from field to field to see
if they were responding to the soil; once a single onion
grew, he might have to sit in his field and wait for someone
to chance by in order that he might try to sell it.

Such was my mother's wedding service business.
After she had helped marry a few others from her various
chat rooms and bulletin boards, once she linked a few
other Home Pages together, she settled down and waited
for those people on line to find her. But it was hard to
make a living. People cruised the Internet, read her pitch,
looked over her graphics, listened to some of the variety of
music to choose from, uploaded a dress or two, maybe an
invitation, then roared away, ready to create their own
weddings. Or people went through with one of my mother's ceremonies and then found themselves dissatisfied.
They demanded she write a divorce page, complete with
arbitration for alimony and custody.

Of course things like divorce, alimony, and custody
were impossible in those early days. The court system was
not on line. The government had plenty of information on
what it liked to call the "Superhighway," but no power of
enforcement. Every user was a kind of renegade, invested
with the superficial power to do anything and everything—from hacking credit to uploading pornography.
Everyone was like a thief; no one was like the law. Almost
anything could be done that could be imagined. And

almost anything could be undone: viruses ran rampant. In fact, it was the huge public computer health crisis that moved us more and more toward a centralized system, toward the Virtual World so many live in today. After all, people wanted the same kind of protection on the Information Superhighway as they had on any of the Interstates. Once the government, together with all the huge telecommunications companies, realized they could make and enforce laws on the computer, they also realized they could make and control people.

It is difficult to explain the leap into Cyberspace as anything but a leap, though there were small steps, incredible preparations, years and years of readying people's minds and hearts for the experiment. Perhaps my mother and my father will serve best as an example of what happened. They were full of enthusiasm and dreams, energy and optimism, but they found themselves unable to become financially solvent in those early Virtual days. They read pamphlets and manuals, they believed in the best in themselves and other people, just as so many Americans had before them. They spent more and more time on the Internet, making friends, visiting the vast array of Home Pages, learning how to shop from the big catalogue companies, how to bank, how to find interesting entertainment—everything from films and television to music and soapbox orations—and how to preview vacations and buy groceries. But it was a time of discouragement. For every wonderful opportunity, there were thousands of people instantly diluting its potential. For every exciting breakthrough, there was a system crash, a new virus, a bug. For every hope, there was despair. Many people, like my own father, longed for days of limited ambition and moderate success. It was in those days that I came wriggling and crying into the world.

That was also about the time when my mother heard about the first Cyberlife experiments. They are well known now, but remember that this was before the Cyberworld became *the* world, before those who followed my mother and father decided to take the great leap into Virtual life. My mother was fascinated with those early projects. And she was ambitious that I have a different life from hers, or from my father's. And of course, she had been interested in managing people, in feeding them on limited resources, in building structures for them to live in. So when the government announced Project Bidwell, wherein it would move a group of people *into* the computer, she convinced my father that this was *the* future and, therefore, it was their future.

They moved into the Virtual town of Bidwell, and embarked on the business of helping the government perfect a Cyberworld so seamless—or should I say so seemfull?—that nobody would feel dissatisfied living there rather than in what so many people so stubbornly insisted on calling the "real" world. Our move took six years, as we were interviewed, readied, deemed fit for the Bidwell experiment.

I remember getting rid of each of our possessions. I was but a boy, and attached to things in the way of a child. It is discouraging how people with so little in the world can grow so fond of each small thing. My mother insisted we were losing nothing, but by the time we entered our shelter—as small as a Munchkin house in *The Wizard of Oz*—we had given up everything we could touch. All that was ours—clothing, photographs of our relatives, pots and pans, souvenirs from our small travels, our automobile, even our pet dog Sunflower—had been scanned in, re-created, had become Virtual things in the Bidwell System.

You see, in a time of limited resources, it makes sense that people might have as rich a life in a computer as in that "real" world—even a richer life—and yet not deplete, nor pollute, precious resources. Our experimental program fed us protein paks while we went to Bidwell's

Virtual restaurant and ordered from the menu; we were
served, we smelled, and we even seemed to taste the rich
food that would have been so expensive to prepare and so
dangerous to our bloodstreams to ingest. We could get
into a Virtual car and take any trip we wanted—the
Bidwell System included the Oregon Coast, the Grand
Canyon, even the long Interstate drive across Kansas—
and of course, we used no gasoline, polluted no air; we did
not wear out a single highway, not to mention the treads
on our nonexistent tires. Think of a world in which one
can do or use anything, and yet nothing is ever used up.

The Bidwell System, with its on-line town, citizens,
and services, had not been written in a day, and took many
days to understand. But my mother, ever ambitious for us
and for our future, rallied our spirits. We were pioneers,
she said, in the great American tradition. The three of us
sat side by side, helmeted, logged-on, keying and mousing
our way through the Cyberworld. We were the first astronauts of Cyberspace. Mother's enthusiasm was so strong it
might have been programmed into the computer, or
flashed as an image into the helmet I wore to replace the
sensory data of the "real" world with the sensory data pro-
jected by the computer. I was, after all, my mother's son. I
don't know what was in my father's helmet, but sometimes
he wearied of it. My mother shook her head disapprov-
ingly whenever he took it off.

One day, he walked out of our small dome and sat on
the ground. I followed him. I remember squinting, squeez-
ing my eyes against the incredibly bright light of the sun.
I approached him until my shadow fell over his bald head.
He looked up at me as though he wasn't certain who I was.

"What's wrong, Father?" I asked.

"I like to be outdoors when I think," he said. "I used to
have my best thoughts when I was cultivating onions,
back before you were born."

"What about now?" I said. I knew how to think: I

thought of things to do, places to venture on the Bidwell System; I had problems to solve in Cyberschool.

"I think," he said. "But I am not thoughtful. Out here, thoughts grow. They are vertical and not horizontal." He held his arms up to me. "Come," he said, "sit in my lap."

I was not used to being held by my father, but I did as he asked. He put his arms around me as though I were the onion and he the earth. He smelled deep and rich with a smell I hadn't experienced for a long time. I shut my eyes and thought of what it would be like to stay in his lap, protected and warm, nothing to do but grow.

"Among the onions," he said, "it was quiet, and sure. Rooted."

My mother came to the door. "Your helmets are beeping," she said. The Bidwell project, the directors had reminded us again and again, would not work were we to slip away from our helmets for long periods of time.

But we could slip off *into* the computer anytime we wanted, and I did. At first, for fun, I would run away into Cyberspace, seeing how far I could travel into the Virtual world before my parents found me. Most of the time, I spent hours making Virtual friends at Cyberschool (it didn't matter when I clicked into that part of the program, though I learned the habits of some of the other children in Bidwell). You see, I was an only child. The son of an only child. I could have created a Cyberbrother, I know, maybe an older one who could show me the way into things, someone I could imitate; or maybe a younger one, someone to boss around, to try to leave behind, stuck on some old key system like a computer before there were mouses. I could have created more pets, too, or found keypals all over the world.

Instead, our small family stayed close together — I sat between my mother, with her ambition for the future, and my father, with his struggle to keep up with her. Although our small domed unit was, at times, claustrophobic — three computers in comfortable chairs downstairs, along with one bathroom, and three beds upstairs—nobody lived in a broader world, nobody could go more places, see more things, learn more quickly than we could. "We live in the mind," my mother said over and over. "Most of life is spent in the mind, anyway, isn't it?"

"An onion is outside the mind," said my father. "It needs care."

"What did Father mean about an onion and care?" I asked my mother later.

"He misses some of his old world," explained my mother. "Don't worry about him. Peel a Cyberonion and see what is there."

I did, and watched layer after layer come off until, on the very inside, there was no inside. It was all layers after all.

"You see," said my mother, "an onion, Cyber or grown in the earth, is perhaps no more real than a computer system. Layers and layers of programming create this non-polluting, resource-saving world. No matter what's inside, it's the layers that are important."

"A Cyberonion," said my father, "is not a real onion." He liked to call one up, peel it, try to enjoy its Cybersmell and Cybertaste. "A real onion can make you cry."

"How can an onion make somebody cry?" I asked my mother.

"Chemical reaction," she said.

"But it takes a real onion," said my father. "And a real somebody."

My father had, he told me, a worker's body, a body that liked to bend to the earth, to dig, to hoe, to pause for a moment and look around, smelling whatever might be on an afternoon breeze, predict the weather. In Bidwell, however, we floated in Cyberspace hour after hour, our minds doing everything—even touching and eating, smelling and tasting—with no stimulus but the simulations made of dots and our memories. Floating, my father did not tire, and as mother and I slept, readying ourselves for a new Cyberday, my father lay awake, his body remembering the long hours with his physical self that had once brought him a need for rest and sleep.

In those long nights when there was little to do, Father had time to think. Often he lay staring at his collection of onions that had grown oddly in the ground. He had carried his jars everywhere with him; they were the only things he refused to have scanned into the Bidwell computer. The government had permitted him to keep his collection in our small dome. These pickled onions were my father's constant reminder of his other world. With them, he remembered how, as a young man, he had become intimate with the nature of the earth and onions. How, when he and Mother first married, the smell of onions was on his hands. He remembered the soreness of a body saturated with work, the satisfying thud of an onion tossed gently into a box, the sharp taste of the raw yellow onion, the sweet purple of the red onion, the crispness of a white onion, its skin flaking like snow. He missed onions.

And the more he stared at his collection, the more they became fixed, permanent, never changing: like Cyberonions. Of course they looked different from their computerized counterparts: in some of the jars were onions with double, triple, even quadruple bulbs—huge things the size of babies' heads; in one jar was an onion with indentations that made it replicate exactly the profile of George Washington; another onion had grown around a small rock so that it looked like an innertube floating in its juice; still another reached up with two stems, like the arms of a man reaching to the sky, asking for rain.

In those long nights, my father grew to hate even these odd onions, for they reminded him that he no longer had the chance to grow other, stranger, more exotic ones.

My father became, during his long nights awake staring at deformed onions, dissatisfied not only with the quality of the Cyberonion, but with the Cyberworld itself.

My mother tried hard to console him. Then she made a suggestion: my father and I might seek the permission of the Bidwell Project Officials to create a better onion, to perfect the Cybersmell and Cybertaste, to match Bidwell onions to the real sensations my father knew so well. With his memory and my computer skills, we might even be allowed to attempt the creation of odd onions, nonuniform, since the ultimate goal of the Cyberworld programmers was to learn to mimic the randomness of the genetic world.

My mother, one of the most enthusiastic of those early Bidwellians, made the plea to the officials for this personal project. "This is the same man who married me in a chat room, who has followed me into Cyberspace, who, though a reluctant pioneer, a hesitant astronaut, will help us move forward, into the beyond that beckons past Bidwell."

And they, loving such rhetoric, granted their permission.

Upon hearing the news, I clicked into the Bidwell Workshop, where the project officials had secured all the tools: from the graphics to stimulate the eye to the impulses that would be delivered to the helmet to make the brain experience taste, texture, smell.

"No," said my father. He took off my helmet and led me to his jars of pickled onions. "First we will study this thing, the onion. I will tell you what I know of it."

My father described onions to me in all their forms. He even wanted me to know of rotting onions, with their distinct pungency and their bruised flesh. He recalled to me the odd molds that lived in onions, folding themselves between layers like sprinkles of pepper. He remembered how the brown, yellow, and white skins flaked from the onion and littered the kitchen of the farmhouse where he'd grown up. He wanted the same thing to happen in the kitchens of Cyberspace. He praised the beauty of the striped effect of a red onion when it was sliced lengthwise. We would, he said, try to re-create it. And the roots: none of the Cyberonions I'd seen had roots, which he told me were once-live, once-soft tendrils that always found what the onion needed and yet, when dry, seemed insubstantial, coarse, as ephemeral as the beard on a goat. He described how the top of an onion might bolt towards its flower, how the stiffest shoot thrusts out of the plant, stops suddenly, and grows from its tip the soft green tendrils, like coarse hairs, each one with a tiny white flower, the flowers together shaped like a small onion, with a deeper smell of onion and earth, like no other smell in all the world, or Cyberworld.

You must remember that I am helping my father as I describe his lessons concerning the onion. I try to allow for his emotion, his enthusiasm. His exact words, if I recall, were something like: "A green shoot, see, and little flowers, bunched up in a ball. Good smell—like soil, like onion. I wish you could smell it." You see, my father's memory of onions far exceeded his ability to describe them, just as my mother's ambitions for us in Cyberspace far outpaced her ability to make us understand just what she envisioned for our future.

Our future, at least for long days and nights in our small, dome-shaped domicile, became the onion: the long attempt to re-create the onion began. We started, of course, with the program the Bidwellians had written to create the Cyberonion. After I examined it, I saw how simple it was, like a child trying to draw the world with a box of six Crayolas. In fact, I began to wonder if all of the Cyberworld I'd grown so used to was equally simple.

"What's in the program to create the *texture* of the onion?" asked my father.

"The same coding they've used for the apple." I did

more research. "And the potato." I visited the programming for other vegetables. "And the carrot, only without as much bite factor."

"Can we use any of it, or shall we start over?" he asked.

I went to my mother. "Remember," she said. "Everything is layers. It's like a chemical formula. Many things are made of carbon, and hydrogen, and oxygen, the simplest building blocks. The *way* they come together can make the simple very complex. Start where they've started, and make a complex onion."

I tried to do as my mother suggested. I tried everything out on my father. He tried everything out on his memory of onions. Each time, I failed.

"Make it fun," said my mother.

"Are you sure they're giving you access to everything?" asked my father.

For weeks and weeks I tried my limited programming abilities. I consulted with others, I examined my father's pickled onions until they haunted my dreams and my waking, I bounced between my mother's exhortations to try and my father's frustration at our failure.

And then, one day, like a Cyberthief, like what in the very old days the authorities called a "hacker," I suddenly found my way onto a screen I had never seen before, in a territory layered inside Bidwell, layered below the Bidwell Workshop, and layered even inside the tools they had given me. I was as close to the center of Cyberspace as I'd ever been. And what I saw helped me to understand why I could not create an onion with my limited tools: I, myself, was being limited.

You see, I was staring at the same programming that controlled the helmet I wore, and my father's helmet, and my mother's, too. I might have been a child in the days before the Cyberworld, looking at a picture of his skeleton on X-ray film.

And when I saw my program, I had a thought I should never have had. I thought that maybe, just maybe I wasn't real at all but a Cyberperson, like my dog Sunflower was now a Cyberdog. Had my parents, I wondered, scanned me into the computer too, as part of the resource-saving, energy-reducing, space-limited Cyberworld? Was the skeleton on the X-ray film only a picture of a child?

I must have screamed, for suddenly my mother and my father tore off their helmets and surrounded me with their concern. I was too upset to explain what I had come to question. But somehow my father understood. Perhaps he was equipped to know my fear best.

He went to his collection of onions, those jars of actual onions in actual vinegar. His eyes gleamed as he shattered a jar against the wall.

"Do you smell that?" he shouted. He reached down for an onion and rubbed it against his pants leg.

"Feel," he commanded. He grabbed my hand and put it on the onion skin. Evaporating vinegar cooled my fingers.

He took a large, crunching bite of the onion. "Taste," he said. He tore off a nibble and put it into my mouth.

I cannot describe this experience, just as my father could not describe his knowledge of onions to me. It was, as I learned later, an experience like faith: something happens, something is there, but how can anyone prove its existence?

"You see," said my father. "If they cannot make a decent Cyberonion, and now you know they cannot, then they cannot make a Cyberboy who could taste a real onion and know the difference."

He began picking up the onions that had rolled into odd places around the room. "You are mine," said my father. "And your mother's. You live in Bidwell, but you are not Bidwellian."

And then he reached into his pants pocket and pulled

out a small packet. He tore an edge from it and shook
some small black grains—they looked like crushed pepper—into his hand.

"Your mother says life is but layer after layer, created
by memory or by a computer—what is the difference? The
Bidwellians want you to believe so, too."

He took me outside to where he used to sit on the
ground. He scratched the surface of the earth. "*This* is different," he said, and he took a small black seed, bent down,
and pushed it gently into the exposed soil.

"Should you try to remove the layers, you would
destroy the life that waits inside here, the life that makes
you, and me, and computers, and all of Bidwell." He covered up the seed and gently stepped on the ground.

My mother watched from the doorway. She didn't
say a word when our computer helmets began to beep. But
my father started back into our small home. I stared after
him.

"Father, wait," I said. "How can we leave this place?"

He turned to me and laughed. "Because it is *not*
Cyberspace. Because it will always be here. Because this
onion seed will grow into an onion, programmed by nothing more than the earth itself. Onion to seed to onion to
seed."

And so we went back to Bidwell, donned our helmets,
and logged into Cyberspace, a place no *more* real, though
increasingly no *less* real, than the small patch of scratched
earth outside the door of our small, domed shelter. We,
like so many of our human counterparts, learned to live in
both worlds: to dream and to wake, to learn and to imagine, to live between two lives, almost like a boy might sit
between a mother and a father, learning to grow, and to
grow onions.

And that, I conclude, represents the complete and
final triumph of the onion, at least as far as my family is
concerned.

Better Be Ready 'Bout Half Past Eight

"I'm changing sex," Zach said.

Byron looked up from his lab notebook. "For the better, I hope."

"This is something I've never discussed with you," Zach said, stepping back and leaning against the cold-room door. "I need to. Do you want to go get a beer or something?"

"I have to transcribe this data," Byron said. "What do you need to discuss?"

"My sexuality," Zach said. "The way I feel trapped in the wrong body."

"Well, I suppose you were right," Byron said.

"Right?" Zach said.

"Not to discuss it with me," Byron said. "It's none of my business, is it?"

"We've been friends a long time," Zach said.

"Have you always felt this way?" Byron said.

Zach nodded. "I didn't know it was this I was feeling," he said. "But I've been in therapy for over a year now, and I'm sure."

23

■

Better
Be
Ready
'Bout
Half
Past
Eight

"You've been seeing Terry about *this*?" Byron had given Zach the name of Terry Wu, whom he himself had once consulted professionally.

Zach nodded again. "He's terrific. He knew the first time he met me what I was."

"What were you?" Byron said.

"A woman," Zach said.

Had there been any signs? Frowning, Byron sat staring at the computer screen. Then he stood, shoved his hands into his pockets, and stared out the window. He could see the sky and the top of the snow-covered hills. On this floor all the windows started at chin level, so you couldn't see the parking lot or the ground outside; you could only see distances, clouds, and sections of sunrise.

He walked up and down the hall for a while. The surrounding labs buzzed with action, students leaning intently over whirring equipment, technicians laughing over coffee. Secretaries clopped through the hall and said, "Hi, Dr. Glass" when they passed him. He could ignore them because he had a reputation for being absentminded; he was absorbed in his research, or perhaps in a new poem. He was well known, particularly in scientific circles, for his poetry. He edited the poetry column of *Science*. He judged many poetry-writing competitions, and he had edited anthologies.

What had he missed?

Worrying about it was useless. Zach's life wasn't *his* concern. "Just as long as it doesn't interfere with work," he would say. "I can't have personal life running amok in the lab."

But in fact he didn't believe in the separation of work and home. "If your love life's screwed up, you're probably going to screw up the science," he'd said more than once when he sent a sobbing technician home, or gave a distraught graduate student the name of a counselor. As a result his workers did sacrifice, to some extent, their personal lives to come in on weekends or at night to see to an experiment. It worked out.

"Go on home," he imagined himself saying to Zach, patting him on the shoulder. "Come back when it's all over."

But that wouldn't work. For one thing, it wouldn't end. For another thing, Zach wouldn't be Zach when he came back. He would be a woman Byron had never met.

"He's putting you on," Emily said. She was sitting at the table, ostensibly editing a paper on the synthesis of mRNA at the transcriptional level in the Drosophila per protein; but whenever the spoon Byron held approached Toby's open mouth, her own mouth opened in anticipation.

"Nope," Byron said, spooning more applesauce from the jar. "He wanted to tell me before he started wearing makeup."

"If Zach thinks that's the definition of women, he's headed for trouble," Emily said. "I suppose he's shaving his legs and getting silicone implants, too."

"Not to mention waxing his bikini line," Byron said.

"Oh, God," Emily said, laughing. "I don't want to hear any more." She handed Byron a washcloth, and Byron carefully wiped applesauce off Toby's chin. "How would you know you were the wrong sex?"

"Woman's intuition?" Byron said.

"Very attractive," he said the next morning, when Zach walked into the lab wearing eye shadow.

"Don't make fun of me, okay?" Zach said.

Byron felt embarrassed. "I didn't mean anything," he said. "I mean, it's subtle, and everything."

25

■
Better
Be
Ready
'Bout
Half
Past
Eight

Zach looked pleased. "I've been practicing," he said. "You know what? My younger brother wears more make-up than I do. Is this a crazy world or what?"

"Yeah," Byron said. He'd met Zach's brother, whose makeup was usually black. "Are you doing this gradually? Or are you sort of going cold turkey? I mean, will you come in in nylons and spike heels some morning?"

"Babe," Zach said, "I've been getting hormones for six months. Don't you notice anything different?"

He put his hands on his hips and turned slowly around, and Byron saw discernible breasts pushing up the cloth of Zach's rugby shirt. Byron felt a little faint, but he managed to say, "You're wearing a bra."

Zach went over to look in the mirror behind the door. He stood on tiptoe, staring intently at his breasts for a moment, and then, as he took his lab coat off the hook, he said, "God, I'm starting to feel good."

"You are?" was all Byron could manage. He was wondering how to say, without hurting Zach's new feelings, Don't call me Babe.

All day he tried not to look at Zach's breasts, but there they were, right in front of him, as Zach bent over the bench, or peered into the microscope, or leaned back with his hands behind his neck, staring at the ceiling, thinking.

"I'm heading out," Byron told Sarah in midafternoon.

"Are you okay?" she said, looking up from the bench. "You look a little peaked."

"I'm fine," Byron said. "I'll be back in the morning."

But once out in the parking lot, sitting in his car, he could think of no place he wanted to go. He hung on to the steering wheel and stared at the Mercedes in front of him, which had a Utah license plate that read IMAQT. A woman, of course.

Well, it's not *my* life, he thought. Nothing has changed for me.

"I haven't had this much trouble with breasts since I was sixteen," he said to Emily as they sat at the kitchen table watching the sunset.

"How big are they?" Emily said.

"Jesus, I don't know," Byron said.

"Bigger than mine?" she said.

Byron looked at Emily's breasts, which were bigger since she'd had Toby. "No," he said. "But I think they've just started."

"You mean he'll just keep taking hormones till they're the size he wants?" Emily said. "I should do that."

"You know," Byron said, "what I don't understand is why it bothers me so much. You'd think he's doing it to spite me."

"Going to meetings will be more expensive," she said.

"What do you mean?" Byron said.

"Honey," Emily said, "if Zach's a woman, you won't be sharing a room. Will you?"

"Oh," Byron said. "Do you think it will make that much difference?"

"You're already obsessed with his breasts," Emily said. "Wait till he's fully equipped."

Byron leaned his head on his hand. He hadn't even *thought* about the surgical procedure.

"I think you're letting this come between us," Zach said the next day.

"What?" Byron said.

"We've been friends a long time. I don't want to lose that."

"Zach," Byron said, "I don't see how things can stay the same."

"But I'm still the same person," Zach said.

Byron was not at all sure of that. "Well, how's it going?" he finally said.

27

■

**Better
Be
Ready
'Bout
Half
Past
Eight**

Zach seemed pleased to be asked. He sat down on the desk and folded his arms. "Really well," he said. "The surgeon says the physiological changes are right on schedule. I'm scheduled for surgery starting next month."

"Starting?" Byron said.

"It's a series of operations," Zach said. "Probably about six, over a couple of months. Cosmetic surgery for the most part."

"Zach," Byron said, "maybe it's none of my business, but don't you feel"—he cast about for the right way to say it—"doesn't it make you feel mutilated?"

Zach shook his head. "That's what it's all about," he said. "It *doesn't*. To tell you the truth, in the last year or two I've come to feel as if my penis is an alien growth on my body. It's my *enemy*, Byron. This surgery's going to liberate me."

Byron crossed his legs. "I don't think I can relate to that," he said.

"I know," Zach said. "My support group says nobody really understands."

"Your support group?"

"Women who've had the operation," Zach said, "or are in the process. We meet every week."

"How many are there?" Byron said.

"More than you'd think," Zach said.

"So," Byron said. "Are you—I mean, should I call you 'she' now?"

Zach grinned. "I've been calling myself 'she' for a while. But so far nobody outside my group has."

"Well," Byron said. He tried to look at Zach and smile, but he couldn't do both at once. He smiled first, and then looked. "I'll work on it," he said. "But it's not exactly easy for me either, you know."

"I know. I really appreciate your trying to understand." Zach stood up. "Back to work," he said. "Oh." He turned around with his hand on the doorknob. "I'm changing my name, too. As of next month, I'll be Zoe."

"Zoe," Byron said.

"It means 'life,'" Zach said. "Mine is finally beginning."

"It means 'life,'" Byron said mincingly to Toby as he pulled the soggy diaper out from under him. "Life, for Christ's sake."

Toby smiled.

"What's he been for thirty-eight years—dead?" Byron said. He dried Toby and sprinkled him with powder, smoothing it into the soft creases. As he lifted Toby's feet to slide a clean diaper underneath him, a stream of pee arced gracefully into the air and hit Byron in the chest, leaving a trail of droplets across Toby's powdered thighs.

"Oh, geez," Byron said. "Couldn't you wait ten seconds?" He reached for the washcloth and wiped the baby off. Then he wiggled the little penis between his thumb and forefinger. "You know what you are, don't you?" he said, leaning over and peering into Toby's face. "A little man. No question about that."

Toby laughed.

After he'd put Toby into the crib, Byron went into the bathroom, pulling his T-shirt off. He caught sight of himself in the mirror and stood still. With the neckband of the shirt stuck on his head, framing his face, the shirt hung from his head like a wig of green hair.

He took his glasses off to blur the details and moved close to the glass, looking at the line of his jaw. Was his jaw strong? Some women who had what were called "strong features" were quite attractive. Byron's mother used to say that Emily was built like a football player, but Byron had always thought she was sexy.

He put his glasses on and stepped back, bending his knees so that only his shoulders showed in the glass. With long hair around his face, and a few hormones to change his shape a little, he'd make a terrific woman.

He opened the medicine cabinet and took out one of

29
.
Better
Be
Ready
'Bout
Half
Past
Eight

Emily's lipsticks. He leaned forward and spread it on his mouth, and as he pressed his lips together, a woman's face materialized in the mirror. Byron's heart came to a standstill.

It was his mother.

"It was the weirdest thing," he said. "I never looked like her before. Never."

"You never cross-dressed before," Zach said, continuing to stare at the video monitor. "What's going on with this data?"

"Of course I never cross-dressed," Byron said. "I still don't cross-dress. I just happened to look in the mirror when my shirt was on my head."

Zach looked up at him and grinned. "And there she was," he said. "You would be amazed what we find out about ourselves when we come to terms with our sexuality."

"Oh, for God's sake," Byron said. "I was taking my shirt off. I wasn't coming to terms with anything."

"That's fairly obvious," Zach said, tapping at the keyboard.

"Jesus!" Byron said. "Do those hormones come complete with bitchiness? Or is your period starting?"

Zach stared at him. "I can't believe you said that," he said.

Byron couldn't believe he'd said it either, but he went on. "Everything's sexuality with you these days," he said crossly. "I'm trying to tell you about my mother and you tell me it's my goddamn sexuality."

Zach stood up and stepped away from the desk. "Look," he said, folding his arms, "it's called the Tiresias syndrome. You're jealous because I understand both sexes. By cross-dressing—whether you go around in Emily's underwear or just pretend you've got a wig on— you're trying to identify with me."

For a long moment Byron was unable to move. "What?" he finally said.

"You can't handle talking about the things that really

matter, can you?" Zach said. "As soon as we get close to personal feelings, you back off."

"Feelings," Byron said.

"You're a typical man when it comes to emotions," Zach said.

"And you're a typical woman," Byron said.

Zach shook his head. "You are in trouble, boy."

"*I'm* in trouble?" Byron said. "Looks to me like you're the one with the problem."

"That's the difference between us," Zach said. "I'm taking steps to correct my problem. You won't even admit yours."

"My problem is you," Byron said. "You are a fucking prick."

"Not for long," Zach said.

"Once a prick, always a prick," Byron shouted.

After Zach walked out the door, Byron sat down at his desk and stared at the data Zach had pulled up on the screen, but its sense eluded him. Finally he spun his chair around and put his feet up on the bookcase behind him, and reached for a legal pad.

He always wrote his poetry on long yellow legal pads. He had once tried to jot down some poetic thoughts on the computer, but they had slipped out of his poem and insinuated themselves into a new idea for a research project, which in fact developed into a grant proposal that was later funded. The experience had scared him.

He stared up at the slice of sky that was visible from where he sat, and held the legal pad on his lap for over an hour, during which he wrote down thirteen words. When Sarah stuck her head into the office and said, "See you tomorrow," he put the pad down and left work for the day.

Driving home he thought about his dead mother, Melba Glass. She had never liked Emily, but once Byron was married, his mother stopped saying snide things about her. She asked them instead. "Honey," she'd say, "isn't Emily a little *strident*?"

"What do you mean, *strident*?" Byron would snarl, and she would say she'd meant nothing at all, really, young women were just *different* these days. Byron would narrow his eyes at her; but later, when he'd driven his mother to the train station and waved her off, the idea would come back to him. Emily *was* vociferous in her opinions. And not particularly tolerant of her mother-in-law's old-fashioned tendencies.

"Why doesn't your mother even fucking *drive*?" she'd say.

"Why should she?" Byron said. "She never needed to."

"She needs to now, doesn't she?" Emily said.

"Why should she?" Byron would repeat; and for a couple of days he would react to everything Emily said as if she was being highly unreasonable, and *strident*.

What would Emily say if he told her that his dead mother had appeared to him? Worse, that he had appeared to himself as his dead mother?

She would lean over Toby's crib in the dark. "I'll be Don Ameche in a taxi, honey," she'd sing. "Better be ready 'bout half past eight."

"How are you? Three of you now. Ha!" Terry Wu said.

"Three of me?" Byron said.

"You have a little baby?" Terry said.

"Oh! Toby! Terrific! And Emily. I see. Sure, we're fine. Really. Everything's terrific."

A concerned look seized Terry Wu's face. "Do you protest too much?" he said, and he leaned forward, pressing his fingertips together.

"Protest?" Byron said. "That's not why I'm here."

"Maybe no, maybe yes," Terry said, but he leaned back again.

"No, it's my, uh, colleague. You know, Zach."

"Ah," Terry said.

"I seem obsessed," Byron said weakly.

"You are obsessed with your colleague?"

"With his sex," Byron said.

"*His* sex?" Terry said.

Byron felt himself blushing. "I can't get used to the idea that he's a woman."

Terry nodded again. "Each one is a mystery."

"No, it's just—why didn't I know?"

"Did you know your wife was pregnant when she conceived?"

"What does that have to do with it?" Byron said.

"Well," Terry said, "you were there when it happened, in fact you did the deed, and yet you didn't know about it."

"Terry, I think that's something else."

Terry shrugged. "Are you in love with your colleague?"

"Of course not." He was getting angry. "What are you getting at?"

"I am trying to elicit a coherent statement from you," Terry said. "So far all you have managed to tell me is that you are obsessed with your colleague and are not in love with her. I am having trouble following your flight of ideas."

"Look." Byron looked down at his feet. "Someone whom I have known for more than twenty years has overnight turned into a woman. It's shaken my understanding of reality. I can no longer trust what I see before my eyes."

"Yet you call yourself a scientist," Terry said thoughtfully. "It is simply a matter of surgery and hormonal therapy, isn't it? Changing one form into another by a well-documented protocol?"

Byron stared at him. "That's not what I mean," he said.

Terry clasped his hands together happily. "Yet there

is a magical process involved as well! An invisible and powerful force! Something that is beyond our understanding! But"—he put his hands on his desk and stared into Byron's eyes—"even your poetic license will not allow you to accept it?"

33

■

Better
Be
Ready
'Bout
Half
Past
Eight

"My poetic license?" Byron said.

"Are man and woman so different, so unrelated, that no transformation is possible? It's this Western culture," Terry said in disgust. "In my country people exchange sexes every day."

Byron wondered if he had understood Terry correctly.

"Suppose your little baby comes to you in twenty years and says, 'Daddy, I am now Chinese.' Will you disown the child, after twenty years of paternity? No! He will still be the son you love."

"Chinese?" Byron said.

"I fear our time is up," Terry said. He stood up and held his hand out. Byron stood, too, and shook it. "Good to see you again. Would you like to resume these discussions on a regular basis? I can see you at this time every week."

"I don't think so," Byron said. "I just wanted this one consultation."

"Glad to be of service," Terry said. "No charge, no charge. Professional courtesy. Someday I may need an experiment!" He chuckled. "Or a poem."

"A shower?" Byron said.

"Isn't it a kick?" Emily said. "Gifts like garter belts and strawberry douches."

"That's sick," he said.

"Oh, come on, honey. His men friends are invited too." She put down the screwdriver she'd been using to put together Toby's Baby Bouncer and leaned over to kiss Byron's knee. "It'll be fun."

"Why don't we just play Red Rover?" Byron said. "All the girls can stand on one side and yell, 'Let Zach come on over.'"

"You act as if you've lost your best friend," Emily said.

"I *am* losing him. I've known him all these years and suddenly I find out he's the opposite of what I thought he was."

"Ah," Emily said, and she sat back against the sofa. "Here we go. Men and women are diametrically opposed."

"Don't you start," he said. "I don't need an attack on the home front."

"I'm supposed to comfort you, I suppose," Emily said. "Sympathize with you because your good buddy's going over to the enemy."

"Well?" Byron said. "Aren't you secretly glad? Having a celebration? Letting him in on all your girlish secrets?"

Emily shook her head. "We're talking about a human being who has suffered for forty years, and you're jealous because we're giving him some lacy underpants? You're welcome to borrow some of mine, if that's what you want." She smiled at him.

"Suffered?" Byron said. "The dire fate of living in a male body? A fate worse than death, clearly."

"Why are you attacking *me*?" Emily said.

"I'm not attacking you," he said. "I'm just upset." He scooted closer to her and put his arms around her, laying his head against her breasts. "What if I lost you, too?"

"Sweetheart," Emily said, "you're stuck with me for the duration."

"I hope so," Byron said. He turned his head and pressed his face against her. "I certainly hope so." His voice, caught in her cleavage, sounded very far away.

"Many, many years ago," Byron said softly, holding Toby in his arms as he rocked in the dark, "when Daddy and Uncle Zach were very young—"

Toby, who was gazing at his eyes as he spoke, flung out his fist.

35

■

Better
Be
Ready
'Bout
Half
Past
Eight

"He was still Uncle Zach at the time," Byron said. He tucked the fist into his armpit. "Anyway, we used to ride out to the quarries to go swimming. You've never been swimming, but it's a lot like bobbing around in Mummy's uterus."

Toby's eyes closed.

"We used to ride our bikes out there after we'd finished our lab work," Byron said. "Riding a bike in the summertime in southern Indiana is a lot like swimming. The air is so full of humidity you can hardly push the sweat out your pores.

"So we would ride out there in the late afternoon, and hide our bikes in the trees, and go out to our favorite jumping-off place," Byron said. "And Daddy and Uncle Zach would take off all their clothes, and take a running start, and jump right off the edge of the cliff into space!"

Toby made a sound.

"Yes, the final frontier," Byron said. "And we would hit the water at the same instant, and sink nearly to the bottom of the bottomless pit, and bob up without any breath. It was so cold."

He frowned. What kind of story was this to tell his son? "That was poetry, son," he whispered. He stood up and lay the sleeping baby on his stomach in the crib. Tomorrow morning Emily would put Toby in his new Baby Bouncer, and Toby Glass would begin to move through the world on his own.

"What are you giving her?" Sarah said.

"Who?" Byron said, looking up from his calculations.

"Zoe," Sarah said. "We're giving her silk underwear from Frederick's of Hollywood. Do you know her bra size?"

"Sarah," Byron said, pushing his chair back and crossing his arms, "why on earth would I know Zach's bra size?"

"Oooh," Sarah said. "Touchy, aren't we? You *are* friends." She stood there watching him as if, Byron thought, she was daring him to deny it.

"There are some things you just don't discuss in the locker room," he said.

"Oh," Sarah said. "Well, what are you getting her?"

"I haven't thought about it," Byron said.

"Don't you think you *ought* to think about it?"

"Mother! I thought you were dead!" Byron said.

"Byron, dear, put your feet down," Melba Glass said. She sat down on the chair at the side of his desk, touching her hair, and looked around. "The janitorial staff doesn't get in here very often, do they?"

"Mother, what are you doing here?" Byron said, swinging his feet off the desk and sitting up straight. "How did you get here?"

"I took a taxi, dear," Melba Glass said. She put her purse on the floor beside her and leaned over to brush some crumbs of Byron's lunch off his blotter. "Now about this gift for your friend. Why not something personal? Intimate? You two have known each other a long time."

"Mom, you don't get something intimate for another guy."

"Oh, Byron, Byron. You should be more flexible, dear. You sound like your father."

"I do?" Byron was rather pleased. "Are you and Dad together up there?"

"Up where, dear?" Melba Glass said.

"Well, heaven," Byron said.

"Heaven! What an idea!" Melba Glass said, and she laughed. "Your father's idea of heaven and mine are very different."

"Oh," Byron said. His mother did not elaborate, so he said, "Did they tell you Emily and I had a baby?" He turned the picture of Toby around so that his mother could see it.

Melba Glass frowned at the picture, then reached into her purse and took out her reading glasses. She peered through them. "Looks like Emily's father," she said "Now. About Zoe."

"What about Zoe?" Byron said.

"What about a nice pair of silk stockings?" Melba Glass said. She folded her hands on her knee and swung her crossed leg. "When I worked at DuPont, they gave us all the stockings we wanted, but they were nylon."

"Mom," Byron said. "I don't want to give him anything."

Melba Glass took off her glasses and looked closely at Byron. "The longer I live, the more surprises I get," she said, shaking her head. "How could I have raised such a reactionary son?"

"Me?" Byron said.

"Byron, it's wonderful what science has done for your friend," Melba Glass said, leaning toward him with an eager face. "This modern world! You should embrace change, son."

She put her glasses back into her purse and stood up. "Just let me tell you this, Byron. If you don't support Zoe at this time in her life, you'll regret it forever." She stepped toward him, shaking her finger at him. "Forever, Byron." She saw the legal pad on the desk and picked it up. "Another poem?" she said. She held it at arm's length, then shook her head. "I can't quite make it out," she said sadly. "You know, I used to write poetry."

"You did?" Byron said.

"Try Dellekamps," Melba Glass said. "They always have nice things."

■

37

■

Better
Be
Ready
'Bout
Half
Past
Eight

"I wonder what happened to all my mother's poems," Byron said.

Emily looked up from the paper she was reading and stared at him thoughtfully, chewing on the end of her red pencil. "It wasn't very *good* poetry," she said.

"How do you know?" he said.

She frowned. "Byron, sometimes I think you live in a cocoon."

"You read it?" Byron said in amazement.

"Sure," she said. "You know, little poems about love, flowers, the moon."

"Why didn't she let me read it?" Byron said. He stared at the television screen, where a black woman was talking about teenage reproductive strategies in abusive households. "Em. What happened to it?"

"She threw it away," Emily said. "She thought it was too embarrassing to keep."

"Why did she talk to *you* about it?" Byron said.

"We had to talk about something," Emily said.

"Maybe your mother is right," Byron said. "Maybe I have no idea what's going on in the world." He peered into the rearview mirror at Toby, who was snoring softly in his car seat and paying no attention.

Byron had thought in the beginning that being a scientist would increase his understanding of the world, and even the world's understanding of itself. But instead, as his work grew more specialized over the years and his expertise became narrower, his brain seemed to be purging its data banks of extraneous information, and shutting down, one after another, his receptors for external stimuli. He had been so caught up in chronicling the minuscule changes taking place in the gels and tubes of his laboratory that the universe had changed its very nature without his even noticing. The world had a new arrangement that everyone else seemed to understand very well; even his poetry had simply served to keep him self-absorbed, oblivious to what must be reality.

39

■

Better
Be
Ready
'Bout
Half
Past
Eight

Actually, he rather liked the idea of living in a cocoon while the world became a wilder and more exotic place. Sirens wailed, cars throbbing with bass notes roared past him with mere children at the wheel, dead women appeared in mirrors, and men changed into women; but Byron and Toby Glass putted across town safe and snug inside a cocoon.

What do *I* know? Byron thought. What *do* I know?

"Can I help you?" said a heavily scented young woman with beige hair. Her lips were a carnivorous shade of red, and her eyelids a remarkable magenta.

"I'm looking for a gift," Byron said.

"For Baby's mother?" the woman said.

"Who?" Byron said.

"Baby's mother," she said, and with a long scarlet fingernail she poked at the Snugli where Toby Glass was sleeping peacefully against Byron's stomach.

"Oh," Byron said. "No. This is for a shower."

"Oh, I love showers!" the woman said. "What kind?"

"Sort of a coming-out shower."

"We don't see many of those," she said. She turned to survey her wares. "Are you close to the young lady?"

"I used to be," Byron said. "But she's changed."

"*Plus ça change*," the woman said. "Something to remember you by. Something in leather?"

"Well, I don't know," Byron said, nervously stroking the warm curve of Toby's back. "I thought maybe stockings?"

The woman frowned. "You mean like pantyhose?"

"I guess not," he said.

"I know." The woman tapped Byron's lower lip with the red fingernail. "Follow me." She led him to the back of the store and leaned down to pull open a drawer. "For our discerning customers. A Merry Widow." She held up a lacy black item covered with ribbons and zippers.

"Wow," Byron said. "I didn't know they still made those."

"They are *hot*," the saleswoman said. She held it up against her body. "Imagine your friend in this!"

"I can't," Byron said.

"Do you know her bra size?" the woman asked.

"I'm not sure it's final yet," Byron said.

"Oh," the woman said. "Well, maybe some perfume." Byron followed her back to the front of the store, where she waved her hand grandly at a locked glass cabinet. "These are very fine perfumes, from the perfume capitals of the world. Paris, Hong Kong, Aspen. This one is very popular—La Différence."

"That's good," Byron said. "I'll take some of that."

"Oh, excellent choice!" The woman patted his cheek before she reached into her cleavage and drew out a golden key to unlock the perfume cabinet.

"While Ginny rings that up, would you like to try on some of our makeup?" said another salesperson.

"No thanks," Byron said.

The woman pouted at him. "You *should*," she said. "Lots of men wear it. Girls go crazy for it." She patted a stool in front of the counter. "Sit down."

Byron sat, and she removed his glasses. "You'll look *terrific*," she said. She leaned toward him, her lips parted, and gently massaged his eyelid with a colorful finger. " 'Scuse me while I kiss the sky," she sang softly, stroking the other one. Then she drew on his eyelid with a long black instrument. "This is Creem-So-Soft," she told him. "It is *so* easy to put on." She drew it across the other eyelid, and finally she brushed his eyelashes with a little brush and stood back. "There," she said. "You are a *killer*."

Toby began to gasp into Byron's shirt. The makeup

woman swooped down. "Oooh," she said. "Little booper's making hungry noises." She lifted her eyes to Byron. "Bet I can stall him."

41

■

Better
Be
Ready
'Bout
Half
Past
Eight

"You can?" Byron said.

"Babies *love* this," she said. She lifted Toby out of the Snugli and sat him down facing her on Byron's lap. She began to sketch on his face with the Creem-So-Soft while Toby stared silently at her nose. "There!" She picked Toby up and held him for Byron to examine.

Toby beamed and waved his limbs. He was adorned with a black mustache and a pointy black goatee.

"Oh, how darling," Ginny said, coming back from the cash register. "Will this be cash or charge?"

Byron looked at the bill she handed him. "Charge," he said. "I thought this store went out of business a long time ago."

"Lots of people say that," Ginny said.

"What have you done to the baby?" Emily said when Byron walked in the door.

"Babies like this," Byron said. "It's a preview of what he'll look like in twenty years."

"He's going to be a beatnik?" Emily said. She took Toby from Byron's arms. "Don't you think you're rushing things a little?"

Byron sighed. "They grow up so fast," he said. He kissed the top of Toby's head, and then kissed Emily. "How do you like the new me?"

Emily looked at him. "Did you get your hair cut?" she said.

"Em, I'm wearing makeup," Byron said.

"Oh," she said. "So you are." She held Toby up and sniffed at his bottom. "Daddy didn't change your dipes," she said, and she carried him off to his room.

Byron went into the bathroom to look at himself. His eyelids were a very bright purple. He picked up Emily's

Barn Red lipstick and carefully covered his lips with it.
Then he took off his glasses.

"You know who you look like?" Emily said, appearing
beside him in the mirror. "Your mother. Honest to God. If
you had one of those curly little perms you could pass for
your own mother."

She looked at herself in the mirror, stretching her
upper lip with her forefinger. "Do you think I should
shave my mustache?"

"No," Byron said. "It's sexy." He slid his hands under
her arms and over her breasts. "Let's go to bed."

"No thanks," Emily said. She picked up her Creem-
So-Soft and started to outline her eyes. "I have no desire
to sleep with your mother."

"You never did like my mother," Byron said.

"Not a lot," Emily said.

"I think I'll go over to the lab," Byron said. He kissed
her cheek, leaving a large red lip print.

"Don't run any red lights," Emily said.

Byron liked weekends at the lab. He liked weekdays, too,
when students and technicians wandered in and out of
each other's labs borrowing chemicals, and all the world
seemed engaged in analyzing the structures and chemical
interactions of various tissues. But weekends—when the
offices were empty and the halls were quiet, and only the
odd student padded back and forth from the bathroom—
had a cozy, private feeling. Byron could think better in the
silence, and he felt close to other scientists, who had given
up time in the outside world to bend lovingly over their
benches and peer into microscopes, hoping to add to the
world's slim store of truth. Both the lab work he did and
the poetry he wrote on weekends seemed to spring from a
deeper level: a place of intuition and hope that was inac-
cessible when he was distracted by bustle. It was on weekends that he caught glimpses of the world he hoped to find,

where poetry and science were one, and could explain the meaning of life.

"The meaning of life," he said aloud, and wrote it down on his legal pad. Then he turned and typed it on the keyboard, and it appeared in amber letters on the screen in front of him. He smiled and pushed back in his chair, and put his feet on the desk. Poem or experiment? Either one!

He felt that he was on the threshold of an important discovery.

43

■

Better
Be
Ready
'Bout
Half
Past
Eight

"Why are you doing this?"

Byron opened his eyes. It was Zoe, leaning against the doorjamb. It was definitely and absolutely Zoe; there was no mistaking her for a man any more. He stared at her; what was it? The hair, the clothes, the jaw, the way the arms were folded: all were utterly familiar. What had happened?

Zoe shook her head impatiently. "The makeup," she said. "You're trying to be something you're not."

Byron had forgotten the makeup he was wearing, but he said, "How do you know what I'm not?"

"It's just that you're so conservative," Zoe said.

"No," he said. "I'm really quite wild. I'm just handicapped by my many fears."

"You?" Zoe said.

He nodded. "But you're wild through and through."

Zoe shook her head. "I'm conservative at the core. That's always been my major problem." She gazed out the window at the white hills. "You know the only thing I regret? I'll never have any children now."

"You could adopt."

She shook her head. "They wouldn't have my genes."

"You never really know your children anyway," Byron said.

Zoe sighed. "Tell me honestly. Did Emily teach you how to put that eyeliner on?"

Byron smiled. "No," he said. "In fact she learned from me."

Zoe narrowed her eyes and stared at him for a moment, then sat down on a stool. "I'm thinking of going to law school."

"Are you serious?" he said. "You'd leave the lab?"

"Sure. Patents is the way to go."

"You'd leave me?"

Zoe reached over and seized the tablet. "Poetry, poetry, poetry," she said. "Always with you it's the poetry. Anyone would think you're too distracted to work."

"You think this is easy?" Byron said.

"None of it is," she said.

They sat together for a while without talking.

"Are you coming to my shower?" Zoe said.

"Aren't showers supposed to be a surprise?" Byron said.

Zoe shrugged. "I hate surprises. I told Sarah she could only give me a shower if she invited men, too."

"I got you a gift." Byron was surprised to feel suddenly shy. "But is there anything you'd really like?"

"Will you come see me in the hospital?"

Byron nodded.

Zoe smiled. "Actually, you look good in makeup," she said. "It redefines your features. You look stronger."

"It's the same old me, though," Byron said.

"I really am thinking of law school," Zoe said. "I need to change my life."

"Changing your sex isn't enough?"

"No. That's who I've been all along."

"Oh," Byron said, and all at once he felt very sad, and exhausted. He put his feet up on the desk, and they sat in silence, gazing at the part of the world they could see through the window.

After a while he told Zoe about Toby's trip to

45

■

Better
Be
Ready
'Bout
Half
Past
Eight

Dellekamps. "And then," he said, "I'm sitting on a bench in the mall giving him his bottle, and I look up and these two old ladies are staring at him. 'That is dis*gust*ing,' one of them says. And then the other one gasps and grabs her arm and points at me. And they both back away looking horrified."

Zoe began to laugh.

"And then this man and a little girl walk by, and the little girl says, 'Daddy, is that a homeless person?' And the father says, 'No, dear, that's a man with problems.'"

"Oh," Zoe gasped, holding her ribs.

Byron wiped the tears from his own cheeks, and when he looked at his hand he saw that it was smeared with mascara. "I had no idea," he said, "no idea why these people were saying these things. I'd forgotten about my makeup. And Toby just looked normal to me."

"Stop," Zoe said, bending over and clutching her stomach.

"And finally a man comes up to me with his hands on his hips and says, 'You ought to be ashamed.'"

"I'm dying," Zoe croaked. "I can't breathe. Oh." She jumped from the stool and ran through the door. "I have to pee."

"You," Byron called after her, "should be ashamed."

He listened to the squeegeeing of her sneakers as she ran down the empty hall, and to the familiar creak of the hinges as she pushed open the door to the men's room.

"Glad you could make it, glad you could make it," Terry Wu said, shaking Byron's hand vigorously.

"Did you think I wouldn't?" Byron said.

"You're a busy man," Terry said. "So often the cells can't wait." He smiled and leaned forward. "I am giving her a vibrator. The muscles of the calves ache very much when one first wears high heels."

"That is so true," Emily said. She smiled at Terry Wu and pulled Byron away. "That guy gives me the creeps," she said.

"Honey, you're being xenophobic," Byron said. "Things are different in his country."

They pushed their way through the crowd, Byron cupping one hand protectively around Toby's head to keep him from being squashed in the Snugli.

"There you are!" Sarah appeared in front of them. "Isn't the turnout great?" She waved her arm at the crowd.

Emily hugged her. "Did you get it?" she said.

Sarah nodded. "I never spent that much on a bra in my life."

"How did you know what size to get?" Byron asked.

"I asked her," Sarah said. She led them over to where Zoe stood beside a gift-covered table. "Here are the Glasses!"

"I'm so glad you could come," Zoe said. She kissed Emily on the cheek and prodded Toby's bottom with a glistening red-tipped forefinger. "How's my little beatnik godbaby?"

"Zoe, you look gorgeous," Emily said. "Really. You look so . . . you."

"Next I'm having electrolysis on my facial hair," Zoe said.

"You look pretty good as you are," Byron said. He wondered when the time would come that Zoe would kiss *his* cheek. "I bought you some perfume, but I ended up giving it to Emily."

"Thank goodness," Zoe said. "I'm allergic to everything but La Différence, anyway."

"One of these days," Byron said, "I'll write you a poem."

"He's never done that for me." Emily waved her hand at the table in front of them. "Look at all this loot."

47

∎

**Better
Be
Ready
'Bout
Half
Past
Eight**

They stared at the pile of presents. "I can't wait to open them," Zoe said. "I've always wanted a shower."

"Isn't it wonderful to get what you always wanted?" Byron put his arm through hers and squeezed it, and he could feel her breast against his triceps as she squeezed back, her muscles hardening briefly against his own.

He felt a rush of pleasure. On his left, Emily reached for a bacon-wrapped chicken liver; on his right, his oldest friend in the world gently disengaged her arm from his to touch the hands of the dozens of people who had come to wish her well; and from his shoulders, like a newly discoverd organ of delight, hung the little bag full of Toby Glass.

Toby Glass, who could grow up to be anything!

The musicians in the string quartet began to tune their instruments, leaning toward each other, listening, nodding gravely. The cellist moved her stool a little closer to the violinist; the violinist held her instrument away from her neck as she shook back her long red hair, and then replaced it firmly under her chin. Suddenly, as if spontaneously, each player lifted her bow and held it poised in the air for a long moment, until at some prearranged and invisible signal they plunged their bows toward the strings of their various instruments and began to play.

The Omma-tidium Minia-tures

A IS FOR APHID. Emmons could never recall his mother without thinking of the ABC books of microscopic phenomena that she had compiled to amuse him during long summer afternoons on Tybee Island. A microscopist of acknowledged creativity, Kathleen Emmons had published one of these books under the off-putting title *An Abecedary of the Near Invisible.* To almost everyone's surprise, it became a best-seller. For the next few years you couldn't find a home with elementary-school-age children anywhere in the country without a copy of her book lying on a coffee table or sticking out of a bookcase.

"*A Is for Aphid,*" it asserted. And on the facing page, looking to young Emmons more like bug-eyed outer-space monsters than like microscopic insects, a herd of potato-shaped aphids elephant-walked the magnified branch of a muscadine vine. Deeper into the picture book, you learned that *D Is for Diatom, M Is for Microchip, R Is for Rotifer,* and you saw the stunning micrographs illustrating these statements. But the siphon-nosed aphids at the outset of his mother's book were the creatures that had fascinated Emmons as a boy, so he'd leapt at the invitation of International MicroDyne and begun preparing for his drop-down. He'd done so not only to test the minute engines of the company's new technologies but also to solder a spiritual link with his past—when *he'd* been little: an embryonic personality struggling to creep out from the shadows of his mother's success and his father's international reputation.

THE INCREDIBLE SHRINKING MAN. On the seventh floor of the IMD Sensor and Actuator Center in a northern suburb of Atlanta, Emmons sat in a conference room watching a video of a 1957 sci-fi film he had previously avoided having to see. Watching the movie was one of the weirder requirements of the field-test training that McKay had masterminded for the pilot of the company's first microremote; and as Scott Carey, the movie's common-man protagonist, shrank to the size of a three-year-old boy, a mouse, and, finally, a bipedal cockroach, Emmons's attention wobbled.

"I can't believe you've never seen this," said McKay, leaning into him in the carpeted dark and flinching when Carey stabbed his straight pin up into the belly of an attacking spider. "It's a certifiable classic."

But Emmons thought it smart to refrain from confessing that he hated the movies, that he had always hated the movies, and that he was grateful to his parents for encouraging him to develop other interests. He kept his eyes—not his mind—on the oversized screen and said nothing. McKay, a personnel rather than a research-and-development specialist, sincerely believed that even MicroDyne's brightest technicians could benefit from the psychological training provided by a sci-fi "classic" like *The Incredible Shrinking Man,* and when an executive of his rank took that tack, what else could you do but comply?

■

TO GOD THERE IS NO ZERO. For now, high on the screen, Scott Carey, who had squeezed into his garden from a window ledge in the basement, was gazing at the impossibly distant stars and all the muddled galaxies. "That existence begins and ends," said the actor Grant Williams in the film's final voice-over narration, "is Man's conception, not nature's. And I felt my body dwindling, melting, becoming nothing. My fears melted away, and in their place came acceptance. All this vast majesty of creation, it had to mean something. And then I meant something, too. Yes, smaller than the smallest, I meant something, too. To God there is no zero. I still exist!"

And B is for bullshit, thought Emmons, for it appeared to him that all he had seen in the film—denial, alienation, degradation, struggle—refuted Carey's concluding cry of existential yea-saying; indeed, Carey's fears about his own insignificance and life's ultimate meaninglessness had been underscored by the fact that he was going to go on shrinking forever.

BEING THERE. McKay had the lights brought up. He still got a boost from the film's upbeat gloss on the existential ramifications of littleness.

"Going down isn't easy," he told Emmons. "It's different from light microscopy, different from electron microscopy, and different from doing hands-on manipulations with a stereo-microscope assist. Being there—down among the dust mites, so to speak—is an *intenser* sort of microscopy, Emmons. Even if, on the literal level, you're operating a tiny waldo, doing watchmaker tasks with silicon pincers the size of an ameoba's paws.

"You have to overcome the possibility of 'dimensional shock' and take your bearings from the point of view of a nematode, say, or a spider colt. You have to learn to see again, at what I like to call 'ground zero.' Theoretically, it seems smart to work your way to the needed redimension-alization slowly. Which is why I've asked you to watch *The Incredible Shrinking Man* and then to discuss it with me."

Emmons discussed the film with McKay, certain that his boss was enjoying their talk—as he had the movie—immeasurably more than Emmons was.

FROGS AND PHILISTINES. During their talk, McKay noted that Science—Emmons could hear the capital S—had long ago declared that certain species of frog could not see anything in their environment inapplicable to their day-to-day existence. They were selectively blind to whatever failed to advance their survival or immediate well-being. The nonessential was invisible to them. A dragonfly at meal-time would loom like a helicopter, but an animal neither edible nor threatening—a wading heifer, for example—could splash by unregarded.

Scowling, McKay noted that some human philistines had a similar trait; namely, an inability to see anything that so much as hinted at parentheticality or irrelevance, e.g., the microscopic.

Emmons's mind cast back to his mother's abe-cedaries: McKay was preaching to the converted. If A wasn't for aphid, then it was for amoeba; if F wasn't for follicle, then it was for flea. The naked human eye could not distinguish two dots less than 0.1 millimeter apart, but from an early age he had trained himself to see all that the human eye *could* see.

How, then, was he either a frog or a philistine?

His mother had helped make him sensitive to the invis-ible—the infusoria in a vial of creek water—and his father, whose namesake Emmons was, had made these lessons stick by seeing to it that he often felt like a mere protozoan. In fact, of late Emmons secretly saw himself as someone whom others did not fully register: a spear carrier in a play or some anonymous urban scarecrow sleeping in the gutter.

■

F IS FOR FATHER, F IS FOR FLEA. The Emmonses' beach house on Tybee Island had always been full of dogs: Newfoundlands, poodles, Russian wolfhounds. It had also been full of fleas.

As McKay lectured, Emmons recalled his father striding shoeless in his tennis whites over the rattan mats on their concrete porch. Fleas jumped from the mats onto the damp cotton of his father's sweat socks, where their hard little bodies took on the instant visibility of commas or periods. His father picked off each flea with his thumb and forefinger and dropped it into the hot tapwater in an otherwise empty fish tank.

Lying on their pinched sides, the fleas kicked pathetically on the surface. Finger-jabbed, they spiraled, still kicking, to the bottom, where, eventually, the kicking ceased.

The elder Emmons, who seldom played very long with his namesake because his son usually netted more shots than he returned, would spend the rest of the morning decoying, seizing, and dunking fleas, moving from spot to spot on the mats to entice fresh generations of vermin to spring onto his socks. This intellectual celebrity, the computer scientist and backdoor cosmologist who had extended and redeemed his once-discredited mentor Edward Fredkin's science of "digital physics," would scold young Emmons for failing to capture fleas, too.

To the world at large, he held up the dictum that the universe is a computer—that atoms, electrons, and other subatomic particles are built from infinitesimal bits of information; that reality is grainy; and that there exists a single underlying programming rule to account for the movement and purpose of each of its constituent grains—but to his twelve-year-old son on Tybee, in the microcosmos of his family's summer retreat, he preached filial devotion, a more disciplined overhead smash, and the philosophical-cum-recreational benefits of flea-tweezering.

MICROSCOPIC RAIN AND A MIDGET'S PARASOL. "In a sense," McKay was saying, "Carey was lucky. He shrank by degrees, with plenty of chances to make adjustments."

Emmons, returned from his flashback, became aware of the dense particulate rain in his boss's strangely appointed office. Decay products from the radioactive gases thrown off by the ceiling tiles and the Sheetrock walls rained down as an invisible but inescapable fallout. The air was afire. It fell in charged veils, sleeting, draping, folding back on itself to repeatedly stipple his boss with iotas of disintegrating matter. Also, the molecules on the surface of McKay's aircraft carrier of a desk were migrating aside to allow the falling particles to penetrate and rape it.

A guilty horror seized Emmons as he watched the rain, a shower clearly imperceptible to McKay, who was jawing about "acclimating declensions" and giving odd examples:

"The smallest adult human being recorded, Emmons, was a Mexican midget called Zuchia Zarate. At seventeen, Señorita Zarate stood two feet and two inches tall and weighed not quite five and a half pounds. This nineteenth-century freak could have stepped from one of the Montgolfiers' balloons, popped a parasol, and floated safely to earth. On her trip down, she could have leisurely scrutinized a torrent of high-altitude plankton: pollen grains, lichen fragments, the spores of fungi, bacteria, algae, and so forth. If MicroDyne could bring off that easy a drop-down, Emmons, you'd have no sweat accepting your littleness."

But Emmons kept thinking how handy the señorita's parasol would have been: a shield against the invisible deluge.

LET'S GET SMALL. McKay's office was a museum of the minute. It contained an elegant miniature of the living room of the Tybee Island beach house—down to a baby baby-grand piano, an itsy-bitsy computer station, a dinky fireplace with even dinkier andirons and grates, a collection of foraminifer shells, and a gallery of framed Kirkuchi patterns (diffraction images of various alloy particles as created and photographed inside a transmission electron microscope) no bigger than postage stamps.

A newt-sized plastic doll of Emmons's canonized father sat in a wicker rocker in this mock-down of their old beach house, gazing at the Kirkuchi patterns and thinking godly thoughts. McKay paid no attention to these items— he'd seen them so many times before—but Emmons knew that this miniature architectural tribute to his father had triggered his flashback as surely as had McKay's jabber about frogs and philistines. The urge seized him to grab the father doll and pop it between his fingernails as if clicking the carapace of a flea—but even as a tiny doll, his father remained a Micromegas in Emmons's view and he couldn't do it.

Elsewhere in McKay's office there were Lilliputian cathedrals, miniature divans, Tinker Toy forts, and a display case containing gnat robots, beetle jeeps, electrostatic motors, and microdozers. The spiders that had draped some of these furnishings with gauze were living creatures, just like Emmons, but everything inanimate in the room mocked him by seeming more cunningly made.

"Ever see a tape of Steve Martin doing his classic 'Let's Get Small' routine?" McKay had just asked. "God, I love that routine. Think 'high' for 'small.' You'll get a grip on microminiaturization as a kind of occupational addiction. Look around. You can see why a shtick like that would appeal to me. . . ."

■

INADEQUACY, IMPOTENCE, INSIGNIFICANCE: A TRACT. That evening, in his apartment, Emmons worried that even his competence as a microremote engineer hadn't given him the sense of self possessed by a pompous company shill like McKay. Would going down—getting smaller—do the trick?

If H isn't for humility (an abstract noun), then it's for hydra (a tube-shaped freshwater polyp with a mouth at one end ringed by tentacles). And another definition of *hydra* is "a multifarious evil not overcome by a single effort." How to cope with the fact that the hydra he'd been struggling to defeat wasn't any sort of evil but rather the achievements of a mother who'd classified over a thousand species of nematodes and a father who'd led the world's scientific community toward the one computational rule governing every nanometer of space and perhaps explaining everything?

Forget that Fredkin's Rule—as his father had dubbed it—was still incompletely teased out. Forget that many scientists still blasted both the elder Emmons and the late Fredkin as, at best, inspired crackpots. *Emmons* was now an Olympian name. Although the son bearing it was proud of his name, he was also cowed by it, mindful of the meagerness of his own efforts in comparison to those of his parents. He seemed doomed by the scale of their reputations to fall on his face in any attempt to match them. He was too small to rival their successes, a bacterium in a life-extinguishing drop of acid: Scott Carey with a Ph.D. in microengineering.

IT'S A DIDINIUM-EAT-PARAMECIUM WORLD. Germaine Bihaly, who lived across the complex's parking lot, showed up at his door with a tray of Cantonese carryout boxes, each one a small soggy chalet packed with steamed chestnuts, sweet-and-sour meats, plump shrimp, and vivid strings of slime defying identification.

"Share?" she said.

Emmons let her in. Bihaly was a travel agent he had met over the telephone while booking a flight to a sensor-and-actuator conference in Berkeley. Later, he had coincidentally found her to be one of his neighbors.

They ate Chinese sitting on the ad sections from the *Atlanta Constitution*. Emmons explained why he felt like the incredible shrinking man and told her how, as part of his training, he'd had to watch an old sci-fi flick and then listen to McKay gab about its applicability to the piloting of microremotes.

Unsympathetic, Bihaly said, "Hey, Emmons, it's a Didinium-eat-Paramecium world," a joke between them ever since he had shown her his mother's sequential micrographs of a predatory ciliate seizing and absorbing another ciliate species nearly twice the Didinium's size. Wasn't he a big boy? Couldn't he take care of himself in the sharkish corporate world?

Later, Emmons, frightened and tentative, hovered over Bihaly's body like a gar above the remains of a hammerhead's kill.

THE NIGHT TESTIMONY OF LEEUWENHOEK. Bihaly stayed anyway, and Emmons dreamed that he was an animalcule in a moist cavern among a population explosion of such creatures, all fidgeting, feeding, and reproducing in a balmy darkness not unlike that of MicroDyne's company pool.

What most upset Emmons about his presence among these nameless microorganisms was the heightening of his own namelessness by their large numbers. The indeterminacy of the Where in which he and all the other tiny beasties multipled also bothered him. But at last a voice spoke over, around, and through him—like God making a proclamation—and he knew that he and the bacteria around him were cliff-dwelling on the speaker's gums.

"I dug some stuff out of the roots of one of my teeth," boomed

the dead Dutch lens grinder and scope maker, Anton van Leeuwenhoek, Emmons's host. *"And in it I found an unbelievably great company of living animalcules, moving more nimbly than I had seen up to now. The biggest sort bent their bodies into curves in going forwards, and the number of animalcules was so extraordinarily great that 'twould take a thousand million of some of them to make up the bulk of a coarse sand grain."*

In his sleep, Emmons shriveled.

"Indeed, all the people living in our United Netherlands are not as many as the living animals I carry in my own mouth." Emmons had once read that Leeuwenhoek attributed his lifelong ruddy health to a hot Ethiop beverage — coffee — that "scalded the animalcules" in his mouth. Emmons's arms reached out for Germaine Bihaly, but they could not find her.

ARTIFICIAL FAUNA IN A DAY-CARE ZOO. For the past seven months, Emmons had stopped nearly every morning on the edge of the day-care courtyard. He watched the kids swarm over the fiberglass backs of pink dinosaurs or the extruded-foam statues of giraffes.

Today he saw a mechanical crane lowering into the courtyard an armored monster so much like a menacing alien crab that most of the kids dashed into the arms of day-care workers to escape it. Emmons knew it for the jungle-gym simulacrum of a dust mite, magnified thousands of times. Its body plates and serrated front claws were gigantic. Detracting from its realism, size aside, was the absence of magnified counterparts for the carpet fibers, hair strands, and skin flakes that cling to living dust mites.

"Educational, don't you think?" said McKay, appearing behind Emmons as if from nowhere.

Emmons stayed mute. He imagined the kids climbing on the dust mite like parasites on parasites, *ad infinitum*. A team of workmen positioned the yawing statue on its base, and Emmons wondered if possibly there weren't a few situations in which it might not be so bad to be parasitized.

THE RELATIVITY OF TIME CONSCIOUSNESS. "When you're down there, Emmons, you'll feel like the Methuselah of the microverse. That's because your eyes and hands will be electronically plugged into the ommatidia and manipulators of your remote. Generations will come and go, but you'll endure.

"Your consciousness—unlike poor Scott Carey's—will be up here in the Sensor and Actuator Center with me, President Sawyer, and the kids out there in the courtyard, but you'll be interacting with critters for whom a second may be an hour and a day a lifetime. That could rattle you."

McKay pointed to the hummingbird feeder on the far edge of the fiberglass zoo and to the rubythroats hovering about it.

"Those guys have a metabolic rate higher than that of any other bird or mammal, Emmons. About twelve times that of a pigeon, about a hundred times that of an elephant. A second for a hummingbird is equivalent to two or three minutes for a whale. Just imagine what an hour down in the microdimensions could be, and remember that as you observe and actuate, okay?

"You've got to have this conception of yourself as being in two places at once, but you've got to subordinate your real-world self to the one on microsafari. Otherwise, you'll screw up. We don't sweat the screw-ups for MicroDyne's sake, Emmons. One day we'll mass-produce microbots in the same kind of volume that the folks in Silicon Valley do microchips. It's *your* well-being we're worried about. We don't want to take a raving loon or a mindless artichoke out of actuator harness."

McKay consulted his watch. Less than two hours to drop-down. It would roll around in either an eyeblink or an ice age, depending on which of his anxieties Emmons set his inner clock by.

TELEMETRY VS. MANNED REDIMENSIONALIZATION. Bihaly could not understand why International MicroDyne, or any other multinational mass-producing flea-sized actuators and invisible sensors, thought it necessary to plug the eyes and mind of a human being into the tiny contraptions that were already evaluating the safety of space-shuttle parts, encoding new functions on gallium-arsenide chips, and overseeing the manufacture of other microbots.

"Hell, Bihaly, to boldly go where no one's ever gone before," Emmons told her. "Why weren't we satisfied to fling only a lander at Mars? Why do our astronauts perform EVAs when a machine could do the job a helluva lot more safely?"

Bihaly continued to object. Emmons wasn't going to shrink, not like that guy in the sf film; in fact, he wasn't going to go bodily to the microdimensions at all. But according to McKay, there was a psychological hazard as forbidding as the prospect of stranding an astronaut on Titan.

"So please tell me," Bihaly said, "why you've chosen to be the first MicroDyne employee to accept the risk?"

"It's pretty simple, really. I want to send back this message to McKay: 'That's one baby step for amoebakind, one gigantic step for yours truly.' Ain't it a shame the lousy drop-down's not going to be televised?"

THE MAP IS NOT THE TERRITORY, THE NAME IS NOT THE THING NAMED. McKay took him into the hermetic, dust-free room in which he was to execute the drop-down and perform his mission. "Dust-free," McKay hurried to qualify, in the sense that only the target area—a bell of clear glass eighteen inches in diameter and six inches high—contained any dust, organic debris, or moisture. As for

Emmons himself, he would not really be in this room but in a nearby operator's booth, jacked into the microremote prototype beneath the glass bell in the center of the otherwise vacant floor of this otherwise featureless chamber. In sterile yellow boots and coveralls, the two men stared down on the bell.

"My Mildendo," Emmons said.

McKay lifted his eyebrows.

"The capital city of Lilliput," Emmons said. He saw that the dome's inner circle had been quartered into pie wedges of jungle, desert, ocean, and a landscape of Mondrianesque microcircuitry. It was a map, a relief map. As a very small boy, he had once taken a Texaco road map from the glove box of his dad's Audi and studied it as if it were a two-dimensional kingdom, convinced that the names of towns were the towns themselves and that dot-sized people really lived there.

A fantasy that his mother's microscopy had given a credibility that even beginning grade school hadn't undermined.

Today the fantasy had come true. The map was the territory (even if the name was still not the thing named.) As he and McKay knelt to examine the bell more closely, Emmons had the unpleasant sensation that he was both a demiurge to this little world and one of its puny inhabitants.

O IS FOR OMMATIDIA. What must it be like to be a gnat gazing up through the bell at McKay and him? Would the ommatidia of one of those tiny insects even register them, or would their images be fragmented into so many repeating split screens that the creature's brain rebelled against the overload?

An ommatidium—as Emmons and half the population of the United States had learned thirty years ago from *An Abecedary of the Near Invisible*—is one of the light-sensitive facets of the compound eye of a fly, a honeybee, or a dragonfly. The dragonfly, his mother's book had said, has more of these honeycomblike optical drupes than does any other insect, nearly thirty thousand.

Emmons loved the word: *Ommatidium*.

Dragonflies saw the world fractured, divvied up, split-screened to infinity, which, of course, was also the way that Emmons lived his life and saw reality. It was the same discontinuous, grainy, particulate world amplified in his father's brilliant reworking of Fredkin's private science, digital physics. And just as thousands of ommatidia working together brought useful information out of the fundamental graininess of the world, so too might Fredkin's Rule precipitate from the countless information bits of the universe one crystalline truth that made perfect sense of the whole.

Emmons said it to himself as a mantra: Ommm-atiddy-*ummm*. Ommm-atiddy-*ummm*. Ommm-atiddy-*ummm*.

"You'll see more when you're down there," McKay said, puffing as he climbed off the floor. "From a human vantage, the bell's pretty damn empty-looking and ordinary-seeming. But there's stuff in there, all right, and you'd best get to it."

Emmons, standing, had a dizzying image of thousands of immense, cockamamie avatars of himself backing away from the dome and fading off into a vast blue muzziness.

INSIDE THE MICROTAUR. Emmons entered the operator's booth and, with McKay's and two businesslike technicians' help, placed himself in harness.

His invisible vehicle—the one at the very center of the sealed dome—was smaller than a weevil nymph, much too tiny for unassisted detection. Its dimensions qualified it as a micro- , rather than a nano- , technological wonder, but it had not been manufactured by the whittle-away process employed for most of MicroDyne's current wares; instead, it had been drexlered—built up atom by atom— from virtual nothingness, so that it had not only a clear exterior shape under the scanning electron microscope but also an intricately made interior, or cockpit, with fine one-to-one correspondences to all the controls in the human-scale operator's cab.

Outwardly, the remote resembled a cross between an armor-plated combat vehicle, moving on treads, and an eight-armed crab. Emmons regarded it as the spider-mite equivalent of a modern tank and the mythological centaur, a kind of high-tech microtaur.

Strapped into his seat and plugged into the vehicle's sensors and actuators, Emmons finally received the signal for drop-down. Obediently, he hit the switches in their proper sequences. *Wham!* Brobdingnagian landscapes bloomed, and he was there, an intruder in the pettiness and majesty of the microdimensions.

DOWN AMONG THE DUST MITES. "That's one baby step for amoeba-kind," Emmons said, but the realization that he was moving forward on tiny caterpillar treads made him cut short the guff. He could float, he could tractor, he could shinny, and, by the unfurling of veil-like wings, he could even fly a little, escaping by a hair the fate of insects so nearly weightless that the Brownian move-ment of random molecular action could buffet them to doom.

What he couldn't do was walk—not as a person walked, anyway—and his first true dimensional shock, all training aside, was the weirdness of this inability. Simulator trials had been helpful but not wholly to the point. After all, the incredible shrinking man had not had to give up his body as he dropped toward the infinitesimal, only the dumb assumption that size bestowed dignity, that whatever was small was willy-nilly of no import. The great whales of the seas and the bacterial populations in the

human gut, Emmons knew, were . . . well, equally mean-
ingless lifeforms.

But not being able to ambulate as human beings usually do—that was a bitch. Down among the dust mites,
you had to motor like dust mites. If you didn't do in Rome
as the Romans did, you could count on going nowhere but
crazy. Frustrated, Emmons slapped at switches like a kid
trying to undercut an upright Babel of ABC blocks.

REVERBERATIONS FROM THE VOICE OF GOD. "Emmons,
you idiot, stop that!" McKay thundered from afar. "I can't
believe you're behaving this way! You haven't done a
blasted thing yet!"

But Emmons could believe it. He was a child again,
overwhelmed by his father's disdain, lost in an utterly mystifying world.

"Easy," God advised, "Caterpillar into Quadrant Dust
Jungle. We'll try the microchip wirings after you've had a
chance to take your bearings there."

Emmons settled down; he headed the microtaur into
Quadrant Dust Jungle, treading through a gray tangle of
pet hairs, grease-coated cotton fibers, cat-flea eggs, pollen
grains, skin scales, severed strands of spider webbing, and
lopsided arches of unidentifiable gunk and fuzz.

Initially, this alien landscape fascinated Emmons
more by its grotesquerie than by its beauty, but the longer
he piloted the microtaur the more grim and monotonous it
seemed. He was reminded of boyhood car trips across the
panhandle of Oklahoma.

Boredom was settling on him when he saw a scale-
freckled dust mite micrometering over the detritus-cob-
bled terrain, and he neared the retiring critter, a sort of
cow-cum-crayfish, just to see what it would do.

It sensed the microtaur and switched directions. Thus
baited, Emmons caterpillared after the mite, careful not to
overtake it in his zeal to enliven things.

Relatively soon, he came among dozens—hundreds—of other such mites grazing through the spun-dust jungle of the quadrant. They were microdimensional cattle, heifers of the waste declensions of the very small.

"Reorient your vehicle and head for the EPROM chips in Quadrant Microprocessor!" demanded God.

Grudgingly, Emmons obeyed.

TAKING THE TOUR. Over a period of days, Emmons's microtaur did a grand promenade of the bell, creeping into the separately sealed Quadrant Microprocessor to perform Herculean cutting, pasting, and wire-connecting labors on the wafers arrayed there and incidentally clabbering them with debris from Dust Mite Territory.

Never mind, said McKay; it was the execution of the preassigned tasks that mattered, not their ultimate results, for under optimum conditions their results were entirely predictable. It was the doing of them by hands-on intervention at "ground zero" that was being tested.

"A is for A-Okay," the godly McKay intoned. "Good job, Emmons."

In the control booth, Emmons took nutrients through I.V. stylets and fatigue-offsetting electrostimulus through the wires externally mapping his nervous system.

His microtaur entered Quadrant Living Desert, where its treads terraced a landscape of sand grains, humus particles, and buried seeds. Beneath this promise squirmed springtails and earthworms, creatures out of the *Dune* books, while beneath them unraveled miles of fungal mycelium and loop snares.

The microtaur's drexlered claws seized nematodes, tardigrades, and Pantagruelian lice. It brought minute soil samples into its collection baskets, then tractored out of Quadrant Living Desert into its final microenvironment, Quadrant Waterworld.

Here, it unshipped flagellate oars to power it through a realm of rotifers, ciliates, and diatoms.

Despite his various energizing hookups, Emmons was exhausted. He hadn't slept for days. If he failed to get some sleep soon, he would begin—even in this hallucinatory realm—to trip out. McKay and MicroDyne were hard taskmasters. He hated them for protracting his mission and for holding him so long in actuator harness. A pox on the bastards.

A RENDEZVOUS WITH *MYTILINA*. Emmons's microtaur sculled through Quadrant Waterworld and all its lightshot, algae-forested grottoes, bucking, releasing ballast, sounding, rising again.

Eventually, it neared a branching filamentous tree, jewel-green in the submarine stillness, on which a single crystal rotifer had gingerly perched. By its thornlike toes resembling paired tails, its red eye-spot like a speck of blood in a minute package of egg white, and its transparent shell or lorica, Emmons knew it for a representative of the genus *Mytilina*.

It bobbed in the currents stirred by the MicroDyne vehicle but otherwise appeared unalarmed even though Emmons understood that the rotifer was aware of his approach. In fact, it actually wished for him to close with it so that they could converse.

"McKay," he said, activating his throat mike, "this is weird. A goddamn rotifer wants to talk with me."

When no one in the Sensor and Actuator Center replied, Emmons knew that the *Mytilina* had willed his isolation from his co-workers and that a meeting with the creature was inevitable.

"Son," it said. "Son, what do you think you're doing?"

HOW CAN THE PERCEIVER KNOW THAT WHICH COMPOSES ITS APPARATUSES OF PERCEPTION? Each separate hairlike process ringing the mouth of the rotifer wiggled at its own ever-altering rate. The sound waves generated by these "smart" vibrations belled out through the water, colliding with, building upon, or subtly damping one another as the *Mytilina* itself required, so that by the time the shaped wave-front struck the sensors of his vehicle, it was— Emmons could think of no other appropriate term—recognizable human speech. On the other hand, Emmons realized that the speaker was actually either God (not McKay & Friends, but the Living God) or his own celebrity father in the guise of a microorganism.

"Maybe this is just my way of trying to help deduce the rule," Emmons replied. "Didn't you always claim that the basic units of reality are very small, that the universe seems continuous only because we can't see the parts from which it's made? It's like a pointillistic painting by Seurat seen from a long way away. Walk closer and you see the dots. The same with the Sunday funnies. Take a magnifying glass and you'll see the specks of colored ink making up Linus's security blanket."

The crimson eye-spot of the bobbing rotifer pulsed, growing and shrinking at the whim of some inner cadence.

"Derek," it said, "can eyes composed of the smallest units in existence perceive those units? Do you really believe such a situation possible or likely?"

(Either the Deity or my dad is scolding me, Emmons thought. Take heed.)

"Remember," the *Mytilina* said, wobbling on its algal perch. "If the universe is a computer, everything happening as a result of its existence is innately incapable of understanding that it runs at the *direction* of that computer. The software, Derek, can't know the hardware—just as ommatidia the size of the smallest grains comprising reality can never see those grains. Put another way, they can never know—perceive—themselves."

KNOW THYSELF. The rotifer talked to Emmons for mind-made ages; the purpose of the mystic computer of the universe—to answer the question posed by its hidden creator—was obvious. But both the answer and the question itself remained obscure to the universe's sentient representatives because the algorithmic program running to provide the answer was still in process. Not even God—as the *Mytilina* itself could attest—had the answer yet, and no one could guess how much longer the program had to run before it burped out its solution.

Emmons's head began to ache. Other wheel animalcules drifted into view, curlicuing toward his father's emerald tree like pixels filling a computer screen.

"Join us, Derek," the rotifer said. "Escape that shell you're hiding in and join us here in Quadrant Waterworld."

It confessed that although he might never learn the question God had posed the universe, being too small to perceive anything that vast and too integral a part of the program in process to have an objective vantage on it, he might yet learn a few things that would repay him for slipping out of harness into the amniotic warmth of the very small.

Emmons, in the submerged microtaur, saw this as the best offer he'd had in years. Doggedly, he started to prise up electrodes, unplug jacks, strip away wiring, and pull out I.V. stylets. Free at last, he would crawl into the ejection tube and shoot himself into the tiny waterworld now harboring both his father and God.

Z IS FOR ZERO, WHICH TO GOD DOES NOT EXIST. McKay ordered two burly technicians into the barricaded control booth. But before they could restrain him, Emmons—sweaty, pop-eyed, thick-tongued—fell back into his padded chair as if siphoned of all memory and will. The operator's cab was a shambles. (His microremote yawed in an emerald orchard of algae and glassy rotifers.) Feverishly, McKay and his cohorts worked to revive Emmons.

Bihaly's appearance wasn't providential—she had been worrying about the drop-down—but McKay's decision to let her in before the company doctor arrived may have been. "Rick," she said, using her private diminutive. "Rick, look at me."

Emmons's eyes opened. Above him, the faces of Bihaly, McKay, and the doctor orbited one another like kaleidoscope jewels. He felt nothing—not relief, gratitude, or panic—only a fine, pervasive nothingness drifting through him like pollen through the foliage of evergreens. So what? Nothingness was okay. It might even be survivable. To God, after all, there was no zero.

Emmons had been down for slightly more than four hours, a fact McKay's blurred watch face withheld from him. Again, no matter. Eventually, his eyes would adjust. Maybe, when they did, Bihaly, who had called him back from that which cannot see itself, would still be there, and with her, he would try to understand all that had ever happened to him.

They're
Made
Out
of
Meat

"They're made out of meat."

"Meat?"

"Meat. They're made out of meat."

"Meat?"

"There's no doubt about it. We picked up several from different parts of the planet, took them aboard our recon vessels, and probed them all the way through. They're completely meat."

"That's impossible. What about the radio signals? The messages to the stars?"

"They use the radio waves to talk, but the signals don't come from them. The signals come from machines."

"So who made the machines? That's who we want to contact."

"*They* made the machines. That's what I'm trying to tell you. Meat made the machines."

"That's ridiculous. How can meat make a machine? You're asking me to believe in sentient meat."

"I'm not asking you. I'm telling you. These creatures

are the only sentient race in that sector, and they're made out of meat."

"Maybe they're like the orfolei. You know, a carbon-based intelligence that goes through a meat stage."

"Nope. They're born meat and they die meat. We studied them for several of their life spans, which didn't take long. Do you have any idea of the life span of meat?"

"Spare me. Okay, maybe they're only part meat. You know, like the weddilei. A meat head with an electron plasma brain inside."

"Nope. We thought of that, since they do have meat heads, like the weddilei. But I told you, we probed them. They're meat all the way through."

"No brain?"

"Oh, there's a brain all right. It's just that the brain is *made out of meat!* That's what I've been trying to tell you."

"So . . . what does the thinking?"

"You're not understanding, are you? You're refusing to deal with what I'm telling you. The brain does the thinking. The meat."

"Thinking meat! You're asking me to believe in thinking meat!"

"Yes, thinking meat! Conscious meat! Loving meat. Dreaming meat. The meat is the whole deal! Are you beginning to get the picture, or do I have to start all over?"

"Omigod. You're serious, then. They're made out of meat."

"Thank you. Finally. Yes. They are indeed made out of meat. And they've been trying to get in touch with us for almost a hundred of their years."

"Omigod. So what does this meat have in mind?"

"First it wants to talk to us. Then I imagine it wants to explore the universe, contact other sentiences, swap ideas and information. The usual."

"We're supposed to talk to meat."

"That's the idea. That's the message they're sending out by radio. 'Hello. Anyone out there? Anybody home?' That sort of thing."

"They actually do talk, then. They use words, ideas, concepts?"

"Oh, yes. Except they do it with meat."

"I thought you just told me they used radio."

"They do, but what do you think is on the radio? Meat sounds. You know how when you slap or flap meat, it makes a noise? They talk by flapping their meat at each other. They can even sing by squirting air through their meat."

"Omigod. Singing meat. This is altogether too much. So what do you advise?"

"Officially or unofficially?"

"Both."

"Officially, we are required to contact, welcome, and log in any and all sentient races or multibeings in this quadrant of the universe, without prejudice, fear, or favor. Unofficially, I advise that we erase the records and forget the whole thing."

"I was hoping you would say that."

"It seems harsh, but there is a limit. Do we really want to make contact with meat?"

"I agree one hundred percent. What's there to say? 'Hello, meat. How's it going?' But will this work? How many planets are we dealing with here?"

"Just one. They can travel to other planets in special meat containers, but they can't live on them. And being meat, they can only travel through C space. Which limits them to the speed of light and makes the possibility of their ever making contact pretty slim. Infinitesimal, in fact."

"So we just pretend there's no one home in the universe."

"That's it."

"Cruel. But you said it yourself, who wants to meet meat? And the ones who have been aboard our vessels, the ones you probed? You're sure they won't remember?"

"They'll be considered crackpots if they do. We went into their heads and smoothed out their meat so that we're just a dream to them."

"A dream to meat!" How strangely appropriate, that we should be meat's dream."

"And we marked the entire sector *unoccupied*."

"Good. Agreed, officially and unofficially. Case closed. Any others? Anyone interesting on that side of the galaxy?"

"Yes, a rather shy but sweet hydrogen core cluster intelligence in a class nine star in G445 zone. Was in contact two galactic rotations ago, wants to be friendly again."

"They always come around."

"And why not? Imagine how unbearably, how unutterably cold the universe would be if one were all alone. . . ."

Tissue
Ablation
and
Variant
Regeneration:
A
Case
Report

At seven A.M. on Thursday morning Mr. Reagan was
wheeled through the swinging doors and down the corridor to operating room six. He was lying flat on the gurney,
and his gaze was fixed on the ceiling; he had the glassy
stare of a man in shock. I was concerned that he had been
given analgesia, but the attendant assured me that he had
not. As we were talking, Mr. Reagan turned his eyes to
me: the pupils were wide, dark as olives, and I recognized
the dilatation of pain and fear. I felt sympathy, but more, I
was relieved that he had not inadvertently been narco-
tized, for it would have delayed the operation for days.

I had yet to scrub and placed my hand on his shoulder to acknowledge his courage. His skin was coarse
beneath the thin sheet that covered him, as the pili erecti
tried in vain to warm the chill we had induced. He shiv-
ered, which was natural, though eventually it would
stop—it must—if we were to proceed with the surgery. I
removed my hand and bent to examine the plastic bag that
hung like a showy organ from the side of the gurney.

There was nearly a liter of pale urine, which assured me that his kidneys were functioning well.

I turned away, and, entering the scrub room, once more conceptualized our plan. There were three teams, one for each pair of extremities and a third for torso and viscera. I headed the latter, which was proper, for the major responsibility for this project was mine. We had chosen to avoid analgesia, the analeptic properties of excruciating pain being well known. There are several well-drawn studies that conclusively demonstrate the superior survival of tissues thus exposed, and I have cited these in a number of my own monographs. In addition, chlorinated hydrocarbons, which still form the bulk of our anesthetics, are tissue-toxic in extremely small quantities. Though these agents clear rapidly in the normal course of post-operative recovery, tissue propagation is too sensitive a phenomenon for us to have risked their use. The patient was offered, routinely, the choice of an Eastern mode of anesthesia, but he demurred. Mr. Reagan has an obdurate faith in things American.

I set the timer above the sink and commenced to scrub. Through the window I watched as the staff went about the final preparations. Two large tables stood along one wall, and on top of them sat the numerous trays of instruments we would use during the operation. Since this was the largest one of its kind any of us at the center had participated in, I had been generous in my estimation of what would be needed. It is always best in such situations to err on the side of caution, and I had ordered duplicates of each pack to be prepared and placed accessibly. Already an enormous quantity of instruments lay unpacked on the tables, divided into general areas of proximity. Thus, uro-logic was placed beside rectal and lower intestinal, and hepatic, splenic, and gastric were grouped together. Thoracic was separate, and orthopedic and vascular were divided into two groups for those teams assigned to the extremities. There were three sets of general instruments—hemostats, forceps, scissors, and the like—and these were on smaller trays that stood close to the operating table. Perched above them, and sorting the instruments chronologically, were the scrub nurses, hooded, masked, and gloves. Behind, and throughout the operating room circulated other, nonsterile personnel, the nurses and technicians who functioned as the extended arm of the team.

75
■
Tissue
Ablation
and
Variant
Regener-
ation:
A
Case
Report

For the dozenth time I scrubbed my cuticles and the space between fingernail and fingertip, then scoured both sides of my forearms to the elbow. The sheet had been removed from Mr. Reagan, and his ventral surface—from neck to foot—was covered by the yellow suds of antiseptic. His pubic parts, chest, and axilla had been shaved earlier, although he had no great plethora of hair to begin with. The artificial light striking his body at that moment recalled to me the jaundiced hue I have seen at times on certain dysfunctional gall bladders, and I looked at my own hands. They seemed brighter, and I rinsed them several times, then backed into the surgical suite.

A nurse approached with a towel, whose corner I grabbed, proceeding to dry methodically each finger. She returned with a glove, spreading the entrance wide as one might the mouth of a fish in order to peer down its throat. I thrust my fingers and thumb into it and she snapped it upon my forearm. She repeated the exchange with the other, and I thanked her, then stood back and waited for the final preparations.

The soap had been removed from his skin, and now Mr. Reagan was being draped with various-sized linens. Two of these were used to fashion a vertical barrier at the mid-point of his neck; behind this, with his head, sat the two anesthesiologists. Since no anesthetic was to be used, their responsibility lay in monitoring his respiratory and cardiovascular status. He would be intubated, and they would make periodic measurements of the carbon dioxide and oxygen content of his blood.

I gave them a nod and they inserted the intracath, through which we would drip a standard, paralytic dose of succinylcholine. We had briefly considered doing without the drug, for its effect, albeit minimal, would still be noticeable on the ablated tissues. Finally, though, we had chosen to use it, reasoning—and experience proved us correct—that we could not rely on the paralysis of pain to immobilize the patient for the duration of the surgery. If there had been a lull, during which time he had chosen to move, hours of careful work might have been destroyed. Prudence dictated a conservative approach.

After initiating the paralytic, Dr. Guevara, the senior anesthesiologist, promptly inserted the endotracheal tube. It passed easily for there was little, if any, muscular resistance. The respirator was turned on and artificial ventilation begun. I told Mr. Reagan, who would be conscious throughout, that we were about to begin.

I stepped to the table and surveyed the body. The chest was exposed, as were the two legs, above which Drs. Ng and Cochise were poised to begin.

"Scalpel," I said, and the tool was slapped into my palm. I transferred it to my other hand. "Forceps."

I bent over the body, mentally drawing a line from the sternal notch to the symphysis pubis. We had studied our approaches for hours, for the incisions were unique and had been used but rarely before. A procedure of this scale required precision in every detail in order that we preserve the maximal amount of viable tissue. I lifted the scalpel and with a firm and steady hand made the first cut.

He had been cooled in part to cause constriction of the small dermal vessels, thus reducing the quantity of blood lost to ooze. We were not, of course, able to use the electric scalpel to cut or coagulate, nor could we tie bleeding vessels, for both would inflict damage to tissue. Within reason, we had chosen planes of incision that avoided major dermal vasculature, and as I retraced my first cut, pressing harder to separate the more stubborn fascial layers, I was reassured by the paucity of blood that was appearing at the margins of the wound. I exchanged my delicate tissue forceps for a larger pair, everting the stratum of skin, fat, and muscle, and continuing my incision until I reached the costochondral junction in the chest and the linea alba in the belly. I made two lateral incisions, one from the pubis, along the inguinal ligament, ending near the anterior superior iliac spine, and the other from the sternal notch, along the inferior border of the clavicle to the anterior edge of the axilla. There was more blood appearing now, and for a moment I aided Dr. Biko in packing the wound. Much of our success at controlling the bleeding depended, however, upon the speed at which I carried out the next stage, and with this in mind, I left him to mop the red fluid and turned to the thorax.

Pectus hypertrophicus occurs perhaps in one in a thousand; Billings, in a recent study of a dozen such cases, links the condition to a congenital aberration of the short arm of chromosome thirteen, and he postulates a correlation between the hypertrophied sternum, a marked preponderance of glabrous skin, and a mild associative cortical defect. He has studied these cases; I have not. Indeed, Mr. Reagan's sternum was only the second in all my experience that would not yield to the Lebsche knife. I asked for the bone snips, and with the help of Dr. Biko was finally able to split the structure. My forehead dripped from the effort, and a circulating nurse dabbed it with a towel.

I applied the wide-armed retractor, and as I ratcheted it apart, I felt a wince of resistance. I asked Dr. Guevara to increase the infusion of muscle relaxant, for we were entering a most crucial part of the operation.

"His pupils are fixed and dilated," he announced.

77

■
Tissue
Ablation
and
Variant
Regener-
ation:
A
Case
Report

I could see his heart, and it was beating normally. "His gases?" I asked.

"O_2 85, CO_2 38, pH 7.37."

"Good," I said. "It's just agony then. Not death." Dr. Guevara nodded above the barrier that separated us, and as he bent to whisper words of encouragement to Mr. Reagan, I looked into the chest. There I paused, as I always seem to do at the sight of that glistening organ. It throbbed and rolled, sensuously, I thought, majestically, and I renewed my vows to treat it kindly. With the tissue forceps I lifted the pericardium and with the curved scissors punctured it. It peeled off smoothly, reminding me fleetingly of the delicate skin that encloses the tip of the male child's penis.

In rapid succession I ligated the inferior vena cava and cross-clamped the descending aorta, just distal to the bronchial arteries. We had decided not to use our bypass system, thus obviating cannulations that would have required lengthy and meticulous suturing. We had opted instead for a complete de-vascularization distal to the thoracic cavity, reasoning that since all the organs and other structures were to be removed anyway, there was no sense in preserving circulation below the heart. I signalled to my colleagues waiting at the lower extremities to begin their dissections.

I isolated the right subclavian artery and vein, ligated them, and did the same on the left. I anastomosed the internal thoracic artery to the ventral surface of the aortic arch, thus providing arterial flow to the chest wall, which we planned to preserve more or less intact. I returned to the descending aorta, choosing 3–0 Ethilon to assure occlusion of the lumen, and oversewed twice. I released the clamp slowly: there was no leakage, and I breathed a sigh of satisfaction. We had completed a crucial stage, isolating the thoracic and cephalic circulation from that of the rest of the body, and the patient's condition remained stable. What was left was the harvesting of his parts.

79
■
Tissue
Ablation
and
Variant
Regener-
ation:
A
Case
Report

I would like to insert here a word on our behalf, aimed not just at the surgical team but at the full technical and administrative apparatus. We had early on agreed that we must approach the dissection assiduously, meaning that in every case we would apply a greater, rather than a lesser, degree of scrupulousness. At the time of the operation no use—other than in transplantation—had been found for many of the organs we were to resect. Such parts as colon, spleen, and vasculature had not then, nor have they yet, struck utilitarian chords in our imaginations. Surely, they will in the future, and with this as our philosophy we determined to discard not even the most seemingly insignificant part. What could not immediately be utilized would be preserved in our banks, waiting for a bright idea to send it to the regeneration tanks.

It was for this reason, and this reason alone, that the operation lasted as long as it did. I would be lying if I claimed that Mr. Reagan was not in constant and excruciating pain. Who would not be to have his skin fileted, his chest cracked, his limbs meticulously dissected and dismembered? In retrospect, I should have carried out a high transection of the spinal cord, thus interrupting most of the nerve fibers to his brain, but I did not think of it beforehand and during the operation was too occupied with other concerns. That he did survive is a testimony to his strength, though I still remember his post-operative shrieks and protestations. We had, of course, already detached his upper limbs, and therefore we ourselves had to dab the streams of tears that flew from his eyes. At that point, there being no further danger of tissue damage, I did order an analgesic.

After I had successfully completed the de-vascularization procedure, thus removing the risk of life-threatening hemorrhage from our fields, I returned to the outer layer of thorax and abdomen. With an Adson forceps I gently retracted the thin sheet of dermis and began to undermine with the scalpel. It was painstaking, but after much time I finally had the entire area freed. It hung limp, drooping like a dewlap, and as I began the final axillary cut that would release it completely, I asked Ms. Narciso, my scrub nurse, to call the technician. He came just as I finished, and I handed him the skin.

I confess that I have less than a full understanding of the technology of organ variation and regeneration. I am a surgeon, not a technologist, and devote the major part of my energies toward refinement and perfection of operative skills. We do, however, live in an age of great scientific achievement, and the iconoclasm of many of my younger colleagues has forced me to cast my gaze more broadly afield. Thus it is that I am not a complete stranger to inductive mitotics and controlled oncogenesis, and I will attempt to convey the fundamentals.

Upon receiving the tissue, the technician transports it to the appropriate room wherein lie the thermo-magnetic protein baths. These are organ specific, distinguished by temperature, pH, magnetic field, and substrate, and designed to suppress cellular activity; specifically, they prolong dormancy at the G1 stage of mitosis. The magnetic field is altered then, such that each cell will arrange itself ninety degrees to it. A concentrated solution of isotonic nucleic and amino acids is then pumped into the tank, and the bath mechanically agitated to diffuse the solute. Several hours are allowed to pass, and the magnetic field is again shifted, attempting to align it with the nucleic loci that govern the latter stages of mitosis. If this is successful, and success is immediately apparent for failure induces rapid and massive necrosis, the organ system will begin to reproduce. This is a macroscopic phenomenon, obvious to the naked eye. I have been present at this critical moment, and it is a simple, yet wondrous, thing to behold.

Different organs regenerate, multiply, in distinctive fashion. In the case of the skin, genesis occurs quite like the polymerization of synthetic fibers, such as nylon and its congeners. The testes grow in a more sequential manner, analogous perhaps to the clustering of grapes along the vine. Muscles seem to laminate, forming thicker and thicker sheets until, if not separated, they collapse upon themselves. Bone propagates as tubules; ligaments, as lianoid strands of great length. All distinct, yet all variations on a theme.

81

■
Tissue
Ablation
and
Variant
Regener-
ation:
A
Case
Report

In the case of our own patient, the outcome, I am pleased to report, was bounteous; this was especially gratifying in light of our guarded prognostications. I was not alone in the skepticism with which I approached the operation, for the tissues and regenerative capacity of an old man are not those of a youngster. During the surgery, when I noticed the friability and general degree of degeneration of his organs, my thoughts were inclined rather pessimistically. I remember wondering, as Dr. Cochise severed the humeral head from the glenoid fossa, inadvertently crushing a quantity of porotic and fragile bone, if our scrupulous planning had not been a waste of effort, that the fruits of our labor would not be commensurate with our toil. Even now, with the benefit of hindsight, I remain astonished at our degree of success. As much as it is a credit to the work of our surgical team, it is, perhaps more so, a tribute to the resilience and fundamental vitality of the human body.

After releasing the dermal layer as described, I proceeded to detach the muscles. The adipose tissue, so slippery and difficult to manipulate, would be removed chemically, thus saving valuable time. As I have mentioned, the risk of hemorrhage—and its threat to Mr. Reagan's life—had been eliminated, but because of the resultant interruption of circulation we were faced with the real possibility of massive tissue necrosis. For this reason we were required to move most expeditiously.

With sweeping but well guided strokes of the scalpel,

I transected the ligamentous origins of Pectoralis Major and Minor, and Serratus Anterior. I located their points of insertion on the scapula and humerus and severed them as well, indicating to Ms. Narciso that we would need the technician responsible for the muscles. She replied that he had already been summoned by Dr. Ng, and I took that moment to peer in his vicinity.

He and Dr. Cochise had been working rapidly, already having completed the spiraling circumferential incisions from groin to toe, thus allowing, in a fashion similar to the peeling of an orange, the removal in toto of the dermal sheath of the leg. The anterior femoral and pelvic musculature had been exposed, and I could see the Sartorius and at least two of the Quadriceps heads dangling. This was good work and I nodded appreciatively, then turned my attention to the abdominal wall.

In terms of time the abdominal muscles presented less of a problem than the thoracic ones, for there were no ribs to contend with. In addition, as long as I was careful not to puncture the viscera, I could enter the peritoneum almost recklessly. I took my scalpel and thrust it upon the xiphoid, near what laymen call the solar plexus, and started the long and penetrating incision down the linea alba, past the umbilicus, to the symphysis pubis. With one hand I lifted the margin of the wound, and with the other delicately sliced the peritoneal membrane. I reflected all the abdominal muscles, the Rectus and Transversus Abdominis, the Obliquus Internus and Externus, and detached them from their bony insertions. Grasping the peritoneum with a long-toothed forceps and peeling it back, I placed two large towel clips in the overlying muscle mass, and then, as an iceman would pick up a block of ice, lifted it above the table, passing it into the hands of the waiting technician. Another was there for the thoracic musculature, and once these were cleared from the table, I turned to the abdominal contents themselves.

83
■
Tissue
Ablation
and
Variant
Regener-
ation:
A
Case
Report

Let me interject a note as to the status of our patient at that time. As deeply as I become involved in the techniques and mechanics of any surgery, I am always, with another part of my mind, aware of the human being who lies at the mercy of the knife. At this juncture in our operation I noticed, by the flaccidity in the muscles on the other half of the abdomen, that the patient was perhaps too deeply relaxed. Always there is a tension in the muscles, and this must be mollified sufficiently to allow the surgeon to operate without undo resistance, but not so much that it endangers the life of the patient. In this case I noted little, if any, resistance, and I asked Dr. Guevara to reduce slightly the rate of infusion of the relaxant. This affected all the muscles, including, of course, the diaphragm and those of the larynx, and Mr. Reagan took the opportunity to attempt to vocalize. Being intubated, he was in no position to do so, yet somehow managed to produce a keening sound that unnerved us all. His face, as reported by Dr. Guevara, became constricted in a horrible rictus, and his eyes seemed to convulse in their sockets. Clearly, he was in excruciating pain, and my heart flew to him as to a valiant soldier.

The agony, I am certain, was not simply corporeal; surely there was a psychological aspect to it, perhaps a psychosis, as he thought upon the systematic dissection and dismemberment of his manifest self. To me, I know it would have been unbearable, and once again I was humbled by his courage and fortitude. And yet there was still so much left to do; neither empathy nor despair were distractions we could afford. Accordingly, I asked Dr. Guevara to increase the infusion rate in order to still Mr. Reagan's cries, and this achieved, I returned my concentration to the table.

By prearrangement Dr. Biko now moved to the opposite side of the patient and began to duplicate there what I had just finished on mine. The sole modification was that he began on the belly wall and proceeded in a cephalad direction, so that by the time I had extirpated the contents of one half of the abdomen, the other would be exposed and ready. With alacrity I began the evisceration.

It would be tedious to chronicle step by step the various dissections, ligations, and severances; these are detailed in a separate monograph, whose reference can be found in the bibliography. Suffice to say that I identified the organs and proceeded with the resections as we had planned. Once freeing the stomach, I was able to remove the spleen and pancreas without much delay. Because of their combined mass, the liver and gall bladder required more time but eventually came out quite nicely. I reflected the proximal small and large intestines downward in order to lay bare the deeper recesses of the upper abdominal cavity and have access to the kidneys and adrenals. I treated gland and organ as a unit, removing each pair together, transecting the ureters high, near the renal pelvices. The big abdominal vessels, vena cava and aorta, were now exposed, and I had to withstand the urge to include them in my dissection. We had previously agreed that this part of the procedure would be assumed by Dr. Biko, who is as skilled and renowned a vascular surgeon as I am an abdominothoracic one, and though they lay temptingly now within my reach, I resisted the lure and turned to accomplish the extirpation of the alimentary tract.

We did not, as many had urged, remove the cavitous segment of the digestive apparatus as a whole. After consultation with our technical staff we determined that it would be more practical and successful if we proceeded segmentally. Thus, we divided the tract into three parts: stomach, including the esophageal segment just distal to the diaphragm; small intestine, from pylorus to ileocecal valve; and colon, from cecum to anus. These were dutifully resected and sent to the holding banks, where they await future purpose and need.

As I harvested the internal abdominal musculature, the Psoas, Iliacus, Quadratus Lumborum, I let my mind wander for a few moments. We were nearing the end of the operation, and I felt the luxury of certain philosophical meditations. I thought about the people of the world, the hungry, the cold, those without shelter or goods to meet the exigencies of daily life. What are our responsibilities to them, we the educated, the skilled, the possessors? It is said, and I believe, that no man stands above any other. What then can one person do for the many? Listen, I suppose. Change.

85

■
Tissue
Ablation
and
Variant
Regener-
ation:
A
Case
Report

I have found in my profession, as I am certain exists in all others, that to not adapt is to become obsolete. I have known many colleagues, who, unwilling or unable to grapple with innovation, have gone the way of the penny. Tenacity, in some an admirable quality, is no substitute for the ability to change, for what in one age might be considered tenacious in another would most certainly be called cowardly. I thought upon our patient, whose fortunes had so altered since the years of my training, and considered further the question of justice. Could an act of great altruism, albeit forced and involuntary, balance a generation of infamy? How does the dedication of one's own body to the masses weigh upon the scales of sin and repentance?

My brow furrowed, for these questions were far more difficult to me than the operation itself, and had it not been for Ms. Narciso, who spoke up in a timely voice, I might have broken the sterile field by wiping with my own hand the perspiration on my forehead.

"Shall we move to the pelvis, Doctor?" she said, breaking my reverie.

"Yes," I replied softly, turning momentarily from the table to recover, while a nurse mopped the moist skin of my face.

The bladder, of course, had been decompressed by the catheter that had been passed prior to surgery, and once I pierced the floor of the peritoneum, it lay beneath my blade like a flat and flaccid tire. I severed it quickly, taking care to include the prostate, seminal vesicles, ureters, and membranous urethra in the resection. A technician carried these to an intermediate room, where a surgeon was standing by to separate the structures before they were taken to their respective tanks. What remained was to take the penis, which was relatively simple, and testes, which required more care so as not to disrupt the delicate tunica that surrounded them. This done, I straightened my back for perhaps the first time since we began and assessed our progress.

When one becomes so engrossed in a task, so keyed and focused that huge chunks of time pass unaware, it is a jarring feeling, akin to waking from a vivid and lifelike dream, to return to reality. I have felt this frequently during surgeries, but never as I did this time. Hours had passed, personnel had changed, perhaps even the moon outside had risen, in a span that for me was marked in moments. I looked for Drs. Ng and Cochise and was informed that they had left the surgical suite some time ago. I recalled this only dimly, but when I looked to their work was pleased to find that it had been performed most adequately. All limbs were gone, and the glenoid fossae, where the shoulders had been de-articulated, were sealed as we had discussed. Across from me Dr. Biko was just completing the abdominal vascular work. I nodded to myself, and using an interior approach, detached the muscles of the lumbar spine, then asked for the bone saw.

We transected the spinal cord between the second and third lumbar vertebrae, thus preserving the major portion of attachments of the diaphragm. This, of course, was vital, if, as we had planned, Mr. Reagan was to retain the ability to respire. It is well known that those who leave surgery still attached to the respirator, which surely would have been the case if we had been sloppy in this last part

87

■
**Tissue
Ablation
and
Variant
Regener-
ation:
A
Case
Report**

of the operation, do poorly thereafter, often dying in the immediate post-operative period. In this case especially, such an outcome would have been particularly heinous, for it would have deprived this brave man of the fate and rewards most deservedly his.

I am nearing the conclusion of our report, and it must be obvious that I have failed to include each and every nerve, ligament, muscle, and vessel that we removed. If it seems a critical error, I can only say that it is a purposeful one, intended to improve the readability of this document. Hopefully, I have made it more accessible to the lay that exist outside the cloister of our medical world, but those who crave more detailed information I refer to the *Archives of Ablative Technique,* vol. 113, number 6, pp. 67–104, or, indeed, to any comprehensive atlas of anatomy.

We sealed the chest wall and sub-diaphragmatic area with a synthetic polymer (XRO 137, by Dow) that is thin but surprisingly durable and impervious to bacterial invasion. We did a towel count to make certain that none were inadvertently left inside the patient, though at that point there was little of him that could escape our attention, then Dr. Guevara inserted the jugular catheter that would be used for nourishment and medication. Dr. Biko fashioned a neat little fistula from the right external carotid artery, which, because we had taken the kidneys, would be used for dialysis. These completed, we did a final blood gas and vital sign check, each of which was acceptable, and I stepped back from the table.

"Thank you all very much," I said, and turned to Mr. Reagan as I peeled back my gloves. He was beginning to recover from the drug-induced paralysis, and his face seemed to recoil from mine as I bent toward him. I have seen this before in surgery, where the strange apparel, the hooded and masked faces, often cause fright in a patient. It is especially common in the immediate post-operative period, when unusual bodily sensations and a frequently marked mental disorientation play such large roles. I was therefore not alarmed to see our patient's features contort as I drew near.

"It is over," I said gently, keeping my words simple and clear. "It went well. We will take the tube from your mouth, but don't try to talk. Your throat will be quite sore for a while, and it will hurt."

I placed a hand on his cheek, which felt clammy even though the skin was flushed, and Dr. Guevara withdrew the tube. By that time the muscle relaxant had worn off completely, and Mr. Reagan responded superbly by beginning to breathe on his own immediately. Shortly thereafter, he began to shriek.

There are some surgeons I know, and many other physicians, who believe in some arcane manner in the strengthening properties of pain. They assert that it fortifies the organism, steeling it, as it were, to the insults of disease. Earlier, I mentioned the positive association between pain and tissue survival, but this obtains solely with respect to ablative surgery. It has not been demonstrated under myriad other circumstances, and this despite literally hundreds of studies to prove it so. The only possible conclusion, the only scientific one, is that pain, apart from its value as a mechanism of warning, has none of those attributes the algophilists ascribe to it. In my mind these practitioners are reprehensible moralists and should be barred from those specialties, such as surgery, where the problem is ubiquitous.

Needless to say, as soon as Mr. Reagan began to cry, I ordered a potent and long-lasting analgesic. For the first time since we began his face quieted and his eyes closed, and though I never questioned him on it, I like to think that his dreams were sweet and proud at what he, one man, had been able to offer thousands.

Save for the appendix, this is the whole of my report. Once again I apologize for omissions and refer the inter-

ested reader to the ample bibliography. We have demonstrated, I believe, the viability of extensive tissue ablation
and its value in providing substrate for inductive and variant mitotics. Although it is an arduous undertaking, I
believe it holds promise for selected patients in the future.

89
■
Tissue
Ablation
and
Variant
Regener-
ation:
A
Case
Report

Appendix

As of the writing of this document, the following items and
respective quantities have been produced by our regeneration systems:

Item	*Source*	*Quantity*
Oil, refined	Testes: seminiferous tubules	3761 liters
Perfumes and scents	Same	162 grams
Meat, including patties, filets, and ground round	Muscles	13,318 kilograms
Storage jugs	Bladder	2732
Balls, inflatable (recreational use)	Same	325
Cord, multi-purposed	Ligaments	1.2 kilometers
Roofing material, e.g., for tents; flexible siding	Skin: full thickness	3.6 sq. kilometers
Prophylactics	Skin: stratum granulosum	18,763 cartons of 10 ea.
Various enzymes, medications, hormones	Pancreas, adrenal glands, hepatic tissue	272 grams
Flexible struts and housing supports	Bone	453 sq. meters

The vast majority of these have been distributed,

principally to countries of the third world but also to impoverished areas of our own nation. A follow-up study to update our data and provide a geographical breakdown by item will be conducted within the year.

Speech Sounds

There was trouble aboard the Washington Boulevard bus. Rye had expected trouble sooner or later in her journey. She had put off going until loneliness and hopelessness drove her out. She believed she might have one group of relatives left alive—a brother and his two children twenty miles away in Pasadena. That was a day's journey one-way, if she were lucky. The unexpected arrival of the bus as she left her Virginia Road home had seemed to be a piece of luck—until the trouble began.

Two young men were involved in a disagreement of some kind, or, more likely, a misunderstanding. They stood in the aisle, grunting and gesturing at each other, each in his own uncertain T stance as the bus lurched over the potholes. The driver seemed to be putting some effort into keeping them off balance. Still, their gestures stopped just short of contact—mock punches, hand games of intimidation to replace lost curses.

People watched the pair, then looked at one another and made small anxious sounds. Two children whimpered.

Rye sat a few feet behind the disputants and across from the back door. She watched the two carefully, knowing the fight would begin when someone's nerve broke or someone's hand slipped or someone came to the end of his limited ability to communicate. These things could happen anytime.

One of them happened as the bus hit an especially large pothole and one man, tall, thin, and sneering, was thrown into his shorter opponent.

Instantly, the shorter man drove his left fist into the disintegrating sneer. He hammered his larger opponent as though he neither had nor needed any weapon other than his left fist. He hit quickly enough, hard enough to batter his opponent down before the taller man could regain his balance or hit back even once.

People screamed or squawked in fear. Those nearby scrambled to get out of the way. Three more young men roared in excitement and gestured wildly. Then, somehow, a second dispute broke out between two of these three—probably because one inadvertently touched or hit the other.

As the second fight scattered frightened passengers, a woman shook the driver's shoulder and grunted as she gestured toward the fighting.

The driver grunted back through bared teeth. Frightened, the woman drew away.

Rye, knowing the methods of bus drivers, braced herself and held on to the crossbar of the seat in front of her. When the driver hit the brakes, she was ready and the combatants were not. They fell over seats and onto screaming passengers, creating even more confusion. At least one more fight started.

The instant the bus came to a full stop, Rye was on her feet, pushing the back door. At the second push, it opened and she jumped out, holding her pack in one arm. Several other passengers followed, but some stayed on the bus. Buses were so rare and irregular now, people rode

when they could, no matter what. There might not be
another bus today — or tomorrow. People started walking,
and if they saw a bus they flagged it down. People making
intercity trips like Rye's from Los Angeles to Pasadena
made plans to camp out, or risked seeking shelter with
locals who might rob or murder them.

The bus did not move, but Rye moved away from it.
She intended to wait until the trouble was over and get on
again, but if there was shooting, she wanted the protection
of a tree. Thus, she was near the curb when a battered blue
Ford on the other side of the street made a U-turn and
pulled up in front of the bus. Cars were rare these days —
as rare as a severe shortage of fuel and of relatively unim-
paired mechanics could make them. Cars that still ran
were as likely to be used as weapons as they were to serve
as transportation. Thus, when the driver of the Ford beckoned to Rye, she moved away warily. The driver got out —
a big man, young, neatly bearded with dark, thick hair. He
wore a long overcoat and a look of wariness that matched
Rye's. She stood several feet from him, waiting to see what
he would do. He looked at the bus, now rocking with the
combat inside, then at the small cluster of passengers who
had gotten off. Finally he looked at Rye again.

She returned his gaze, very much aware of the old
forty-five automatic her jacket concealed. She watched his
hands.

He pointed with his left hand toward the bus. The
dark-tinted windows prevented him from seeing what was
happening inside.

His use of the left hand interested Rye more than his
obvious question. Left-handed people tended to be less
impaired, more reasonable and comprehending, less driven by frustration, confusion, and anger.

She imitated his gesture, pointing toward the bus
with her own left hand, then punching the air with both
fists.

The man took off his coat, revealing a Los Angeles Police Department uniform complete with baton and service revolver.

Rye took another step back from him. There was no more LAPD, no more *any* large organization, governmental or private. There were neighborhood patrols and armed individuals. That was all.

The man took something from his coat pocket, then threw the coat into the car. Then he gestured Rye back, back toward the rear of the bus. He had something made of plastic in his hand. Rye did not understand what he wanted until he went to the rear door of the bus and beckoned her to stand there. She obeyed mainly out of curiosity. Cop or not, maybe he could do something to stop the stupid fighting.

He walked around the front of the bus, to the street side where the driver's window was open. There, she thought she saw him throw something into the bus. She was still trying to peer through the tinted glass when people began stumbling out the rear door, choking and weeping. Gas.

Rye caught an old woman who would have fallen, lifted two little children down when they were in danger of being knocked down and trampled. She could see the bearded man helping people at the front door. She caught a thin old man shoved out by one of the combatants. Staggered by the old man's weight, she was barely able to get out of the way as the last of the young men pushed his way out. This one, bleeding from nose and mouth, stumbled into another and they grappled blindly, still sobbing from the gas.

The bearded man helped the bus driver out through the front door, though the driver did not seem to appreciate his help. For a moment, Rye thought there would be another fight. The bearded man stepped back and watched the driver gesture threateningly, watched him shout in wordless anger.

The bearded man stood still, made no sound, refused to respond to clearly obscene gestures. The least impaired people tended to do this—stand back unless they were physically threatened and let those with less control scream and jump around. It was as though they felt it beneath them to be as touchy as the less comprehending. This was an attitude of superiority and that was the way people like the bus driver perceived it. Such "superiority" was frequently punished by beatings, even by death. Rye had had close calls of her own. As a result, she never went unarmed. And in this world where the only likely common language was body language, being armed was often enough. She had rarely had to draw her gun or even display it.

The bearded man's revolver was on constant display. Apparently that was enough for the bus driver. The driver spat in disgust, glared at the bearded man for a moment longer, then strode back to his gas-filled bus. He stared at it for a moment, clearly wanting to get in, but the gas was still too strong. Of the windows, only his tiny driver's window actually opened. The front door was open, but the rear door would not stay open unless someone held it. Of course, the air conditioning had failed long ago. The bus would take some time to clear. It was the driver's property, his livelihood. He had pasted old magazine pictures of items he would accept as fare on its sides. Then he would use what he collected to feed his family or to trade. If his bus did not run, he did not eat. On the other hand, if the inside of his bus was torn apart by senseless fighting, he would not eat very well either. He was apparently unable to perceive this. All he could see was that it would be some time before he could use his bus again. He shook his fist at the bearded man and shouted. There seemed to be words in his shout, but Rye could not understand them. She did not know whether this was his fault or hers. She had heard so little coherent human speech for the past three years, she was no longer certain how well she recognized it, no longer certain of the degree of her own impairment.

The bearded man sighed. He glanced toward his car, then beckoned to Rye. He was ready to leave, but he wanted something from her first. No. No, he wanted her to leave with him. Risk getting into his car when, in spite of his uniform, law and order were nothing—not even words any longer.

She shook her head in a universally understood negative, but the man continued to beckon.

She waved him away. He was doing what the less-impaired rarely did—drawing potentially negative attention to another of his kind. People from the bus had begun to look at her.

One of the men who had been fighting tapped another on the arm, then pointed from the bearded man to Rye, and finally held up the first two fingers of his right hand as though giving two-thirds of a Boy Scout salute. The gesture was very quick, its meaning obvious even at a distance. She had been grouped with the bearded man. Now what?

The man who had made the gesture started toward her.

She had no idea what he intended, but she stood her ground. The man was half a foot taller than she was and perhaps ten years younger. She did not imagine she could outrun him. Nor did she expect anyone to help her if she needed help. The people around her were all strangers.

She gestured once—a clear indication to the man to stop. She did not intend to repeat the gesture. Fortunately, the man obeyed. He gestured obscenely and several other men laughed. Loss of verbal language had spawned a whole new set of obscene gestures. The man, with stark simplicity, had accused her of sex with the bearded man and had suggested she accommodate the other men present—beginning with him.

Rye watched him wearily. People might very well stand by and watch if he tried to rape her. They would also stand and watch her shoot him. Would he push things that far?

He did not. After a series of obscene gestures that brought him no closer to her, he turned contemptuously and walked away.

And the bearded man still waited. He had removed her service revolver, holster and all. He beckoned again, both hands empty. No doubt his gun was in the car and within easy reach, but his taking it off impressed her. Maybe he was all right. Maybe he was just alone. She had been alone herself for three years. The illness had stripped her, killing her children one by one, killing her husband, her sister, her parents . . .

The illness, if it was an illness, had cut even the living off from one another. As it swept over the country, people hardly had time to lay blame on the Soviets (though they were falling silent along with the rest of the world), on a new virus, a new pollutant, radiation, divine retribution. . . . The illness was stroke-swift in the way it cut people down and stroke-like in some of its effects. But it was highly specific. Language was always lost or severely impaired. It was never regained. Often there was also paralysis, intellectual impairment, death.

Rye walked toward the bearded man, ignoring the whistling and applauding of two of the young men and their thumbs-up signs to the bearded man. If he had smiled at them or acknowledged them in any way, she would almost certainly have changed her mind. If she had let herself think of the possible deadly consequences of getting into a stranger's car, she would have changed her mind. Instead, she thought of the man who lived across the street from her. He rarely washed since his bout with the illness. And he had gotten into the habit of urinating wherever he happened to be. He had two women already—one tending each of his large gardens. They put up with him in exchange for his protection. He had made it clear that he wanted Rye to become his third woman.

She got into the car and the bearded man shut the door. She watched as he walked around to the driver's door—watched for his sake because his gun was on the seat beside her. And the bus driver and a pair of young men had come a few steps closer. They did nothing, though, until the bearded man was in the car. Then one of them threw a rock. Others followed his example, and as the car drove away, several rocks bounced off harmlessly.

When the bus was some distance behind them, Rye wiped sweat from her forehead and longed to relax. The bus would have taken her more than halfway to Pasadena. She would have had only ten miles to walk. She wondered how far she would have to walk now—and wondered if walking a long distance would be her only problem.

At Figueroa and Washington, where the bus normally made a left turn, the bearded man stopped, looked at her, and indicated that she should choose a direction. When she directed him left and he actually turned left, she began to relax. If he was willing to go where she directed, perhaps he was safe.

As they passed blocks of burned, abandoned buildings, empty lots, and wrecked or stripped cars, he slipped a gold chain over his head and handed it to her. The pendant attached to it was a smooth, glassy, black rock. Obsidian. His name might be Rock or Peter or Black, but she decided to think of him as Obsidian. Even her sometimes useless memory would retain a name like Obsidian.

She handed him her own name symbol—a pin in the shape of a large golden stalk of wheat. She had bought it long before the illness and the silence began. Now she wore it, thinking it was as close as she was likely to come to Rye. People like Obsidian who had not known her before probably thought of her as Wheat. Not that it mattered. She would never hear her name spoken again.

Obsidian handed her pin back to her. He caught her hand as she reached for it and rubbed his thumb over her calluses.

He stopped at First Street and asked which way again. Then, after turning right as she had indicated, he parked near the Music Center. There, he took a folded paper from the dashboard and unfolded it. Rye recognized it as a street map, though the writing on it meant nothing to her. He flattened the map, took her hand again, and put her index finger on one spot. He touched her, touched himself, poined toward the floor. In effect, "We are here." She knew he wanted to know where she was going. She wanted to tell him, but she shook her head sadly. She had lost reading and writing. That was her most serious impairment and her most painful. She had taught history at UCLA. She had done freelance writing. Now she could not even read her own manuscripts. She had a houseful of books that she could neither read nor bring herself to use as fuel. And she had a memory that would not bring back to her much of what she had read before.

She stared at the map, trying to calculate. She had been born in Pasadena, had lived for fifteen years in Los Angeles. Now she was near L.A. Civic Center. She knew the relative positions of the two cities, knew streets, directions, even knew to stay away from freeways which might be blocked by wrecked cars and destroyed overpasses. She ought to know how to point out Pasadena even though she could not recognize the word.

Hesitantly, she placed her hand over a pale orange patch in the upper right corner of the map. That should be right. Pasadena.

Obsidian lifted her hand and looked under it, then

folded the map and put it back on the dashboard. He could read, she realized belatedly. He could probably write, too. Abruptly, she hated him—deep, bitter hatred. What did literacy mean to him—a grown man who played cops and robbers? But he was literate and she was not. She never would be. She felt sick to her stomach with hatred, frustration, and jealousy. And only a few inches from her hand was a loaded gun.

She held herself still, staring at him, almost seeing his blood. But her rage crested and ebbed and she did nothing.

Obsidian reached for her hand with hesitant familiarity. She looked at him. Her face had already revealed too much. No person still living in what was left of human society could fail to recognize that expression, that jealousy.

She closed her eyes wearily, drew a deep breath. She had experienced longing for the past, hatred of the present, growing hopelessness, purposelessness, but she had never experienced such a powerful urge to kill another person. She had left her home, finally, because she had come near to killing herself. She had found no reason to stay alive. Perhaps that was why she had gotten into Obsidian's car. She had never before done such a thing.

He touched her mouth and made chatter motions with thumb and fingers. Could she speak?

She nodded and watched his milder envy come and go. Now both had admitted what it was not safe to admit, and there had been no violence. He tapped his mouth and forehead and shook his head. He did not speak or comprehend spoken language. The illness had played with them, taking away, she suspected, what each valued most.

She plucked at his sleeve, wondering why he had decided on his own to keep the LAPD alive with what he had left. He was sane enough otherwise. Why wasn't he at home raising corn, rabbits, and children? But she did not know how to ask. Then he put his hand on her thigh and she had another question to deal with.

She shook her head. Disease, pregnancy, helpless, solitary agony . . . no.

He massaged her thigh gently and smiled in obvious disbelief.

No one had touched her for three years. She had not wanted anyone to touch her. What kind of world was this to chance bringing a child into even if the father were willing to stay and help raise it? It was too bad, though. Obsidian could not know how attractive he was to her — young, probably younger than she was, clean, asking for what he wanted rather than demanding it. But none of that mattered. What were a few moments of pleasure measured against a lifetime of consequences?

He pulled her closer to him and for a moment she let herself enjoy the closeness. He smelled good — male and good. She pulled away reluctantly.

He sighed, reached toward the glove compartment. She stiffened, not knowing what to expect, but all he took out was a small box. The writing on it meant nothing to her. She did not understand until he broke the seal, opened the box, and took out a condom. He looked at her and she first looked away in surprise. Then she giggled. She could not remember when she had last giggled.

He grinned, gestured toward the backseat, and she laughed aloud. Even in her teens, she had disliked backseats of cars. But she looked around at the empty streets and ruined buildings, then she got out and into the backseat. He let her put the condom on him, then seemed surprised at her eagerness.

Sometime later, they sat together, covered by his coat, unwilling to become clothed near-strangers again just yet. He made rock-the-baby gestures and looked questioningly at her.

She swallowed, shook her head. She did not know how to tell him her children were dead.

He took her hand and drew a cross in it with his

index finger, then made his baby-rocking gesture again.

She nodded, held up three fingers, then turned away, trying to shut out a sudden flood of memories. She had told herself that the children growing up now were to be pitied. They would run through the downtown canyons with no real memory of what the buildings had been or even how they had come to be. Today's children gathered books as well as wood to be burned as fuel. They ran through the streets chasing one another and hooting like chimpanzees. They had no future. They were now all they would ever be.

He put his hand on her shoulder and she turned suddenly, fumbling for his small box, then urging him to make love to her again. He could give her forgetfulness and pleasure. Until now, nothing had been able to do that. Until now, every day had brought her closer to the time when she would do what she had left home to avoid doing: putting her gun in her mouth and pulling the trigger.

She asked Obsidian if he would come home with her, stay with her.

He looked surprised and pleased once he understood. But he did not answer at once. Finally he shook his head as she had feared he might. He was probably having too much fun playing cops and robbers and picking up women.

She dressed in silent disappointment, unable to feel any anger toward him. Perhaps he already had a wife and a home. That was likely. The illness had been harder on men than on women—had killed more men, had left male survivors more severely impaired. Men like Obsidian were rare. Women either settled for less or stayed alone. If they found an Obsidian, they did what they could to keep him. Rye suspected he had someone younger, prettier keeping him.

He touched her while she was strapping her gun on and asked with a complicated series of gestures whether it was loaded.

She nodded grimly.

He patted her arm.

She asked once more if he would come home with her, this time using a different series of gestures. He had seemed hesitant. Perhaps he could be courted.

He got out and into the front seat without responding.

She took her place in front again, watching him. Now he plucked at his uniform and looked at her. She thought she was being asked something, but did not know what it was.

He took off his badge, tapped it with one finger, then tapped his chest. Of course.

She took the badge from his hand and pinned her wheat stalk to it. If playing cops and robbers was his only insanity, let him play. She would take him, uniform and all. It occurred to her that she might eventually lose him to someone he would meet as he had met her. But she would have him for a while.

He took the street map down again, tapped it, pointed vaguely northeast toward Pasadena, then looked at her.

She shrugged, tapped his shoulder, then her own, and held up her index and second fingers tight together, just to be sure.

He grasped the two fingers and nodded. He was with her.

She took the map from him and threw it onto the dashboard. She pointed back southwest—back toward home. Now she did not have to go to Pasadena. Now she could go on having a brother there and two nephews— three right-handed males. Now she did not have to find out for certain whether she was as alone as she feared. Now she was not alone.

Obsidian took Hill Street south, then Washington west, and she leaned back, wondering what it would be like to have someone again. With what she had scavenged, what she had preserved, and what she grew, there was easily enough food for them. There was certainly room enough in a four-bedroom house. He could move his possessions in. Best of all, the animal across the street would pull back and possibly not force her to kill him.

Obsidian had drawn her closer to him and she had put her head on his shoulder when suddenly he braked hard, almost throwing her off the seat. Out of the corner of her eye, she saw that someone had run across the street in front of the car. One car on the street and someone had to run in front of it.

Straightening up, Rye saw that the runner was a woman, fleeing from an old frame house to a boarded-up storefront. She ran silently, but the man who followed her a moment later shouted what sounded like garbled words as he ran. He had something in his hand. Not a gun. A knife, perhaps.

The woman tried a door, found it locked, looked around desperately, finally snatched up a fragment of glass broken from the storefront window. With this she turned to face her pursuer. Rye thought she would be more likely to cut her own hand than to hurt anyone else with the glass.

Obsidian jumped from the car, shouting. It was the first time Rye had heard his voice—deep and hoarse from disuse. He made the same sound over and over the way some speechless people did, "Da, da, da!"

Rye got out of the car as Obsidian ran toward the couple. He had drawn his gun. Fearful, she drew her own and released the safety. She looked around to see who else might be attracted to the scene. She saw the man glance at Obsidian, then suddenly lunge at the woman. The woman jabbed his face with her glass, but he caught her arm and managed to stab her twice before Obsidian shot him.

The man doubled, then toppled, clutching his abdomen. Obsidian shouted, then gestured Rye over to help the woman.

Rye moved to the woman's side, remembering that she had little more than bandages and antiseptic in her pack. But the woman was beyond help. She had been stabbed with a long, slender boning knife.

She touched Obsidian to let him know the woman was dead. He had bent to check the wounded man who lay still and also seemed dead. But as Obsidian looked around to see what Rye wanted, the man opened his eyes. Face contorted, he seized Obsidian's just-holstered revolver and fired. The bullet caught Obsidian in the temple and he collapsed.

It happened just that simply, just that fast. An instant later, Rye shot the wounded man as he was turning the gun on her.

And Rye was alone—with three corpses.

She knelt beside Obsidian, dry-eyed, frowning, trying to understand why everything had suddenly changed. Obsidian was gone. He had died and left her—like everyone else.

Two very small children came out of the house from which the man and woman had run—a boy and girl perhaps three years old. Holding hands, they crossed the street toward Rye. They stared at her, then edged past her and went to the dead woman. The girl shook the woman's arm as though trying to wake her.

This was too much. Rye got up, feeling sick to her stomach with grief and anger. If the children began to cry, she thought she would vomit.

They were on their own, those two kids. They were old enough to scavenge. She did not need any more grief. She did not need a stranger's children who would grow up to be hairless chimps.

She went back to the car. She could drive home, at least. She remembered how to drive.

The thought that Obsidian should be buried occurred to her before she reached the car, and she did vomit.

She had found and lost the man so quickly. It was as

though she had been snatched from comfort and security and given a sudden, inexplicable beating. Her head would not clear. She could not think.

Somehow, she made herself go back to him, look at him. She found herself on her knees beside him with no memory of having knelt. She stroked his face, his beard. One of the children made a noise and she looked at them, at the woman who was probably their mother. The children looked back at her, obviously frightened. Perhaps it was their fear that reached her finally.

She had been about to drive away and leave them. She had almost done it, almost left two toddlers to die. Surely there had been enough dying. She would have to take the children home with her. She would not be able to live with any other decision. She looked around for a place to bury three bodies. Or two. She wondered if the murderer were the children's father. Before the silence, the police had always said some of the most dangerous calls they went out on were domestic disturbance calls. Obsidian should have known that—not that the knowledge would have kept him in the car. It would not have held her back either. She could not have watched the woman murdered and done nothing.

She dragged Obsidian toward the car. She had nothing to dig with her, and no one to guard for her while she dug. Better to take the bodies with her and bury them next to her husband and her children. Obsidian would come home with her after all.

When she had gotten him onto the floor in the back, she returned for the woman. The little girl, thin, dirty, solemn, stood up and unknowingly gave Rye a gift. As Rye began to drag the woman by her arms, the little girl screamed, "No!"

Rye dropped the woman and stared at the girl.

"No!" the girl repeated. She came to stand beside the woman. "Go away!" she told Rye.

"Don't talk," the little boy said to her. There was no blurring or confusing of sounds. Both children had spoken and Rye had understood. The boy looked at the dead murderer and moved further from him. He took the girl's hand. "Be quiet," he whispered.

Fluent speech! Had the woman died because she could talk and had taught her children to talk? Had she been killed by a husband's festering anger or by a stranger's jealous rage? And the children . . . they must have been born after the silence. Had the disease run its course, then? Or were these children simply immune? Certainly they had had time to fall sick and silent. Rye's mind leaped ahead. What if children of three or fewer years were safe and able to learn language? What if all they needed were teachers? Teachers and protectors.

Rye glanced at the dead murderer. To her shame, she thought she could understand some of the passions that must have driven him, whoever he was. Anger, frustration, hopelessness, insane jealousy . . . how many more of him were there—people willing to destroy what they could not have?

Obsidian had been the protector, had chosen that role for who knew what reason. Perhaps putting on an obsolete uniform and patrolling the empty streets had been what he did instead of putting a gun into his mouth. And now that there was something worth protecting, he was gone.

She had been a teacher. A good one. She had been a protector, too, though only of herself. She had kept herself alive when she had no reason to live. If the illness let these children alone, she could keep them alive.

Somehow she lifted the dead woman into her arms and placed her on the backseat of the car. The children began to cry, but she knelt on the broken pavement and whispered to them, fearful of frightening them with the harshness of her long-unused voice.

"It's all right," she told them. "You're going with us, too. Come on." She lifted them both, one in each arm. They were so light. Had they been getting enough to eat?

The boy covered her mouth with his hand, but she moved her face away. "It's all right for me to talk," she told him. "As long as no one's around, it's all right." She put the boy down on the front seat of the car and he moved over without being told to, to make room for the girl. When they were both in the car Rye leaned against the window, looking at them, seeing that they were less afraid now, that they watched her with at least as much curiosity as fear.

"I'm Valerie Rye," she said, savoring the words. "It's all right for you to talk to me."

STEPHEN DIXON

4

The
Hole

The City Planetarium blew up. I was sitting across the street on a park bench at the time. The blast shook the area so hard that my tie and newspaper flew in my face. When I peeled them away I saw pieces of the planetarium's gilded dome dropping around me and flames shooting out of the now domeless theater, in seconds disintegrating the upper branches of the city's oldest and tallest trees.

A woman ran across the street from Planetarium Square. "Two men," she said. "I saw them myself light the dynamite and drive off in a big car. They wore hats and didn't care who was hurt, who was inside," and she beat on her temples and collapsed into my arms.

I took down her name, address, and the information she gave, and tried consoling her. But the tighter I held her and the more comforting words I used, the more hysterically she sobbed.

"Excuse me," I said, "but I'm a policeman. On vacation now, which accounts for my civilian dress. But technically on duty all the time, so I have to get over there to

see how I can help," and I sat her on the bench and started to cross the street.

Behind me she yelled "Don't leave—I'm afraid. Your
duty is as much to protect me as to help them. Because
who knows where those men might strike next. Maybe
right here," and she jumped off the bench. "Or even down
there," and she jumped off the subway grating and darted
into the street. "Or even here, or over here, or right here,"
and she jumped from the sidewalk to the street to the
sidewalk again before she ran screaming into the park.

The fire in the planetarium theater had leveled off to
a small steady blaze. The building was made of poured
concrete, so once the theater seats, carpet and wall paint
went up, there wasn't much left to burn but the wood
floor.

The planetarium guard told me the children now
trapped in the basement cafeteria were having their lunch
when the explosion occurred. "For now," he said, "they're
probably safe from the fire. Their teacher and two of the
kitchen help were with them. And the basement, surrounded by thick sturdy walls, has enough open air ducts
to keep them alive. But once the theater floor over them
goes and the smoke pours in, then the most useful thing we
can do for them is step back from the heat and pray out
our hearts for their souls."

The one approachable entrance to the cafeteria was in
the lobby through a door completely covered with debris.
I flashed my badge to the crowd there and said "Dig.
We've all got to dig for those kids," but only the sickly old
guard and myself began pulling away the rubble that
sealed up the door. I wasn't sure what was keeping the
others back. One man said there might be more dynamite
behind the door and a woman said she was scared of the
young human parts she might find. And there were too
many people to cow with the guard's gun as he was urging
me to do to get them to help.

The police and fire departments arrived with the best digging, firefighting and rescue equipment the city had. In minutes they reached the door leading to the cafeteria and pried it open. Behind it wasn't the empty circular stairway the planetarium director told us to expect, but what looked like a large hole filled to the top with sand, concrete chips and slabs and bits and twists of metal mesh.

"You'll never free them in time," the guard said. "It's too far down—sixteen steps to the cafeteria exact. I know. I've trudged up and down those stairs on my lunch and coffee breaks maybe ten times a day for the past twenty years."

The power-run excavating tools worked rapidly and well till the stair's halfway landing, then became too large and cumbersome when the stairway curved, and the digging stopped.

"Blast the stairway open," a sergeant in Rescue Operations said. He held the explosives, blasting cap, and primer cord and was ready to use them the moment the captain gave the command.

"Blast it open," the fire chief said, "and you'll weaken the building's structure entirely, which will cave in the ceiling long before the fire can."

The sergeant said "No offense meant, but I know what I'm talking about also. I've been on more entombments of this kind than I want to recall. Those seven priests buried alive in the Holy Cathedral dynamiting last month, for example. Those forty ballplayers suffocated to death in the locker rooms at the City Stadium bombing last week, for instance."

The captain decided to dig out the trapped people with manual tools. "That way, even if we're unable to rescue them, at least we won't be charged and be saddled with the guilt of having caused the deaths of those children with an unnecessary blast."

There was space for three men in the stairway. I volunteered and was chosen to be part of the second team, which would work when the primary team came up to rest. The one-to-two buddy system of digging was to be used: one man dislodging the embedded slabs while the other men hauled the freed slabs and metal mesh and pails of fragments and earth around the stairway landing to the sling, which when filled would be hoisted out of the hole by a tackle.

The primary team, working on their bellies and knees, dug out the rest of the halfway landing and two of the remaining eight steps to the cafeteria. Then our team went down and was working past a third step when we heard children screaming.

"They're alive," we all yelled, and a roar went off above the ground that I'm sure was loud enough to be heard by the children. We continued to dig and load, the ground beneath us becoming looser and studded with fewer and smaller slabs. After clearing a fourth step I was able to poke a lance to the bottom of the stairs. I flashed a light down the hole and saw three wiggling fingers, then a mustache and mouth.

It was the teacher. He said there were thirty-five children and two elderly female cafeteria employees with him and all were in reasonably good spirits and health. We sent down penlights, chisels, and sanitation bags. Then we widened the hole from above while he chipped away at it from below, till the captain came down and said the hole seemed large enough for the smallest of the third-graders to crawl through.

"Make the hole wider so we can all crawl through," the teacher said.

"We'll widen it some more once the kids still down there can't fit through the hole we've already made," the captain said. "That way, we'll at least be sure to get some survivors, as the firemen don't know if they can douse the fire before the ceiling falls."

The teacher said he wouldn't let anyone through till the hole was wide enough for everyone to leave. "I don't see why I should be the one who has the best chance of being left behind in this progressively expanding digging system you've developed, just because I'm by far the largest of my group," and he began widening the hole with the lance and spade we'd sent down and ordering his students and the kitchen ladies to carry the rubble to the other side of the room.

The captain said he didn't think anything would change the teacher's mind right now and ordered the primary team back into the hole.

The primary team dug the hole wide enough for their lead man to squirm through. When he made it to the bottom of the stairs and stuck his head past the mouth of the hole into the cafeteria, the teacher told him to either boost himself back to the top or get a lance in his throat, as he wanted to make sure he could get through the hole himself before he let anyone inside.

The lead man squirmed back up and crawled to the halfway landing with the two haulers. The teacher started to crawl up the stairway hole. But because he was too broad-shouldered when he tried to make it up frontways and big-bottomed when he tried to push himself up hindways, he couldn't get more than a few feet up the hole.

"The hole still needs some widening," he said. "And don't be trying to bully your way down here with any of your thinner police, as my threat to that man before holds true for anyone else barging in. But to encourage you to widen the hole further, and repay you for the good work you've already done, I'm sending up my five smallest students."

Each child emerging from the hole was immediately wrapped in a blanket and carried to the waiting ambulance. None of them seemed sick or in the slightest state of shock. All complained that the blankets were too itchy and warm for them on this hot day, especially after they'd been so long in that hot temperature and stuffiness down there, and what they wanted most was to run around on the cool grass without any shoes or clothes on and breathe fresh air. But they were forcibly held down in the blankets, strapped to the ambulance stretchers, and driven to the hospital.

Our team went into the hole again. "How goes it in there?" I asked the teacher, only a few feet from him now and both of us digging away furiously to widen the hole.

He said, "Sticky, stifling, nearly suffocating—what do you think? There's also a little smoke leaking through these ceiling cracks, which means we haven't got long down here if you don't get me out fast."

"Try it now," I said, convinced the hole was wide enough for him. We edged back to the halfway landing as he told us to. He advanced a few feet more than he had the last time, then said he felt as sorry as we must be, but the hole was still too narrow for him to get through.

"Listen," I said. "What'd certainly be worse than dying by yourself in there would be to die with all those kids and kitchen ladies dying around you."

"Listen yourself," he said. "If I know anything about human nature it's that you men will dig a lot harder for me while the kids are down here than if they've all been released. And especially now when you think you know what kind of man you'd be digging out if I happened to end up being stuck alone in here. But I will let the women and some more students up, though not as a digging inducement or rewarding ploy anymore. But because nobody's going to dig a whit harder for two ancient cooking ladies, so I might as well free them to put a stop to their constant nagging and save on the little air we have. And the boys I'm letting out are the ones who always gave me the most trouble in class: puking and bawling now and inciting the rest of my children into an increasingly unmanageable disobedience and maybe a mass physical attack on me soon or total hysteria."

First the cafeteria women came up, looking very frazzled and reviling the police who helped them out of the hole for allowing what they called "that inhuman madman down there" to keep them in that inferno so long. Then seven boys came up. Their faces smudged, bodies limp, hacking and gasping from the smoke in their lungs, all of them fell to the ground when they reached the lobby. One boy yelled to his mother in the crowd. She ducked under the police barrier, clutched her son and screamed into the hole "Butcher . . . murderer . . . you'll get yours quick enough if you ever get up here alive." She fainted and was put on a stretcher alongside the one her son was on, and both were carried to the same ambulance.

"Maybe we better hold up on her," a doctor said, directing the bearers to take her out of the ambulance. "We'll need every stretcher and hospital bed if the kids still down there are suddenly let go."

The woman was lifted off the stretcher and set down on the grass. Several mothers of children still in the cafeteria administered aid to her: holding her hand, massaging her ankles, telling her how lucky she was knowing her son was alive, though she remained unconscious. Her son and the other boys and the cafeteria women were driven to the hospital in a convoy of ambulances and police escorts.

A few hundred people had gathered behind police barriers on the grassy area past the planetarium's driveway. Many of them were calling the police cowards for not forcing their way down the hole to arrest the teacher, and idiots for not shooting him in the hole when they had the chance. The captain said through a bullhorn that any policeman entering the cafeteria wouldn't have had any defense against being lanced as the teacher had sworn to do. "As for shooting him before, an off-target or flesh-exiting bullet could have easily ricocheted into the cafeteria and killed one of the children," but he had to end his explanation because of the jeers from the crowd.

I was sitting on the grass during my rest period when a man standing near me said that today's bombing might wind up producing the city's first lynching in a hundred years. A woman next to him asked if that was a historical fact. "I mean about the possibility of it being the first lynching in a hundred years. I'm a civics professor at the university here, so I'd naturally like to know."

"Two hundred years — even three hundred if you like. What do I know from how long ago the last one was? All I'm saying is it doesn't look like anything could stop this mob from stringing him up. And five gets you the same the police will even be in on it because of the threat to them before. Or at least won't do anything to hold us back — right, Officer?" and he patted my back.

I told him that I for one wouldn't take part in any unlawful execution and in fact would do everything in my power to see the teacher got to jail unharmed and order prevail. The man laughed. The professor said she hoped all the police here felt as I did.

The primary team told the teacher to try the hole again. They moved back to the lobby as he instructed. The teacher crawled to the top of the hole, said, "Fine job, very well constructed, we all thank you very much," and returned to the cafeteria and started sending the children up, smallest ones first.

Tired, disheveled, but emotionally calm children were either reunited in the arms of their parents or bundled up in blankets and dispatched to the hospital. Now only the teacher remained. Our team was sent down to assist him or find out what was keeping him from coming up on his own. Near the bottom of the hole we could still hear the parents in the lobby and spectators on the grass screaming for the teacher's neck.

"Will you please halt where you are?" the teacher said from the cafeteria opening, when I told him we wanted to get him out quick as the ceiling was about to cave in. "And no matter how horrible it is for me in here, sounds as if it'll be worse for me upstairs. But the children and ladies are all right, am I correct in assuming that? Nobody hurt. Everybody alive. A few minor eye and lung ailments which ought to be cleared up in a week. And not only did I preserve the required order down here till everyone was rescued, but my students also learned a vital lesson about life I never could have taught them in class on how to stay alive and deal with their fellow human beings in an emergency situation. Plus an auxiliary lesson related to the city's brotherhood program this week, about how no person should be discriminated against because of his or her age, sex, color, religion, thoughts, health, physiognomy, ethnic, political, geographical, or employment group. What I'm ostensibly saying, Officer, is that I hope no person or assembly upstairs thinks itself justified in playing jury and executioner with me before I've had my rightful due in the proper courts of law."

"The police will do everything possible to see you get booked and arraigned without incident. Now will you please come along?"

Just then a loud crash came from the cafeteria. Smoke looped around the teacher and up the stairway hole. "That was the ceiling that went," he yelled, "so get, you got to get—I said move."

Our team scurried up the hole into the lobby. Part of the crowd had broken through police lines and were waiting for us at the door, clamoring to kill the teacher the moment he appeared. We thought the teacher was right behind us. But he yelled from the halfway landing that he had decided to stay where he was, lance in hand, till he felt certain his chances for survival were better above ground than below.

"A little gas will get him up," the sergeant in Rescue Operations told the captain, and he loaded a tear gas canister into a gun.

"Force him up before we're sure we can handle this mob," I said, "and we might be delivering him to his killers rather than protecting him from them."

We pushed the crowd back behind the barriers. Many people continued to chant for the teacher's death and threatened to bowl over any police who might try to stop them. The captain told us to let the teacher stay put for the time being. "The mob will have shot its rage and disbanded for their homes and bars in an hour, and then we can get him up without further trouble and over to jail. But if he shows before we tell him it's safe, then all we can conclude is that out of a deep feeling of remorse or something, he intentionally crawled out of the hole to get himself killed."

I was thanked for a job well done and released from emergency duty. I went home and sat for a while at the kitchen table, but wouldn't eat. My mother asked what was disturbing me so much that I couldn't even touch my favorite dinner.

I told her I didn't share the captain's optimism about getting the teacher to jail. "I know something about crowd control and collective violence, and a lot of those people didn't look like they'd leave till they had manipulated the others into helping them lynch him. And this might make me a bad policeman, Mom. But realistically, no healthy, sane person wants to get himself killed if he can help it without seriously harming or killing someone else, and that teacher turned out to be the only right one among us after all. Nobody got really hurt or killed. And though I detest his threats against the police, I'm sure we did dig twice as hard because those kids were still with him, which means he would have been buried alive if he'd let them all go all those times we asked him to. And then he wasn't responsible for the bombing or their being entombed. So no matter how evil the mob thinks his motives and methods were, they should at least feel he's gone through enough mishaps and hardships to warrant getting a fair trial."

"Then go back and do what you can for him, since you'll never enjoy your food and vacation the way you are," and I said she was right, phoned the station house, and was told the teacher was still in the hole, got my revolver, kept my civies on as I wasn't allowed to be in uniform unless assigned to duty and when going to and from work, and drove to Planetarium Square, hoping the incident would be over by the time I got there and the teacher unharmed and safe in jail.

He was still down there. A crowd a little larger than when I'd left it was still hoping for his neck. The fire was out and the firemen were gone and the captain had been replaced by a lieutenant and most of the police company had been transferred to City Concert Hall across town, as a bomb had exploded there an hour ago and some three hundred people were still trapped in the debris.

I asked the lieutenant if there was anything I could do. He introduced me to the teacher's son and asked if I'd mind accompanying the young man down the hole so he could try to coax his father up. "I don't want him going in alone. He might leave provisions or clothing on the sly or even stay down there himself, making it even tougher getting the teacher up later on. Now's the most opportune time to get him out too. The darkness should conceal his escape movements if we can avoid tipping off the mob with any scuffling or squabbling sounds from below. If we wait till morning I'm afraid the mob will be larger and doubly intent on getting revenge on him for his treatment of his students before and this new rash of bombings and now all those deaths at Concert Hall. But this is a volunteer assignment, you understand. You're still on vacation. I wouldn't order any man to risk facing a lance while on his chest. But since the teacher seemed to trust you most and you know the hole better than anyone else around, you're the most suitable man for the job."

We entered the hole. The son, lagging behind me,

complained about his knees being scraped and brand-new sandals and slacks getting torn, then apologized for his self-centeredness and said anything was worth ripping and ruining to save his dad. We both carried flashlights and spoke softly as we crawled.

"We're coming, Dad."

"Though please don't make any fuss or objections about it," I said.

"We want you to come out quietly with us for your own good."

"I'm the officer who was the lead man for that backup digging team."

"He's very sympathetic to you and came with me only to help."

"Your son will confirm that now's the best chance you'll have for ditching that mob upstairs."

"It's true, Dad."

"I'm armed. But to show my good faith, I'll leave the gun behind me anytime you say."

The teacher never answered. We crawled to the end of the stairway without finding him. The ceiling caving in before had blocked the cafeteria entrance again. We checked and rechecked the entire hole with our flashlights till I spotted a tiny aperture in the wall where the stairway curved. We broke through the wall, enlarged the opening wide enough to fit through. Behind it was an empty basement corridor still lit by electric lights and seemingly untouched by the explosion and fire. It was about thirty feet long and had a door at either end of it.

I opened one door and found nothing behind it but soap powder and cleaning equipment. The son ran and stood in front of the other door. "Come on," he said. "What's the harm if we let him get out on his own?"

"The harm's that I was sent down to get him up safely, not let him escape."

"He'll be escaping from the mob, not the police. He'll

turn himself in tomorrow when he's sure it's safe enough.
I know my old man. He's extremely legal-conscious, has
an unflagging respect for the law. He'll want to face up to
all the charges brought against him, and if guilty, he'll
gladly serve his time."

"I promise to do everything I can to see he gets to
court. Now will you please let me get on with my job?" I
pushed him aside, opened the door, and found the room or
passageway behind it packed with rubble. We searched
the corridor and utility closet for an exit the teacher might
have gone through, but there were no other door, vents, or
tiny holes.

"He couldn't have just vanished," I said.

"What are we going to tell them upstairs?"

"That he couldn't have just vanished."

"They'll never believe us. Both the mob and the police
will say we were in on the escape. And the longer we stay
down here, the less they'll believe he got away on his own.
We have to think up some airtight excuse right away. What
about that he fell down a shaft made by the bombing before
and which then crumbled apart and buried him?"

"And if he turns up tomorrow as you say?"

"Maybe his great respect for the law and its court system has finally wavered."

"No. The lieutenant will send some men down to try
and dig him out."

"Then what about that he took your gun and made us
dig through the cafeteria entrance and got out some way
through there?"

"No. They'll want to know why we filled in the hole
after him."

"So we did it at gunpoint or he filled it up himself."

"Then they'll want to know why I still have my gun on
me."

"We'll say he threw it back just before he put the last
stone in the hole."

"No. They'll dig through the cafeteria entrance and probably find there isn't another escape route through there."

"How do we know? Maybe there is. But the reason he couldn't find it before is because for most of his time in the cafeteria he had no light."

"The kitchen ladies would have told him of another exit when they were with him."

"Then a new hole or old sealed one they didn't know about could have been opened by the explosion."

"It's too farfetched."

"It'll get us off the hook for now. What about that he went through that second corridor door when he saw us breaking through the wall, and which immediately caved in behind him just as he got past?"

"The lieutenant will get the floor plans. And that door might lead to nothing but a storage room and freezer locker and lavatory and another utility closet with no other way out of these rooms but the doors leading to the room with the door to the corridor that he came through."

"Then what about that he fell down a shaft made by the bombing before and which then crumbled apart and buried him?"

We gave up trying to find a plausible excuse and returned to the lobby and told the lieutenant the truth.

"No chance," he said. He sent several men into the hole to find the teacher or the exit he used. "And this time," he yelled down the stairway to the men, "shoot to disable if he won't come up nice and sweetlike by himself. We're through pussyfooting around that guy just to prevent the unlikely prospect of his getting beaten up or lynched."

The men came up an hour later saying they discovered a chute in the utility closet that led down to a small room that had nothing in it but dirty table linen and uniforms and a door plugged up with impassable debris. Other men were sent down to look for possible escape routes in the laundry room and chute, utility closet, corridor, and stairway hole, but all they could come up with were two six-inch-across air ducts filled with concrete chips and sand.

"How are we going to explain this to the mob?" I asked the lieutenant.

"Very simply that he got away through an opening we've yet to uncover."

"Think they'll believe that?"

"What do I care what they believe? As long as they can mull it over for a while and I get them off my back."

"But they'll say we're still holding him till they leave."

"Then we'll let a few crowd representatives into the hole to inspect the stairway and laundry room."

"When they don't find him they'll say we knowingly let him go to avert disorder."

"So we'll tell them we smuggled the teacher through the lobby as we'd first planned to, and he's now in a downtown jail."

"They'll find out later tonight or tomorrow we don't have him. And when the papers get wind of it we'll be in even worse trouble with a bigger mob, with the jail liable to get destroyed."

"Then we'll tell them exactly what happened, because we haven't any more time to think up an excuse. There was a bombing at City Art Museum a half hour ago and we're all needed there to dig out the night guards and works of art."

He ordered his men into the police vans. Two policemen were kept behind to guard the stairway, just in case the teacher had been hiding someplace in the hole all this time and was waiting to leave through the lobby after everyone had gone. I was asked to make sure the son got home all right and then to resume what the lieutenant called my much-interfered-with-though-more-than-ever-now-well-earned vacation.

He addressed the crowd, told them of the most recent bombing and of his new assignment and that the teacher had apparently given the police the slip. "Though nobody should worry any about it, as we've excellent photos and fingerprints of the man, so it won't be more than a day or two before he's caught. So break it up, everybody. We don't want total chaos and terror becoming the rule of our city. Go back to your homes or jobs or to a quiet bar if you can find one, as there's just no sensible reason left to stick around," and satisfied the crowd was splitting up and leaving, he and his unit drove to the museum.

The crowd quickly re-formed. A group of men bulldozed its way past the two policemen and went into the hole. The son and I stood in the dark behind a parked car nearby in case the teacher turned up. The group came out and said they'd found nothing new downstairs but a trapdoor in the laundry chute that tunneled through to a sewer pipe that wasn't wide enough to fit a kitten in.

The son and I crossed the street and were hailing a cab coming out of the park when a woman shouted "Why are you letting the cop get off free? Wasn't he the one who was so chummy with the teacher, and for all we know came back here to sneak him past us and the police?"

"That's not quite true," I said, when the crowd began forming around us and the cab. "I'll admit I did come back here to see what I could do to get him past you all and safe in jail, but I had no specific plan as to how I'd bring it off. And I only went into the hole a second time because the lieutenant felt the best way to get the teacher to jail without any police and civilians getting hurt was for the teacher's son and I to quietly coax him up into a police van, though we never saw a trace of him."

"His son?" a man said. "Then he's the one we ought to be getting. He's got the same kind of blood in his veins, so he'll be doing the same thing to our kids his dad did if he ever gets the chance. We'll be doing a favor to a whole slew of people in the future by doing away with him now."

The son bolted through the crowd. I yelled "Don't run, you fool, you'll only provoke them more." The cab drove off with its back doors flapping and people pounding its sides with sticks. Some men chased after the son. I drew my revolver, was grabbed from behind, knocked to the ground, and sat on while part of the crowd disarmed the policemen who tried to help me. They caught the son, dragged him back, kicked at his head and body till it seemed all his limbs, ribs, and face were broken, then hung him upside down by his feet from one of the tree branches that had survived the fire. They continued to spit at him and some women pulled out patches of his hair and beat his already unrecognizable face with their handbags, till one of the policemen said, "All right, folks. I think you did everything you could do to him short of setting him on fire, so why don't you go home." Someone lit a match to the son's shirtsleeve, but the policemen slapped the fire out.

The crowd broke up. One of the men who'd been sitting on me said "Just thank your lucky stars you told us the truth." Some people as they walked away from the square turned around every few seconds to give the body dirty looks.

I cut the rope holding the son: he came down on his head. The policemen put him in a canvas sack and that sack into the trunk of their squad car. No charges were brought against anyone for the son's death. The following day the newspapers said the son had died from a fall inside the stairway hole while looking for his father, who was still being sought by the police. The police, the articles said, were still trying to determine the causes and persons responsible for the planetarium bombing and other related explosions. So far they've had no success.

AUDREY FERBER

Drapes
and
Folds

For Ilene

The hermadoor slid open. My friend Diana was the antithesis of NewSociety fashion. Peasant blouse, gauzy floor-length skirt, and a messy yellow-white braid that hung halfway down her back. She hiked her shoulder.

I hiked in response. She was a flat, had lost both breasts to cancer in the Women's Epidemic in 2022. I was a slant; I'd lost only one. Women developed the shoulder hike greeting during the Epidemic to emphasize our chests and our unity.

"Pearl, what's going on?" she asked, kissing my cheek. "I heard you from outside."

"I was screaming at the read-out." Every NewSociety dwelling was equipped with a digitalized word ribbon, a revolving loop of oppressive slandertrash.

"AND IN ADDITION TO THE ELIMINATION OF ALL PEPLUMS, PLEATS, COLLARS, AND CUFFS, THERE IS TO BE ABOUT THE BODY AND DWELLING NO DRAPED OR FOLDED CLOTH . . ." I read the glowy blue-green words aloud.

"I'm sorry, kid." Diana slid her hand over my smooth

head. I'd lost all my hair during my first ultra-chemo, decades ago, and it had never grown back. "Why is the collection out? This place is a mess."

I'd been busy strewing Russian shawls over the backs of modules, draping Indian mirror cloth and batik spreads to disguise the diamonite berths. I'd covered all the work surfaces with lace and bistro-checked cloths and wore my ancient Fab Four beach towel around my shoulders like a stole. The crowning touch was my purple and white kimono. The sleeves fitted across the nipple bar on the wall, leaving the body of the silk robe to cascade down like water.

"Tomorrow's my hundreth birthday. I'm through licking the Powers' vinyline asses. Whatever time I have left, I want to spend with my fabric. I want to adorn my body, dress my home. I want to be who I am."

"You are who you are. Who else could you be? But the point is that fabric is against the law and it hardly seems worth throwing your life away for a few scraps of cloth." Diana's voice sounded tired, flat.

"Cloth is my life! My context, my warp, my woof. I don't know what's happened to you, Diana. You used to be so angry . . ."

She sighed. "Let's not fight . . . here, this is for your birthday."

She threw me something tied in a Niagara Falls kerchief. When I undid the ends, a ten-inch lamina tablex of the FabricLaws fell to the floor.

"What is this, a joke?" I picked up the tablet.

The Diana I knew opposed the FabricLaws with every fiber of her being. There were rules against trim and closures. Stitches had to be hidden, as they were deemed "ornamental," and pockets were outlawed for what they could hide. The Powers saw sumptuous clothing and fabric as part of the "anarchic individualism" that had poisoned the last half of the twentieth century. Dashikis and gang colors, they'd insisted, were part of the multiculture tribalism that had led to Race War 2000.

She shrugged. "How about some TasteLik?" Diana kicked off her wide cork-soled sandals and crossed to the wall.

She still had the erect carriage and turned-out walk of a dancer, her profession before all that had been outlawed. I stared at her feet: bunions, varicose veins, yellowed toenails. They were her rebellion. I'd had mine replaced with moulded volymer OrthoPeds or "wheelies," as the kids called them, decades ago.

"But thanks for the scarf." I pulled it through the clasp of my uni, pressed my wrist pad to my thigh, and sped to her side. "It's great." I kissed her cheek. "Are you all right?"

She shrugged me off, asking: "Did you get that sweet and sour fixed?" Then she pulled the kimono off the wall and clamped onto a nipple.

ANP, the NewSociety's Approved Nutritional Procedure, attaching at the navel to a sup-pump and filling up, provided adequate fuel. But those of us old enough to remember the caress of melted cheese, the ecstatic crackle of garlic-infused chicken skin, craved taste. So a group of elders developed TasteLik, a system of synthetic flavor delivery. Most persons over sixty had a unit, wall-mounted nipples or a simple flavor board, with tastes like Texas barbecue, school cafeteria, Thai, Thanksgiving.

"I could go for a little hot and sour," I said, joining her at the nipples.

"Hot and sour? Never heard of it."

Very odd. Hot and sour was one of our little jokes, a Chinese soup that had been popular ages ago, right before "foreign" foods had been disallowed. We'd loved the tangy fungus-filled broth, the fermented bean curd, the slippery strands of mucousy egg. The textures and odd floating shapes were so distant from the NewSociety conception of food as pap, it had become our code for everything that we missed. If Diana didn't remember hot and sour, something was definitely wrong. But before I could question her, Xera, my birthdaughter Casey's NewOne, glided by.

"Oh no, Old Putrid Flesh," Xera vevved in her androgenous robotic voice. "Disgusting nipple suck again? Sup-pump usage, please . . ."

NewOnes, NewSociety citizens farmed after the year 2025, were a ghastly mix of human and roboid. In Xera's batch, the use of human eyes was being studied. So in her rigid, volymer face, real light blue eyes quivered like jellies. She wasn't being cruel when she called me Old Putrid Flesh. Her olfactory apparatus was so sensitive, she could literally smell parts of me decaying.

"That's it. I've had enough," Diana said abruptly, detaching from the nipples.

"What? No buttered rum? It's your favorite . . ." Diana was the original TasteQueen. Usually she likked until she passed out. "How about fruit salad?"

"Don't make me vetch," Xera bleated, speeding past us, three strands of beads clacking her wheelies.

"Why is she wearing ankle bracelets?" Diana asked when Xera was out of the room. "She's always been so observant. A FabricLaw fanatic. 'Utility or Futility,' unadorned simplicity in all things . . ."

"Adolescent rebellion." I slumped on the rest berth. "Or maybe she's a little like her Gran . . ."

That word held deep and pleasant memories for me. I closed my eyes and pictured my mother's mother and the afternoons we'd spent in her millinery shop. I remembered sifting through buckets of buttons, letting the cool shapes slide between my fingers, pressing opalescent sequins onto my skin. We sat close together, up to our knees in feathers, the walls thick with rolls of rick-rack, grosgrain, satin, and French ribbon, lengths of maribou, strings of pearls. She'd taught me about fabric and fashion, each trim, each color an aspect of her depth and love.

Maybe that's when it started for me, connecting warmth and affection with texture and design. Or maybe my need to express myself in cloth was inborn. I'd so wanted to teach those same lessons to some young person, to be a vibrant inspiration, to give to Xera all that had been given to me. But when I talked to her about trapunto or crewelwork, her eyes glazed over. And when I'd asked her, begged her to call me Gran, she'd told me that she wasn't programmed for that word.

The loop gave off a hum, a sound wave we experienced as a mild shock, a subliminal compulsion to view the message. ". . . WE HAVE BEGUN AN ORDERLY TRANSITION. A NATIONWIDE PROGRAM TO INSTALL THE BRACIE IS NOW IN PLACE . . ."

"No!" I gasped and sank lower on the berth. "This is the end."

"Have you ever thought about trying one?" Diana sat next to me.

"Of course not! Bracies are conformity, annihilation, the end of clothing as we've known it."

The hosed-on sludge-colored bodysuits favored by the Powers employed hydraulics to eliminate individual morphs. All bodies were reduced to one bland, universal form.

"Maybe it would feel nice. Like a big support stocking, an elastic glove. I could use a little lift . . ." She sputtered a weak laugh.

"Diana! What's going on?"

"Listen, Pearl." She looked over her shoulder. "The other night, while I was sleeping . . ." She lowered her voice. "They gave me a sweep."

"No." I grabbed her forearm.

"They said that preliminary monitoring had shown hardening, an extreme hardening, that the inside of my head was as dry and hard as a rock . . ."

"You let them do it?"

"They didn't ask permission."

"They've invaded you, stolen what was inside your brain." My words came out in short blustery puffs as I roller-paced the floor.

"Well, if they took anything I don't care because I can't remember what it was. Really, I'm okay. I feel lighter, cleaner. They said it was like a moisturizer for my brain."

"Stop it!" I reached down and shook her shoulders, "You're not yourself."

"Now I'm thinking less is more, and it would be good to pare down. For you too. Get rid of your collection, Pearl." She grabbed my wrist. "Give it up." She stood and started lifting cloth off the modules, folding and making neat piles. "Don't you ever get tired of these old things, all this history . . ."

"Put down that mirror cloth."

"You can't fight this, Pearl. They're too powerful. Life's much simpler without all these memories."

"I remember everything." I pounded my thigh. "Standing in my crib with a blanket draped around me like a strapless sheath . . ."

"You remember pictures, stories people told you . . ."

"Every piece of clothing I made for my dolls. Five-pocket jeans, hand-knit sweaters, and wetsuits cut from a kitchen sponge. And I remember meeting you. We were twelve years old."

"Oh, I remember that too. I was interested in boys and you were spinning and carding wool. You were very peculiar . . ."

"I thought you liked me because I was different . . . Diana, put that tablecloth down." She let the checked cloth fall to the floor.

"All right. I won't try to help. They'll cart you off somewhere and I'll never see you again. You never cared about anyone but yourself. Not Casey, not Xera, not me . . ."

"Casey's been gone for more than eight months.

Europe, or one of the other adult theme-parks. Xera's a box on wheels. And you and me, we're almost gone . . ."

The hum. Then a metallic twitch in my upper thigh. We both stopped and read. ". . . SECTOR EIGHTEEN. PREPARE YOUR DWELLING FOR DE-FABRICATION. THE REMOVAL OF ALL CLOTH DETRITUS. MONITORS WILL VISIT YOUR SECTOR TODAY . . ."

"You've left me before. I'll get used to it again." Diana spoke as soon as she'd finished scanning the lines.

"I can't believe you're still upset about something that happened in the year twenty ten. Don't you understand? I couldn't stay here. I hated what this country had become." I collapsed onto the rest berth.

"And you thought Japan, island of toxic waste, would be better?" Diana sat next to me and lifted her braid. Decades ago, she'd been on the wrong end of a hormone protocol and still suffered hot flashbacks.

"No, not really." I blew on the back of her neck. "The truth is, I fell in love with the kimono."

"You left me and everything you knew for a robe?"

"It was perfect. Comfortable, unisex, and the most self-expressive garment in fashion history."

My particular innovation was the addition of a plasticene back panel. One day I'd place flowers in mine, the next day a poem or political tract. The panel gave each wearer a voice previously unheard in clothing.

"Millions of women were dying, and you were on an island silkscreening robes . . ."

I'd returned to the States as soon as I'd heard. Diana was waiting for me at the terminal. As she told me about the Women's Epidemic, I noticed that her tunic was bunched and empty on one side, that her lavaliere hung off kilter. She'd already lost one breast. The disease was so virulent that in less than six months I had lost a breast as well. Later, it was discovered that the lack of fat in our diets, vacuum-cleaner exhaust, and cosmetic slurry were all precipitating factors. Women's reproductive organs | 133

■
Drapes
and
Folds

were attacked as well. In the same week that Diana lost
her second breast, hormonal irregularities were noted in
my dailies. Estrogen pump panties were prescribed to
counteract the sparseness of my vagostatic fluids.

"There was never any talking to you when you were
creating . . ." But before she finished her complaint, I doubled over in a pain that felt like barbed wire being pulled
through my veins. We read together:

"SECTOR EIGHTEEN, COORDINATE TWELVE, DWELLING
OF THE ELDER, PEARL, AND THE NEWONE, XERA. WE WILL
ENTER YOUR DOMICILE IN THE NEXT HOUR. BE PREPARED
TO ABANDON ALL OLD WORLD CLOTHING AND RELATED
PARAPHERNALIA: FOOTWEAR, JEWELRY, LINENS, AND
HOMEFASHIONS. NO ITEMS, WE REPEAT, NO ITEMS MAY BE
KEPT FOR ARCHIVAL OR PERSONAL USE."

Diana sprang up, her braid slapping her back. "Okay,
this is it. Don't worry. I'll help you get everything ready."
She whipped the indigo batik off the seating module. "If all
the cloth is folded and ready when they get here, they'll think
you're making an effort, that you're willing to go along . . ."

"Screw them! It's you that I'm worried about. They've
taken my friend and left a chicken, a yellow-bellied traitor,
in her place!" I tried to wrest the cloth from her hands.

"I am not a chicken," she said, pulling it in the opposite direction.

Back and forth, we tugged and grunted, until I heard
the unmistakable sound of ripping fabric. As the worn
material split in two, we fell back onto the rest berth,
looked at each other, and started to laugh.

"Do you remember the Chicken Years?" I asked, wiping the tears from my eyes.

"When was it, twenty twenty-three, twenty twenty-
five? All that lovely chicken . . ."

"Lovely chicken?"

For five years, the national diet had been based

entirely on the boneless, skinless chicken breast. Poultry tea, chicken milk, and the chocolate substitute chickilate . . . Everyone hated it, the manipulation, the boredom. When Diana and I were laughing, for a moment, it had felt like old times. But if she'd forgotten the misery of the Chicken Years, there was no hope.

"And your beautiful babies . . ."

"Diana, they were poultry infants. My little girl had no brain, and the boy was born menstruating, with fully developed female breasts."

The Powers had ripped them from my arms, called them "ThrowAways," recycled them for their usable parts. It was years before they admitted that the hormones they'd used to create ninety-pound, six-breasted chickens had deformed thousands of citizens.

"All children find their place in the NewSociety." Diane stroked my cheek.

She was clearly delusional. Her fingers felt papery on my skin. I slipped to the floor, my polymette swivel joints creaking as badly as the knees they'd replaced. I pulled the utility bin out from under the berth. Under the sup-pump tubing, replacement wheelies, and arnica shields, I burrowed my hands. Deeper and deeper, I let them find their pleasure between the layers of challis and pongee slub.

"After the chicken, what came next?" she asked dreamily.

"The Pasta Project." I twisted my hands until they were bandaged in the beautiful cloth.

"Oh yes, pasta. Italian. Very romantic."

"No, Diana, not romantic at all." I sighed. "After all the soil boosting and genetic engineering, most of us had developed an allergy to wheat. We were so sick and angry, we almost rebelled."

"How awful."

"No! It was wonderful. You held secret meetings,

organized the Food Cabal. Don't you remember? You were our leader."

"Oh no, you must be thinking of someone else."

"You were outraged! Couldn't believe that so many citizens would give up food and taste without a fight."

"Sup-pumps are efficient. Balanced fuel on demand . . ."

As Diana repeated the party line, I realized that my friend was truly gone. With just one sweep, they'd filled her head with revisionist pseudo-history and robbed us of the past we'd shared. But I kept talking, as if words could give us back what we had lost.

"Think, Diana. Try and remember." I sat next to her again and took her hands in mine. "After the pasta, that's when I had my Casey . . ."

Out of the corner of my eye, I saw Xera roll by, one of my ancient silk stockings bunched into a rosette and attached to her bracie. She'd never shown any interest in my collection before, but I was too distracted to react. "Xera, come sit. We're talking about your mother."

Usually she avoided Diana, claimed that her feet made her vetch, but Xera joined us on the berth.

"I was in my forties," I continued. "I could have mail-ordered from Petrie's Dish or used one of those Grow Your Own home-creation kits, but the more sterile the NewSociety became, the more I wanted to experience the blood of RealBirth."

"Primitive." Xera repulsed, rotating her head.

"What soft skin you have," Diana said, patting Xera's cold, lifeless hand.

"It was a long shot, with my cancer treatments and thin fluids. But I was lucky with a turkey baster and a vial of banked semen and became pregnant with your mother on my first try."

Xera blinked. It was only a mechanical gesture, but to me she looked curious and intent.

"It's hard to explain, the urge to procreate, to see some

part of yourself continue, to pass on your hopes and dreams . . . It happened to your mother too. When Casey neared forty, her hormones exploded. And the Farmers promised: 'A NewOne with all modern conveniences plus the pleasing familiarity of inherited traits.' So she sent them a fingernail clipping and ordered a bouncing baby NewBlood imprinted with her own genetic code."

"Traits . . ." Xera repeated, her head spinning three full revolutions. Was she disgusted? Alarmed? I was never sure if she felt anything at all. Then she stood and sped from the room.

"Pearl's career took off after that. You should have seen her, Xera. She was the darling of the Bureau. BOFD."

Diana was too fuddled to notice that she was talking to herself, but what she said was true. In the midst of all that horror, I found true fulfillment in designing clothing for other slants and flats. Using lush fabrics, versions of my beloved velvets and chenilles, I fashioned the uni, a jaunty, affirmative garment that encouraged full move-ment and complimented the body, whatever its shape and size. We dyed the cloth in retro food tones, shades of per-simmon, avocado, blackberry, and wine, in homage to the tastes that we still craved.

News of my designs spread. I received orders from all over the country. I became a minor celebrity, a spokes-woman for slants and flats. But as my profile heightened, my run-ins with the Powers began. I was contacted by the Bureau of Fabric Discipline, BOFD, and brought in for a "meeting."

They took me on a tour of the FabricLabs. It was hard not to be impressed with BioKil, the fabric that fought off viral infection; Endorpha, the pleasure fiber; and Interferex, the cloth that had put an end to cancer. The artist in me itched to work with that cloth, but the tradeoffs were too great. Their "designers" were already working on the bracie. They didn't care about clothing. They were germ-warfare specialists, microbe engineers.

Xera rolled by again, a pair of jeans tied aound her waist.

"Bran," she generated in a wobbly voice.

"Where did you learn the name of that ancient food-stuff?" I asked. Her vocal apparatus was obviously mal-functioning.

She pulled the nylon stocking rosette off her bracie and added it and the jeans to the pile Diana had started on the floor.

"Fran," Xera bleated, circling the berth slowly.

"Do you suppose we could have some of that chick-en?" Diana asked, folding the jeans Xera had thrown on the floor.

"What do you want, Xera?"

She pointed to the hermadoor and I felt a hum in the pit of my stomach. Then a shock so violent, I was thrown, writhing, to the floor. When it ended, I was drenched with sweat. I lifted my head to read.

"SECTOR EIGHTEEN, DWELLING TWO, HOME OF PEARL AND THE NEWONE, XERA. MONITORS ARE NOW ENTERING YOUR GRID. BE PREPARED TO GIVE UP ALL CLOTH ITEMS. THERE ARE NO LONGER ANY EXCEPTIONS, WE REPEAT, NO EXCEPTIONS TO THIS RULE."

The moment I'd been dreading had arrived. Our free-dom of fashion had been taken away. I pulled myself up and raced the periphery. With Diana's sustaining friend-ship, life in the NewSociety had been bleak but tolerable. Without her, there was no reason to go on.

I surveyed my room. A suicide's nightmare. Like a nursery, all rounded and modular, no place to hang a noose, nothing sharp to tear the skin. Xera skittered for-ward, then backward, holding something behind her back.

"What has she got? What is she hiding?" Diana demanded.

Xera vevved something unintelligible, then held out a small drawstring bag I'd pieced together in Japan. It was made from remnants of my earliest kimonos, fabric patterned with bamboo, lotus, hats and fans, and part of a plasticene back panel with my own haiku:

Early morning rain,
acid-laced, toxic dew. Trees
are the only hope.

Oh, the handwork was crude, the poetry poor, but it brought tears to my eyes. Of all my work, this reminder of my early days in Japan felt closest to my heart. When I'd shown it to Xera years ago, she'd seemed uninterested. But to know that she'd kept it all these years . . .

"They can take everything but this," I said, pressing it to my chest.

"Utility or futility. Utility or futility," Diana chanted, marching in a small circle.

Then I heard the whooshing halt of the gray needle-nosed collection vehicle outside my dwelling.

"Gran," Xera vevved. Oh, that word! The word I'd waited so long to hear! It warmed me like a flannel gown. But as I moved to embrace my dear girl, she rolled backwards and popped her right arm out of its socket. "Bag," she said. "In here."

"Bag?" I repeated, paralyzed by the sight of her holding her limb.

"Oh, give it here." Diana grabbed the arm and tried to stuff the pouch inside.

"No. Shoulder. Hurry." Xera's voice was unwinding like a tired toy.

Diana followed her instructions and fitted it in the hollow beneath Xera's clavicle. Who knows what PowerFailure allowed her to help me, what bit of loyal memory their sweep had missed? But as always, Diana remained my true friend. She popped Xera's arm back into place.

Three monitors in PowerBracies, with inflated shoulders and breastplates, entered and photo-lasered the room. As they riffled through the bins, I realized that they could laser Xera as well. If they found the bag, we'd all be done for. But they moved to the back room.

They returned with armloads of flapper dresses and a minor spin-off collection of old sports uniforms. "Have we discovered all outlawed cloth?" they generated simultaneously, adding the clothing to the pile on the floor.

"Yes, you've taken everything." My arm shot out towards my collection involuntarily, but Diana eased it down. Xera flanked my other side.

"You will report to the distribution center tomorrow, to be fitted for the bracie. The old one, Diana, as well." Then, they tied my life's work in two enormous Belgian lace tablecloths, slung them over their shoulders, and were gone.

"We'll be there," Diana said as the hermadoor slid shut.

I leaned my head on my granddaughter's shoulder. Yes, for in those few minutes, that's what she had become. Beneath the cool volymer, beneath her tiny extruded seams, she carried my message. I pulsed inside her, warm as blood.

KAREN JOY FOWLER

The
Poplar
Street
Study

The 600 block of Poplar Street was known for its nice lawns. The Desmonds, who lived on the corner, had the very nicest—a tasteful display of seasonal flowers under the arch of an oriental bridge. The Narrs next door worked endlessly to keep the Desmonds' grass out of their ornamental strawberries, but this irritation had never blossomed into gunfire the way the Simpson/Martin dog-fight had.

Two years ago the Martins had acquired a dog—a nervous terrier who never stopped barking. People farther down the street were able to ignore the noise. It was so steady it became no more troublesome than the occasional jet overhead, or the comforting sound of power mowers on a Sunday morning. But the Simpsons, who shared a fence with the Martins, compared it to Chinese water torture. One night Mr. Simpson hysterically demanded a solution. Mr. Martin, who really had tried to train the dog, responded nastily that the only thing he could do was to shoot it. "The blood will be on your hands," he said coldly, closing the door on Mr. Simpson's hysteria. He walked calmly into the backyard and discharged a pistol into the air. He enjoyed it, picturing the guilt Mr. Simpson must be suffering, but the terrier, who had stopped barking in surprise at the sounds of the gunshot, resumed its noise almost immediately, so the tableau was not really a convincing one.

Two months later the Simpsons moved out and the Andersons moved in. The Andersons were both black and Jewish, a nice family with two boys and a dog of their own. The barking seemed to trouble them less, although they did tell the Aldritches that the Simpsons had not mentioned the dog to them during the sale of the house and had described the neighborhood as "quiet." Mrs. Aldritch imagined this was a complaint, although nothing in Mrs. Anderson's tone suggested it.

At this point the trouble center of the block shifted to the Kramer house. Everyone knew that the Kramers' marriage, which had survived for twenty miserable years, was gasping its last few breaths. Mr. Kramer had told them so. "A man has certain needs," he hinted. Mr. Kramer had a drinking problem, which he displayed at every opportunity. He was overweight, balding, and flirtatious. Mrs. Kramer was a saint. Everyone said so.

The people of the 600 block knew each other without actually being friends. They were, for the most part, professionals, gone all day and tired at night. They took pride in their homes and protected their privacy.

There were only a few children: the Anderson boys, David and Joey, who were ten and eight years old; Sunny Aldritch, age eight; Tommy and Maureen Martin, eight and two; and the Evert baby, who was too little to count.

Once a year on the fourth of July they closed both ends of the street and had a block party with volleyball. The Kramers and the Andersons sometimes played bridge together and groups sometimes watched the World Series or the Superbowl at the Narrs', where reception was inexplicably better. When the Simpsons had gone for four weeks without cutting their grass, Mrs. Desmond had organized a neighborhood improvement committee to deal with them. But for the most part, the 600 block was not a social unit. Only the children were really friends, and spent the weekends riding their bicycles together, up and down the street.

The first indication of crisis that Poplar Street had was the six o'clock news, which wasn't on. Mr. Anderson turned on his television to see how the Padres were doing and got "Father Knows Best" reruns instead. On every channel. He went next door to check the Martins' TV, but the Martins were eating and Mr. Martin said, rather shortly, that they never watched television during the dinner hour. Later Tommy Martin came to see if David and Joey could play, and interrupted the Andersons' dinner. Mr. Anderson thought it was deliberate and told his wife that Mr. Martin was a bigot with a lot of repressed hostility. He tried to call and tell him so, but the phone was dead.

Mrs. Narr discovered that her phone was out of order at about the same time. She went to the Desmonds next door, planning to call the phone company and report it, but their phone didn't work either. It was cocktail hour at the Desmonds and they persuaded her to stay and join them. Mrs. Desmond and Mrs. Narr got along well, in spite of their warring gardens. They were both attractive, well-groomed, ambitious women in their thirties. They were both married to older, admiring men. Mrs. Desmond worked in city government and Mrs. Narr sold real estate. Confident that someone else would eventually report the phones, they sipped martinis and complained about the Aldritches, who lived on the other side of the Narrs, but had so many cars they continually parked the oldest one in front of the Narrs' house. "There's a grease spot there nothing will ever remove," Mrs. Narr said.

The Aldritches were a young couple with strange friends. Mrs. Aldritch must have been a child bride and she was totally ineffectual in controlling her daughter, Sunny, whose real name was Sunshine and who knew an astounding number of vulgar expressions. The Desmonds were sympathetic to Mrs. Narr's complaints and sent her home with the comfortable feeling that she had been heard. Mrs. Desmond had even spoken of rejuvenating the Neighborhood Improvement Society, "if push came to shove," she said. Mrs. Narr went to bed happy, one of the last on Poplar Street to turn out her light.

Only Mr. Kramer remained awake, having a solitary scotch and thinking that something was different. He thought of his wife, already asleep, and had another drink, still puzzling over the change until, at last, it came to him. It was amazingly quiet out. No planes. No trains. Even the Martins' dog seemed muted. He sat out on the back patio for a long time, listening to the whisper of the natural world.

Friday morning came early to the 600 block, with so many people trying to get to so many offices, schools, and childcare centers on time. Mrs. Aldritch discovered she had no banana for Sunny's cereal. She had raisins, but Sunny didn't really like raisins, and Mrs. Aldritch thought she had time to get to the store if she took the car and made only the one purchase. She drove to the end of the block, then, suddenly, the car went dead. "Damn," she thought. It had started up smoothly enough, although she had noticed it dripping oil. Mrs. Aldritch got out with the intention of looking under the hood, but was immediately distracted by an enormous presence on the Desmonds' lawn. "My god, look at that!" she said to herself. At one end of the oriental bridge sat what appeared to be a piece of modern sculpture, huge, iridescent, with an obsidian slickness that made it appear permanently wet. "The Desmonds were the ones," she thought, "who made that huge fuss when the Kramers wanted to put those little gnomes in their yard and now they go and put up something like this." The sculpture resembled an eight-foot mood ring. She could hardly wait to go home and tell her husband about it.

She turned, but peripherally she saw a slight tremor and looked back. Now there were two sculptured pieces and they began to grow horizontally in a movement which became the lifting of many arms. Suddenly the bulges at the top were clearly clusters of eyes, and she could make out, she thought, lips, too, rolled back to display drooping incisors. Each creature held an object in front of it in a single hand. The objects were identical, small, metallic boxes, perfectly square, and they extended them toward Mrs. Aldritch, making her scream and then freeze as still as her car.

The sound of her scream brought the Desmonds to their front door and Mr. Anderson to her side. Mr. Andersons's morning paper had not been delivered and the early news had been replaced by a Dean Martin/Jerry Lewis movie. Mr. Anderson had come outside with the intention of finding out what in hell was going on when he heard Mrs. Aldritch. He stood beside her now, his hand floating just above her shoulder, his mouth still open for the question he'd never asked. The creatures responded to his presence by waving their arms wildly and rubbing them together. The friction of their arms created a high, hollow sound, like a flute far off in the distance. Then a mechanical voice, lisping slightly and off-pitch like a record played a bit too fast, came from within the boxes. "Retain your composure if possible," it said. "No one is going to be hurt."

Down the street a door slammed and Sunny's plaintive voice was heard. "Mommy! I thought you were making my breakfast! I'm starving to death . . ." She appeared in front of the Aldritch house, caught sight of her mother, and began to run toward her. Mrs. Aldritch whirled, calling to Sunny to get back in the house *instantly* and to stay there. Sunny did not even pause and her mother caught her as she came, wrapping her arms about the child protectively. From inside her mother's clutch, Sunny located the creatures. "Gross out," she said. "Really."

They heard Mr. Kramer's car pull out and head in the opposite direction. At the end of the block it went dead, and moments later, Mr. Kramer ran toward them, white-faced and panting. Mr. Anderson caught his arm as he went past, slowing Mr. Kramer sufficiently to notice the creatures in his way. "My god," sobbed Mr. Kramer. "My god. We're surrounded."

The 600 block of Poplar Street lived inside for two whole days. Mr. Martin and Mr. Aldritch, independently, tried to climb their back fences. They found that they froze upon reaching the top, and then some irresistible force gently pushed them back. Mr. Aldritch kept trying until he sprained his wrist. He had an over-the-fence acquaintance with his rear neighbors and tried to call to them. Mr. Anderson stood in *his* backyard and signaled repeated SOSes with bathtowels and flashlights. Neither received any response. As nearly as they could tell, the blocks on every side of them were deserted.

The Narrs began to run out of food. Saturday had always been their big shopping day. Sunny, David, Joey, and Tommy began to find it tiresome indoors. They were active children, used to running and bicycling, and being children, they found it impossible to sustain an atmosphere of alarm. The creatures had remained on the corners and made no attempt to enter the block itself. "The Best of Johnny Carson" was the only show on television.

Sunny was the first child to defy her parents and venture outdoors. She rode her bicycle enticingly back and forth in front of the Andersons' until David and Joey joined her and soon the Martin children were out, too, pedaling around as though it were a normal weekend. They discovered a wonderful new game. If they rode as hard as they could into the Poplar/Maxwell intersection, the bicycle would freeze up suddenly, then be spit back into Poplar Street. The Anderson boys rigged a jump so that they could be aloft at the moment of freezing.

The creatures arm-wrestled at the corners and ignored them. Mrs. Desmond watched from her window. At last she made herself open the door. She walked by the creatures, catching a quick whiff of an odor rather like tuna fish, forcing herself not to move too fast. The Narrs' door opened just enough to let her in.

Mrs. Narr wanted to talk about food. The Desmonds had purchased catastrophe supplies of dried foods when Reagan became president. Mrs. Desmond chose not to mention these now, but listened to Mrs. Narr's concerns as though she shared them. "Why are they here?" said Mrs. Narr at last, and her voice went hoarse as she said it. "What do they want with us?"

Mrs. Desmond, with her greater political awareness, suggested that the Andersons might be the key. She tried to explain the quota system to Mrs. Narr, who didn't listen. The conversation about familiar issues and complaints began to soothe Mrs. Desmond. She was a professional; she was used to being in charge. Her self-confidence began to return to her. "Well, why don't we just ask them?" she said in a voice almost girlish.

But Mrs. Narr refused to join her. Not that she didn't think it was a good idea. But it struck her as rash. Mrs. Narr never behaved rashly, she reminded Mrs. Desmond. Unless she was certain the occasion called for it.

This was irritating and shook Mrs. Desmond's resolve slightly. But only slightly. She pointed out to herself that she had to pass right by the creatures to get home anyway. She smiled politely and told herself Mrs. Narr was a wimp. She took a deep breath, holding herself very straight, and opened the door. It was her lawn they were camped out on, after all. She was entitled to an explanation. She attempted a confident, purposeful stride and wished she had dressed with more care. What were her clothes saying about her?

The creatures watched her approach, beginning to wave their arms. She heard a faint sound like wind chimes. The tuna odor intensified. That and their sleek skins reminded her of the seal pool at Marine World.

"I believe I speak for the entire neighborhood," she said formally, "when I say I think we have a right to know what's going on."

There was a pause, then the boxes answered. The synthetic voices reminded her of Alvin, the singing chipmunk. "Information will be provided as it is purposeful," they answered.

What did that mean? Mrs. Desmond wondered. She grew more specific; her tone was aggressive. "How long are we to be kept here?" she asked. "I have a job to go to. We're in the middle of budgeting and I really cannot be spared. The children have school."

She waited for the response. "These things are no longer necessary," she was told.

It chilled Mrs. Desmond. She was suddenly aware of her husband, watching her through the window. His silent support brought an unprofessional quaver to her voice. She lost her courage all at once. "We cannot stay here indefinitely," she forced herself to say. "We are running out of food."

"We are prepared to assume responsibility for your nutritional needs."

The teeth which loomed above her were so clearly carnivorous. The wet skin suggested a fatty diet. Mrs. Desmond felt faint. She began to cry. "You've no right to keep us here," she said. "What are you going to do to us?"

"No one will be hurt," the boxes answered. "Information will be provided as needed." The two creatures sank back into the lawn, lowered the metallic boxes. Their arms intertwined.

Mrs. Desmond went into her house and let her husband put his arms around her. "I've made you a cup of coffee," he said. "I'll go and get it."

He looked so concerned Mrs. Desmond forced herself to smile. "Put some powdered milk in it," she told him. "We might as well get used to dried foods."

She took a long time over her coffee. If she had been at work she would have been drinking coffee just like this. She would have been making decisions, red-penciling the glut out of proposed expenditures, drafting memos. She sipped her drink. "Honey," she said. "We all need to talk. Don't you think? I mean the whole neighborhood. We need to have a meeting.

"Will they let us?"

"Let's see. Are you with me? We'll go knock on doors."

"I'm with you," her husband told her. "Whatever you say."

"Or—" Mrs. Desmond's voice was thoughtful. "If we all put on our swimsuits we could say we were going to the Kramers' for a swim. That would be even better. We could say we do it every Sunday."

Mr. Desmond thought she was clever and said so. He went to slip into his suit and flipflops. But at the last moment Mrs. Desmond chose a sundress for herself. It had occurred to her that she could easily dominate a group of people in swimsuits if she dressed appropriately. And leadership was going to be critical now. A unified response. One leader.

The creatures seemed to pay no attention to them as they stepped outside, but had a disconcerting ability to look in many directions at once, each eye independent of

the others. Mr. Desmond waved his towel in their direction. "Pool party," he called and proceeded hastily to the
Narrs' front door.

Sunny Aldritch came skidding up on her bicycle.
"Did they invite us to go swimming?" she asked excitedly.
"Really? I'll get my suit. Far out! I'll go tell my Mom. She
didn't think they were *ever* going to ask us."

The Everts wouldn't answer their door, but the rest of the
neighborhood assembled quickly at the Kramers'. A quantity of beer was produced—to help with the cover—and
they began to drink it. Mrs. Desmond opened a can and
looked for a place to throw the fliptop. "We must be thinking about escape," she said. "After all, there are only four
of them."

Sunny Aldritch took a sip of her mother's beer. "Oh,
there are lots more than that," she said.

"What do you mean, sweetheart?" said Mrs.
Desmond icily. "Two in front of my house, two down by
the Everts'."

"But not always the same two," said Sunny. "The two
at your house now are different than the first two we saw."

Mrs. Desmond felt something bitter rise in her throat.
"Are you sure? How can you be sure? They all look alike."

"Not to me," said Sunny saucily.

"Even if there were only four," said Mr. Anderson.
"What good would it do us? We're webbed in here. We're
no match for them."

"It's a force field," said Mr. Aldritch knowledgeably.
"I've seen them on 'Star Trek.' What we have to do is find
out how they generate it. A picked team of us will have
to turn it off at the source while the rest of us create a
diversion."

"What if the source is outside the field?" asked Mr.
Anderson.

"The key is those little boxes," said Mr. Kramer. "One

of them pointed that at me and I went weak all over. We have to get those little boxes."

The children began a game of Marco Polo in the pool. Mrs. Desmond felt the meeting was slipping away from her. "What kind of weapons do we have?" she asked.

There was a pause. "Mr. Martin has a gun," said Mr. Desmond. "We all know that. And Mr. Narr has a hunting rifle."

"Three rifles," Mr. Narr told them.

Mr. Aldritch nodded. "Keep those ready. They might be just the diversion we need." He sipped his beer. "Aliens invade suburban neighborhood," he said. "I saw it on 'Twilight Zone.' The important thing now is that we don't begin to turn on each other."

"Why?" said Mrs. Narr.

"Why what?"

"Why did aliens invade a suburban neighborhood?"

Mr. Aldritch shrugged. "For entertainment? For research?" He lowered his voice so the children wouldn't hear. "For food."

Mrs. Narr sniffled slightly. "Suppose we could get off the block," she said. "Have you looked at the houses behind us? The grass is growing, but no one mows it. No one lives in those houses anymore."

"We haven't been mowing our lawns, but we're still here," Mr. Martin objected.

Mr. Anderson finished his beer. "But Mrs. Narr is right. Those houses are deserted. No noise, no lights. Our radios don't work. They may be holding the whole city."

"So what can we do?" asked Mrs. Desmond. "That's what we have to decide."

"Mommy!" Sunny's voice was loud and indignant. "Tommy keeps opening his eyes underwater."

"Am not," said Tommy.

"Are, too."

"You're just a baby. Can't stand to get caught."

"Can, too!"

"Can not."

"I wish we could signal," said Mrs. Aldritch quietly.
There was a pause while the neighbors thought nostalgically about the Simpsons' CB radio, which had so infuriated everyone by interfering with prime time television reception. "We have flares in the car trunk," Mrs. Desmond said at last.

"Oh, so do we," said Mrs. Aldritch. "In all the car trunks."

"We can set some out tonight," Mr. Anderson agreed.

Mr. Kramer reached for the last Coors. They were down to the light beer now. "I wonder how the Padres are doing," he said.

"Do you think they're playing?" said Mr. Anderson. "They were scheduled against the Braves today. And what are we getting? Did you look this morning? 'Gilligan's Island.' " His wife moved in closer to him. She thought he was beginning to get drunk. "You know Garry Templeton, the shortstop?" Mr. Anderson continued. "Did I tell you he went to the same high school I did?" There was a long silence. "Damn it! It irks me to just sit here." Mr. Anderson stood up. "I'm going to go find out what's what."

Mrs. Desmond rose, too, one hand on her husband's arm, pulling him to his feet at the same time. "We'll come," she said.

"And us," said Mr. Aldritch, "except for Sunny." Sunny climbed out of the pool instantly and came to drip on his shoes.

"Except for Sunny what?" she asked.

The other neighbors looked uncomfortably away. It was a small and silent delegation. Mr. Anderson's anger propelled them down the street. "I want some questions answered," he told the two sentries in the Desmonds' yard. They had draped themselved over the oriental bridge which, as a result, was creaking in the center. The creatures straightened and began to rub their arms together. Mr. Anderson paid no attention to the faint music. "And I want them answered now," he said.

"Information will be provided as it is purposeful," the boxes answered. The creatures were not even holding them today, but had them slung about their bodies like tourist cameras.

"We want to contact our friends and family outside."

"Regretfully, we cannot permit it."

"I—" Mr. Anderson's voice was dangerously quiet and distinct. Beer and baseball, thought Mrs. Desmond irritatedly, that's what it takes to get a man to act like a man. "*I*," repeated Mr. Anderson, "refuse to be kept here."

The boxes made their customary pause. The sound of the creatures' arms rose in pitch. "We have no interest in interfering in your life," they said. "Please continue to function normally."

"Normally! Normally!" Mr. Anderson's voice rose to match the boxes. "Do you imagine any part of the last few days has been normal for us? You imprison us in our homes. Cut us off from our friends. Deprive us of our sources of food and information. Even the television is nothing but reruns."

There was a longer pause. Then the boxes responded like a choir of dwarves. "We have continued the television," they said, "because we believe it to be an integral part of your routine. We welcome programming suggestions."

Mr. Anderson sneered. *"Invasion of the Body Snatchers,"* he said.

"The Invaders," said Mrs. Aldritch.

"War of the Worlds," said Mr. Aldritch.

" 'Joanie Loves Chachi,' " said Sunny.

The next day the aliens delivered the first shipment of food. Four additional aliens appeared to distribute it. They greeted each other with a weaving of arms which was almost sexual, Mrs. Desmond thought, and somewhat disgusting. When the boxes were opened they contained small, hard pellets like dog food.

"Do you believe this?" Mrs. Desmond asked. She was anxious to reestablish her authority. She felt Mr. Anderson's actions after the pool party had threatened it slightly. "Are we supposed to eat this?" she asked the alien next to her. It focused three of its jellied eyes on her, but did not respond.

Mr. Aldritch picked up a pellet and tasted it. "It tastes just like it looks," he told them.

"It looks like the food you buy in the zoo for animals," said Mrs. Desmond.

"It looks like shit," said Sunny. "Rat shit. I'm not eating it."

The voice boxes spoke. "The foodstuffs are of a high quality. They are noncarcinogenic and contain slight doses of fluoride in addition to vitamins. . . ."

"We need a variety of foods," said Mrs. Narr despairingly.

"No, these will meet your nutritional needs."

"We like a variety of foods."

Mr. Evert had joined them today. He looked wan and unsteady. "The baby can't chew these," he pointed out.

"The food has been sorted according to residence. In the box labeled with the number of your residence you will find a powdered variant which may be mixed with water." Mrs. Desmond began to pass out the packages. The aliens retreated back down the street to their usual corners. "Starting tomorrow," the voice boxes chorused, "we will expect you to take weekly physicals."

Mr. Kramer's mouth went dry. "Physicals?" he said.

"We are taking care of you. We have assumed responsibility for you." The voices grew faster. "Check your televisions. There is a film festival on."

Mr. Anderson picked up a handful of food and let it

slip through his fingers. "Rat *food*," he said. "Lab rats. That's it. It's a study."

Eight additional aliens appeared in the morning for the physicals. Each could wield several instruments at once so things went very fast. Despite Mr. Kramer's premonitions, the physicals were just physicals. Tissue samples, blood, urine, mucus, and stool samples were collected from each neighbor. Each neighbor was weighed and measured, their voice pitches were recorded, their posture was analyzed. There were balance tests, reflex tests and questionnaires. " 'I have the feeling people are out to get me,' " Mr. Anderson read aloud off his personality profile. " 'Usually true, sometimes true, rarely true.' Jesus Christ!"

At the end of the week the aliens made another announcement. The rubbing of their arms was particularly harmonious. They had brought five boxes of Whitman's candies as a special treat.

"Great," said Mr. Narr. "When do we get them?"

The synthetic voices were annoyingly even. "They've been hidden. You must hunt for them."

There was a long dumbfounded silence. "You must be kidding," said Mr. Anderson. He felt a clutch inside him, a furious contraction "We've cooperated with your physicals; we've answered your questionnaires. But we're not going to hunt for chocolates."

"I will," said Sunny. "And I bet I find them."

The children fanned out, leaving behind an angry and bewildered group of adults. "This is to humiliate us," said Mrs. Desmond. "This is a psychological ploy to break us completely. Mr. Martin, get your gun. Enough is enough."

Mr. Martin reached slowly into his shirt. "It won't work," he said. "I've already tried it."

He handed the pistol to Mrs. Desmond, who aimed in the direction of her front yard. The creatures gave no sign of noticing. "Not like this," said Mr. Anderson. "We need a plan, we need the boxes . . ." His voice faded as Mrs. Desmond pulled the trigger and heard dead air.

"Are you sure . . .?" she began.

"Oh, it's loaded," said Mr. Martin.

"Let me try." Mr. Kramer reached for the gun. His hand shook violently and left a sweaty film on Mrs. Desmond's own dry skin. Mr. Kramer had been looking quite ill recently. His flirtatious, easy manner had vanished with the last of the alcohol. Now, in one sharp movement, he pointed the gun to his forehead and pulled the trigger. The silence continued. "Damn," said Mr. Kramer, beginning to cry. "Damn."

Sunny came racing back down the street. "I found one box in the Andersons' ivy," she called. "And another under our car. I get all the chocolate creams."

David Anderson appeared with a Whitman sampler. "Here, Mom," he said.

Mrs. Anderson opened the box. "There's a rum chocolate," she said. "You take it, Mr. Kramer." She passed the rest around.

Mrs. Narr took a caramel. "David is a good boy," she said quietly to Mrs. Aldritch, who nodded, chewing thoughtfully.

"A nice kid," Mrs. Aldritch said. "But just a little repressed. You'll never see Sunny stifled like that."

"No," Mrs. Narr agreed. "I know I won't."

After that the creatures began to hide the daily food supplies and to time the hunts. One day the neighbors couldn't find the food at all. They appealed to the creatures for help, but were told to look harder. A week later they came across the missing boxes in the Aldritches' garage.

"I'm surprised we *ever* found them," said Mr. Martin nastily. "It's lucky you've got the whole street to park along. It's lucky you don't have to try and fit a car in here."

Mrs. Desmond took charge of the extra food—their insurance against another failed search. She felt she was the most trustworthy since she and her husband still had their dried foods, but she did not explain this to the neighbors. The fact that the Desmonds were still drinking coffee was something they kept just between the two of them.

In the third week Mr. Anderson was asked to remain at the physicals for additional testing. A single alien did the extra work-up; it was the first time Mr. Anderson had seen one alone. He had begun to notice differences in the individual creatures—enough to know that Sunny was right. There were a great many of them. They even smelled different at times. The one drawing blood samples from him now had the customary tuna odor with a sort of garlic overlay. Mr. Anderson supposed that *their* diets varied. He tried to count up exactly how many there were, but couldn't. He thought of the hopeless flares they had lit, night after night, when there were no humans in the air to see them. He felt completely dispirited.

The voice box spoke in its high-pitched, expressionless way. "You seem to have an abnormality in your ability to use sugar."

"You're talking about diabetes," said Mr. Anderson. "No, I'm not diabetic."

"Our tests confirm that you are."

"I would have thought we were on a pretty low-sugar diet. But, if you're right, I'll need insulin."

"There are a number of possible treatments. Each one necessitates greater contact between you and us than we can allow. Such intercourse may contaminate the control group. It will be necessary to remove you."

Mr. Anderson felt cold. "The control group?" he asked, his own voice high and false somehow. "We're the control group?" There was no answer. "Don't take me," he said. "Please."

"It is regrettable. You were one of the brighter subjects. We have always enjoyed your questionnaires. And you have assumed some leadership. Someone else must replace you. That, in itself, will be interesting to see. Mrs. Aldritch, perhaps? Or Mr. Kramer?"

This was more than any of the creatures had ever said to Mr. Anderson. In the sheer volume of information he was receiving, Mr. Anderson saw the hopelessness of his position. He was not going back. Not even to say good-bye. There was no reason not to be frank with him. "My family is there," he pleaded. "My children."

"The children are proving adaptable to anything. The important element is the integrity of the control. None of our other experiments can be evaluated without it."

Mr. Anderson maneuvered himself closer to the alien. Its arms were nearly around him, the smell was very intense. Almost, he was out of the creature's line of vision, almost too close to be seen. The eyes loomed above him like clusters of fish eggs. He grabbed for the voice box, held on to it though it burned his hand. It became shape-less, melted into his palm, and his last hopes melted with it. The creature ignored this action, merely grasped him gently by the shoulders and lower down the arms, thrust-ing him out farther away. The mountain of eyes focused on him.

"You're all wrong," said Mr. Anderson. "If you imag-ine that you've created a control situation in there. It's laughable, really." He felt his cheeks go wet, his nose fill. He wiped it. "I mean if you think for a moment what's going on out there is normal." The creature created a gen-tle friction with its arms, like wind in the trees. What it meant, Mr. Anderson didn't know, but he thought, he imagined, that the fishy eyes were looking at him intently, and that the movement of the arms was thoughtful.

Five years passed before they saw him on Poplar Street again. The creatures had been mistaken in their predic-tions. Neither Mrs. Aldritch, nor Mr. Kramer, nor Mrs.

Desmond despite her hopes and plans had emerged as the natural block leader. It was Sunny who mediated between the neighbors and the creatures, organized the foodhunts, and planned holidays for their entertainment. She discovered quite quickly that there were patterns to the ways in which the food was hidden, and although the patterns changed, twenty minutes was the longest she ever had to hunt. She used this expertise to bully the reluctant grownups into doing what she wished. Gradually the resentment disappeared and it began to seem natural to listen to Sunny and agree with Sunny and do what Sunny said. When the Martins' dog died in a hysterical fit and Sunny wanted the entire neighborhood to attend a burial in the Martins' backyard, everyone did so.

Mrs. Narr let her garden go to weed and learned to make dandelion salads, which were enjoyed with the same ardor as the occasional Whitman's candies. Mr. Kramer began an evening tradition of story-telling, in which his stories were acknowledged the best. They were, Mrs. Aldritch told him wistfully, as good as the soaps.

He was continuing an old favorite, a tale about warriors as slender as reeds who lived in glass houses on green hills at the end of the world, on the evening when Mr. Anderson reappeared. When they first saw him, in the last light of the day, he was magnificent. His skin gleamed moistly, he waved his arms when he talked and his words were a kind of singing. He had been living with aliens, he told them. But now he was back. They thought he was some sort of Messiah come to lead them to their freedom. He even thought so, himself. Unless it was another experiment. There was really no way to be sure.

The Logical Legend of Heliopause and Cyberfiddle

Outside is dust. Dust, and a fell wind, and a scatter of malcontents, and the dilapidated leavings of some singularity or other. Therefore: begin Inside, where there is no dust at all. Scan these bits, and wonder.

Inside the Warren labors Pryer. Pryer is chambered, neurojacked, hard-wired. He is an ectomorph crawling through the nest of a circuitry bird, if there were any birds anymore in the wide pointless world. Pryer is good bioware, a proud remnant, half awake.

Pryer labors on Carmen Memoranda.

Who is Carmen Memoranda?

Carmen Memoranda is: looking for something lost. Which may be such as a pair of spectacles we saw through in our youth. Which may be the word spoken we didn't take back. Which may be a map given us by a strange woman we didn't know which we misplaced in the glove compartment of a bucket of bolts we drove too fast.

Carmen Memoranda is: a dedicated project, a datadate, a shadow workalike defined by perimeters of labor, taking shape through the accrual of data. Carmen Memoranda's algorithm is: sifting for the misstep. Prowling for the moment Humanity flipped its wig. Playing the transcript back to hear when the villain confesses. Carmen Memoranda is not a bioperson, an archaic solo isoware.

So Pryer dandles backlook databits, seeking some ancient text.doc to fulfill Carmen Memoranda's dreams. It's that or sink heavymetal into comahead.

But Pryer is not always a datajock with a hardwired hacker's hook. Not at all. Ten cubed cycles <ago> he is a rocketjock, a fulljacked pilot in actuality. For Pryer is on the crew that meets Heliopause.

Imagine this:

A starship.

Pryer nestled into a strong interface, fingers itching to veer the interstellar hydrogen streams. His crew arrayed about him, cryobionic, biocybernetic, organomech. This is the first, the interstellar oneshot, Starship *Stellar Kowalski*, a whitewater trip on hydrogen rivers, the only way to fly.

For behold, spacetime is checkered with stress fractures. Down these cracks cascades hydrogen, splitting around whirlpools of sun, a runable river, Cosmic Class Five. And here across the gravity beach rumbles *Stellar Kowalski*, quantum prow agleam. Pryer flexes his cyberpaddles.

■

But Heliopause awaits them.

161

∎

The
Logical
Legend
of
Helio-
pause
and
Cyber-
fiddle

And what is Heliopause?

Imagine this: Space is bread: Time is bread: but: Light is peanut butter, if there were any bread and peanut butter anymore in the wide bitter world. Heliopause signifies where the Sun's work is done, where its gravlight approaches as close to zero as is necessary and sufficient, where it cannot relevantly diminish further. At Heliopause, human will fails. Artifact distresses. Cyberlogic garbles.

Pryer reaches heliopause. He becomes immobilized. He is wracked with inexplicable sorrow. He is negative with virtual fear. He tries to snap a neurolink, but the potential vectors are filled with wailing. Pryer wants to hibernate. Pryer wants to lobernate. He tries everything. He sneaks up on himself. He stuffs his virtual ears with beeswax. All to no avail. They cannot pass Heliopause. Heliopause cannot be passed.

Stellar Kowalski turns, as if steered, along the inside surface of the sphere of Heliopause. There is a xenologic here they cannot override. They turn back, shamed, tears on their faces if they have faces, fear and sorrow in their hearts if they have hearts. Later other crews recapitulate, with the same result. No human thing can pass Heliopause. Heliopause is implacable. Humans are stuck at home, grounded, no wheels, flat broke.

But meanwhile, whither the biosphere? Metacycles of techgnash have toxied the place. Nobody has bothered to houseclean. Nobody does windows. Heavywinds blow, acidwaters flow. Earth is trashed and now there's nowhere to go. Humans sit sadly on the ground and stare at each other. *The long romp is over*, someone says. They've burned their bridges. They can't live on Earth, and *Stellar Kowalski* says they can't leave. Heliopause means no Sunday drive. Heliopause means sitting inside on a gigalong acidrainy afternoon. Where can they go? What can they do?

They assemble the Warren, slink inside, and slam the door. Warren Beatty, the only game in town.

Humans are melancholy babies. They toy listless in their electronic slums. They ignore the Outside, as it slides into nullity. They suckle at fusion nipples. They fribble at naught games. They diminish to a handful and don't care.

Enter Carmen Memoranda. A few humans entertain the idea there is an answer to this puzzle, if only they look carefully enough. Somewhere is surely a datachunk hiding the clue. Therefore: here is Pryer, sifting databits like crazy, seeking cybersalvation for the sad sequestered remnants of the Human deluge. It's that or sink heavymetal into comahead.

But wait!

Behold: Quasi-now Pryer is nanotiks from landing the Big One, the Wholly Data Grail, a freefax to Avalon, the winning realnumber in the cyberlottery.

See: Pryer makes a find. A most palpable find. Something that really rings his virtual bell, something that totally toots his simhorn, something that absolutely bites his biobutt.

It is a *Manual* Pryer has found. Wow! A *Manual* entitled: "Building the Cremonian Violin, After the Innovations of Antonio Stradivari—A Manual of Instruction, With Additional Material on Bow Construction." Wow!

163

■
The
Logical
Legend
of
Helio-
pause
and
Cyber-
fiddle

Pryer has trouble coging a few items. And there is no rea-son why he *should* be able to cog a thing such as this thing. It is old, would be moldy and dusty, if any dust were allowed Inside. What ancient archivist, long since shuffled off to the recyclers, could have converted it to bright biopixels? This is an old-fashioned how-to cut-here glue-there manual. There is a hardcopyness about it that flouts Pryer's logic. Who uploads by iota? Who links mindword to handeye by railroad?

Pryer skitters to Webwordster's. *Manual: from the arcspeak <manum>, meaning hand, therefore something done to applause*, says Webwordster. *Violin: an acoustic musical instrument of the cordophone group, held in the hands and prodded by means of a bowed stick into emitting noise for the pleasure and edification of live listeners*, says Webwordster.

Pryer knows neural soundlinks. He knows somatic bassicks. His aural canals prickle this very moment with retrograde audiotactile muzakbits. But he does not grok this other business. So why does he feel this stirring in his breast? He has forgotten he even has a breast. Something is happening, but he doesn't know what it is, does he MrJones?

Imagine this:

Pryer as a sprat: ten to the fourth cycles ago.
— *These buildings on my screen, Teacher, what were they for?*
— *They were government buildings, Student Pryer,* answers Teacher. *In use, they housed those who were supported by the public. In return, the government made all the decisions for everyone. That was before Instavote, before Kwikno.*
— *What was it like then, Teacher? What was it like to walk those corridors, and breathe that unprocessed air, and use those*

strange things, and not be linked or cyphed or anything?
— Those are silly questions, Student Pryer.

Now that old black magic has Pryer in its spell, that old black magic he forgot he knows so well. Round and round he goes. Here is the litany he scans: *Wood. Glue. Horsehair. Gut.* A mantrum indeed. *Wood. Glue. Horsehair. Gut.* What are these things? He wishes he knew, who has never wished anything since he wished for the stars and got stuffed by Heliopause.

Pryer uploads, then overloads. He goes to viz and meths himself and stays awake two seeks straight to actually wordread "Building the Cremonian Violin, After the Innovations of Antonio Stradivari — A Manual of Instruction, With Additional Material on Bow Construction." Then he cancels his thirtyseek date with his sexmate Squish, and reads it again. Wordreads! Word by word. The logicmatrix reels.

To facilitate his reading, Pryer disses his reticular soundlinks. He disses his Billgram Lights. His neurizon sits empty and he hears his own thoughts unwinding. He thinks he can feel an Ancient uncurling in his cells, reaching out toward his fingertips and toetips. What is this thing, he wonders, this "Building the Cremonian Violin, After the Innovations of Antonio Stradivari — A Manual of Instruction, With Additional Material on Bow Construction," that it should ruffle his ment so noncog? Is it an engagement ring for sweet virgin Carmen Memoranda? Is it a handle he must grasp? Is it a telescope he must peer through?

Or is it just a flood of anachronistic metaphor?

■

165

•

The
Logical
Legend
of
Helio-
pause
and
Cyber-
fiddle

There comes a glister of psychedelia on Pryer's simhelm horizon. An idea is coalescing in his mind. A look of determination flits over and finally roosts on Pryer's features, where they are not covered by his simhelm. He outflips the manual, and holos it, and then he is holding something very much like something that has not been seen in real-space in megacycles, which is to say, a book.

How can this be?

Imagine this:

Again, Pryer the sprat: arguing.
—*But Teacher, why is cybereality so much better? Why is what we do better than what the Ancients did?*
—*Because, young Pryer, there is an inevitable progression from the concrete to the abstract, from the material to the ethereal, from the mechanical to the conceptual, from the gross to the nano. For example, our progenitors took directly from the natural world. Then our industrial ancestors learned to transmogrify raw materials into primitive synthetics and derivatives. Now we eschew materials entirely. We tangible the pure energy of the universe. The sounds of our music, the colors of our art, come from pure concept. We are free at last to develop the world of the mind: Bureaucraty, Ponderation, Introspectic, and all the other great arts of our time.*
—*But Teacher, didn't the Ancients roam the whole wide world and call it their home?*
—*Bummer nonsense,* scoffs Teacher, and it severs the com-link and vanishes into the vortex of polarity in which it resides.

Pryer musters Melt and Smudge and Clack and Cookie, the fingertips and eyelashes and earlobes of Carmen Memoranda. Pryer himself is her lower lip, stuck out petulantly. He quants them "Building the Cremonian Violin, After the Innovations of Antonio Stradivari—A Manual of Instruction, With Additional Material on Bow Construction."

—Eureka. It is the sparkle in Carmen Memoranda's eye. Pryer beams, running simnaked.
— What why? This arcjunk? Silly. Misguided. Melt.
—Mistaken. Clack
—Erroneous. Cookie.
—Blunder. Botch. Boner. Smudge.
— Timesmog. This is a false alarm. We will diss now. Melt finalizes.

Cursors of frustration tweedle Pryer's neurizon. He pounds his console with his balled right fist, then looks in surprise at his hand. The sprat lives.

—Dedicated intent. I wish to fabricate a violin.
— What why? Melt grumbles.
—Melt is Carmen Memoranda's Mom. She should understand.
— What is fabricate?
—Skitter. Pryer skitters.

Construct, build, assemble, fashion, produce, shape, says Webwordster.

—Nonsane. Sim one. Synth one. Holo one. Why fabricate?
— To extrapolize data? Pryer webmutters lamely.

Carmen Memoranda is flabbergasted. She goes vox.

"But to physically construct this thing!" dithers Melt. "Why in the Warren? Data defines itself, as Runnel apts it."

"What is real?" asks Pryer reasonably. "What does Carmen Memoranda's real voice sound like?"

167

■
The
Logical
Legend
of
Helio-
pause
and
Cyber-
fiddle

"Vulgar!" gasps Smudge. "Pryer has no sense of bureaucratic esthetics. What is the value of a primitive soundbox? How can it compare to the electrosynth or empathomat or ramrom?"

"There has not been a violin in ten to the tenth cycles," points out Pryer.

"No doubt there is a good reason for that," splutters Clack.

"We would pay homage to those who came before," says Pryer.

"As if they could care," scoffs Cookie.

"I'm going to make a violin," continues Pryer. "And then I will play it." Pryer is waxing vertebrate.

—*Acknowledged*, grudges Melt. *And Carmen Memoranda will attend. It better be good. Break!*
—*Break.* Smudge disses.
—*Break.* Clack disses.
—*Break.* Cookie disses.

Thus does Pryer put himself into the calloused ancient hands of the anonymous author of "Building the Cremonian Violin, After the Innovations of Antonio Stradivari—A Manual of Instruction, With Additional Material on Bow Construction."

Assemble your tools, says the Manual. *Clear your workbench. Get your life in order. Then you can truly begin.*

Tools. Pryer needs tools.

He finds a list of these at the beginning of the Manual. The tools are steel, with wooden handles. This is two problems in one. First, no one has used ore-based metals in megacycles. Why would they, instead of quasicrystal? Second is the wood, which is a bridge of a different color when he gets to it.

Pryer rings the Turing Company. He needs an Electrotekie to discuss this with. A mandelbrot of cyberdendrites snakes out from Pryer's simhelm and snares rabbits from all the database in Warren Beatty.

—*Yes? Electrotekie here. What's up?*
—*I need to make steel tools.*
—*I grok them. But why steel? Sudokrome would be stronger and sharper. Look nicer too.*
—*They have to be steel.*
—*Look, be a snap to just holo them.*
—*But I want to use them, to make something else. A violin.*
—*Excuse me? I must have insufficient data here. Why not just have me sim the violin? Or synth it, if you must.*
—*Well, because . . . well . . . I don't know.* And Pryer goes diss.

—*Don't sulk. If you want steel, steel you get. You're the Human. However, there are a zillion recipes for steel. Perhaps I might suggest a nice unassuming carbonsteel, with just a hint of molybdenum? Playful, yet erudite.*

Pryer agrees and it is done. For handles, he selects durasim, because why not? Comes a tatter in the possibility curve of Pryer's verity port. Comes a little parade of anachrony.

First here is Pryer's new workbench, which he must clear, also fabbed of durasim. Actually, Pryer did not mean to fab a workbench at all, assuming the Manual to have been engaging in metaphor, but here it is. He and Electrotekie didn't realize the attached vise is a separate and removable tool. But now he is glad, because he has a place to lay his new tools.

169
▪
The
Logical
Legend
of
Helio-
pause
and
Cyber-
fiddle

Here they lie, bright as baby pixels. Small grinning saws, convex-footed planes in descending sizes, like little race cars, if there were any cars anymore in the wide silent world. Spokeshaves, and an array of tiny knives in different shapes, and chisels, and gouges, and drills, and clamps. Pryer is pleased. The ancient inside him is pleased. Carmen Memoranda may or may not be pleased.

Now for the wood. Wood is why he has made all these *wood-working* tools. Time to cross the rolling horse.

You must select your wood carefully, says the Manual. *It is the foundation upon which you build. As is the beginning, so is the end.*

But Pryer really is not quite sure what wood is. Skitter.

The dried cellular skeleton of members of the arboreal families of order <vegetalia>, says Webwordster. *Worked with tools in ancient times to produce <artifacts>,* says Webwordster. *Pieces of <trees>.*

Pryer discusses this with Electrotekie.
—*Can I cut pieces off the trees in Undergarden?*
—*Sure. If you don't mind being fried by the lazercops. It's their religion. No picking the flowers. Keep off the grass. Besides, your watchamacallit, your Manual, calls for specific kinds of woods. Those are different species in Undergarden.*
—*So where can I get the wood?*
—*From trees.*
—*Where do I find the trees? The right kinds of trees?*
—*Outside. There are Bummers Outside who tend a few wretched, leftover trees. At least, that's what I hear.*

Therefore a proximate seek finds Pryer rising from his conform. He disses his linklines. He disses his handjack neuroprobes. It has been ten squared cycles since he's been mobe, but the myoshakers have kept his body functional. He approaches his chamber iris and it opens with a cough. He steps into the Hall of Warren Beatty.

Pryer is alone. Closed irises slumber into vanishment along the Hall perspective. A whisper of virtual reality seeps and glitters from behind each pupil. The Hall echoes with electric breezes. Pryer finds a Paul Newmoslide and zips to Undergarden. Undergarden is empty also, except for the trees and shrubs. Autogardners keep them flourishing.

Pryer gazes over the deserted plantscape. He sees rococo conforms, and movietiles and colorpanels galore, and stimlites winking. There are yumstik dolers. Pryer grabs a lamsuit node from a doler and slides it over his simhelm. It snuggles him. He boards a heinleinbelt.

Empty halls.

Comes a blur in Hall interstice. A subpsychic hum pervades. End concepts pester the Hall perspective.

The Door.

Pryer slides up.
—*Approaching Door,* says the Door. *Please neuroload lock procedure if you intend to exit. You must be wearing a lamsuit.*
—*I'm suited. I'm loaded.*
—*Farout. Delock.*

Pryer's simhelm prickles with terminality. Colorbands traverse Hall matrix. Quasicrystals retract and the Hallwall dilates. Pryer floats in on realization clusters and the Hallwall regroups behind him.

— *Go for it,* says the Door.

A doorbud forms. It opens. Pryer pops out like pollen. For the first time since *Stellar Kowalski,* Pryer stands Outside. Alone. Pryer and his Wounded Planet Sing the Blues.

Comes a temporal dedux.

Before him lay a dry valley, dust swirling across it like rotten lace curtains. A few clumps of coarse green-gray grass encrusted the ground here and there. Plants they were, but certainly not trees. The sky was bilious yellow. Pryer poked irritably at his lamsuit mask, and a little finger of outside air weaseled in and made him cough. He screened the desolation, arid dust-bowls like scabs, and fanged air. Behind him lurked the possibility field of Warren Beatty, dense with almost. He powertrudged down the unwholesome little valley, in seach of Bummers, those gripey outcasts, those sleazy misfits, those dirty scowls in the shadow of the bright Warren Beatty smile.

Winking through the haze flickered a little red eye. Pryer mooched toward it, bouncing on his heelwheels. As he got closer he could see the eye was an eye of flames. *Fire,* his simhelm told him. Wood fire. Pryer just knew it was wood fire. By the fire hunched a drab of a figure. Pryer wheeled up and the figure turned toward him, stood. It came to Pryer's waist. *Child,* Pryer's simhelm told him. *A Bummer.* Pryer stared at the wizened scabrous skin of the *Bummer,* at the corrugated poxy face, at the leaky muddy eyes of it.

What would Pryer know of children?

■

Imagine this:

Pryer the sprat again: Wistful.
— *Where do I come from, Teacher?*
— *You are coming from there now, Student Pryer. How are we but
the vortex of possibility?*
— *Then my body, Teacher. Where does it come from?*
— *Grown in the biotank, Student Pryer, like all bioparts.*
— *Why, Teacher?*
— *To pilot* Stellar Kowalski, *as you very well know. Two is com-
pany, and three is a crowd. Therefore many are called, but few
are grown.*

Now Pryer scanned this Bummer child, heaped with
scabs, crusty with raunch, lumped and bumped and scaly.
The Bummer eyed Pryer.

"Mumble, mumble," gritted the Bummer, and Pryer's
simhelm cleared its throat.

"I knew you would come some time," said Pryer's
simhelm.

"Are you really a Bummer?" asked Pryer.

"Mumble, mumble," gritted the simhelm.

"I'm a Stayer," said the Bummer, through the simhelm.

What are Stayers? Pryer asked his simhelm. *Or Bummers, for
that matter? Are they monsters?*

No, said the simhelm. *They are simply Humans who do not
live in Warren Beatty. They are discontent antis. They did not
want* Stellar Kowalski, *now they do not want Warren Beatty.
They say all Humans should live Outside. When Humankind
came to live in Warren Beatty, they stayed Outside. They live
Outside now, but they do not live long.*

"Why do you say you knew I would come?" Pryer
asked the Bummer via simhelm.

173

■

The
Logical
Legend
of
Helio-
pause
and
Cyber-
fiddle

"It was told," said the Bummer, sitting down again by the fire. "I'm the last. I'm the last Keeper."

"What do you keep?" asked Pryer.

"The Trees," answered the Bummer. "I kept the last Trees."

Pryer felt a thrill go through him. The lamsuit med-text quickly took his vital signs. "Trees?" he said. "Trees are why I came Outside."

"The Trees are all dead," said the Bummer.

"Dead?" said Pryer. "Dead? But I need wood."

"There is wood," said the little Bummer. "All the Trees have died. Strong oak. Sweet cherry. Crazy cottonwood. Sharp cedar. Now they are wood."

"I still don't understand," said Pryer.

The Bummer stirred his fire with a stick. Red sparks dashed up into the thick air. "The Trees are dead. Now they are wood," he said again. "You have come. There are no more Trees to keep, and no more Stayers to keep them. I am the last." The Bummer bowed his head and sat slumped before the flames dancing in the fire of his last wood.

Pryer retracted his heelwheels and paced around the fire. He could feel the heat through his lamsuit samplers. "I made a list." He lidded his simhelm sec. "I need pine," he read, "maple, willow, and ebony."

"I have those, and more," said the Bummer. "Tall pine. Graceful willow. Stout maple. Ebony I do not have. Hot ebony. Ebony never lived here, and died long ago. But you must take all the wood. It is told." He sat without moving, staring, lost in the fire. Pryer waited.

"The wood," Pryer finally reminded him.

"How much wood would a woodchuck chuck if a woodchuck would chuck wood?" asked the Bummer fiercely. He got up and shuffled away from the fire. Pryer followed him. Square black shapes loomed up through the haze, stacks of thick logs. The Bummer leaned himself against a stack, rubbing his cheek against the wood. A black tear furrowed down his face. "Goodbye, wood, my sweet Trees," he said. He turned angrily toward Pryer. Pryer's lamsuit bristled minizaps. "You take the wood, as it was told," said the Bummer. "But also it was told Insiders would make it live again. You must make it live again."

Pryer reached out and put his hand on the wood. His samplers palpated it. "Which is mine?" he asked.

"You must take it all," said the Bummer. "It was told. But here is pine, here willow. That is maple." He indicated a stack, another. A third. Pryer psychlipped a subwhistle and in a few moments a gravdolly came sailing out of the fog. It rounded up all the stacks of wood and looped them with a mollyrope.

Pryer turned to the Bummer, standing alone in the empty place where the wood had been stacked. "Well, thank you," he said awkwardly. "Goodbye."

"Mumble, mumble," said Pryer's simhelm.

"Mumble," said the Bummer, looking at the ground.

"Incoherent," explained the simhelm.

Pryer powertrudged back to the possibility field of the Warren. The gravdolly sailed behind.

Comes a temporal redux.

Pryer intentions implosion. A doorbud flowers. The gravdolly sails within, and Pryer enrolls behind. Just as he is about to ensconce, a small figure appears hazeward. It is the Bummer. He has followed Pryer.

Dedux. Redux.

"I'm the last," says the little Bummer in a small voice. Mumble, mumble. "I have always wished I could see Inside. Just once."

■

175

■
The
Logical
Legend
of
Helio-
pause
and
Cyber-
fiddle

He attempts to put his foot gently through the intention wave of the doorbud.

—*Say, you're not a resident,* says the Door.

A bright orange beam stabs down from a lazerlens. The Bummer crackles and turns black like a bug on a heat coil, if there were any bugs anymore in the wide tedious world. Pryer turns pale and upchucks. His lamsuit fades away and the Door microsweeps him clean.

—*All right,* says the Door. *Welcome back.*

Pryer's scrim seethes with auld lang zymes. Quasicrystals devolve and Pryer is standing in Warren Beatty Hall, the gravdolly teetering beside him. He subwhistles the gravdolly to follow and flees Paul Newmoslide chamberward. Zip.

Pryer offloads the gravdolly in the Hall near his chamber iris. He flings a stasis around the wood so the autosans will leave it alone. This is something new. Trash in the Hall. The neighborhood is going to hell. Chambered, Pryer cons everything. He needs to recover from his Actuality Adventure Outside. He maxes neurolinks, blams his Billgrams.

But Pryer's tools are calling out to him from the workbench in thin steely voices. Finally he gives in, goes diss, goes mobe. Time to build him some violin.

Now. Imagine *this:*

Pryer as he works: In his singleminded concentration, he is like another Antonio Stradivari, if Stradivari had ever dressed in a poly singlet and worked in a plastic room devoid of any object that ever grew upon the green Earth.

See Pryer heft a section of maple log onto his workbench. See him cut with saw. See him exhausted. See him shrug and wield a laser cutter. He removes a plank wedge-cut on the quarter, as his Manual insists. The plank cracks. He cuts another. See him scraping and shaping and thinning, with shavers and chisels and planes. He ruins the work, and begins again. He pours over formulas and has his verity port brew some glue and a bottle to put it in.

There comes a seek when he stares in dumb admiration at a violin-shaped piece of maple wood made of two pieces glued together and only millies thick. This is the back of Pryer's instrument. He runs his hands erotically around the curve of the bouts. Then he begins yet again, for the belly.

See Pryer soaking wet as he steams and bends pine strips for the sides of the violin. His verity port is a mess. He spends tenseeks like H_2O carving scroll, pegs, fingerboard, tailpiece, bow. He uses oak, since he has no ebony, and the Manual agrees oak is a reasonable substitute. He hums as the irritated verity port simulates gut for strings, horsehair for the bow. He touches with alert fingers a piece of maple he means to carve into the bridge. He thinks he feels the living grain of it, even though it is not alive. Look at him, bent like a gargoyle over a whisker-thin strip of stained willow which he has laboriously cut by hand with a knife and which he is now inserting into a narrow gouge around the perimeter of the violin. This is the purfling, the decorative edging. Pryer's breathing is slow and deep, his hands steady.

You must clear your mind when making this cut, says the

Manual. *You must clear your breath. Otherwise, how can your cut be pure?*

177

■

**The
Logical
Legend
of
Helio-
pause
and
Cyber-
fiddle**

Now: Finally: Behold: Pryer stands with bent head before his stained and dented bench. And on the bench lies a violin, varnished a rich red, its strings strung and ready, and beside it lies a bow. To Pryer the violin appears to be breathing, even though it is not alive either. Inside the E string f-hole he can see a P with a circle around it. He has burned this on the inside, just like old Antonio used to do.

It is time to play. Time to take the old fiddle out for a spin. He knows how to hold it and what to do to play it—there are pictures in the Manual. He reaches for the violin. But wait. This is not something to do alone. He needs witnesses, a quorum, a minyan. A gathering of fellow pilgrims.

Pryer musters Carmen Memoranda, Melt and Smudge and Clack and Cookie, her body parts. It has been many seeks since Carmen Memoranda has gathered herself together. There is webcackle, Carmen gossip.

—*Rumors of Pryer recycled.*
—*Rumors that Central disses Squish, Pryer's sexmate.*
—*Fribble. I have built it. I have built the violin.*

He quants them a shining holo of the violin. Carmen Memoranda swoons, maidenly hand to brow. *Lewd*, she webs in four voices.

—*Gather. Proof is in the pudding.* Pryer <shrugs>.
—*Acknowledged. Here comes Carmen. She is all ears. Your place or mine?*
—*Neither. Undergarden.*
—*Undergarden?*
—*Undergarden.* Pryer confirms.

—*Break.* Carmen Memoranda goes diss.

Pryer polishes the violin with a piece of red poly, synthed for the occasion, until the wood assumes a deep and moody gleam. He wraps the violin in the poly and Paul Newmozips to Undergarden. He knows the way. He's been around the block a time or two.

In Undergarden he finds a conform and stands on it. Worried lazercops hover nearby. In a few moments there is scrimshimmer and four possibilities gape the near horizon. Melt and Clack and Smudge and Cookie come holo, bristling circuitry.

Pryer whips the poly off and brandishes the violin at them, a grin leaking around his simhelm. They blink at this veritability.

—*Please ∂off neurolinks,* says Pryer, proudly and lewdly. *The show is about to begin.*

The cells of Carmen Memoranda blink again and diss a few links. That's all Pryer is going to get.

With visions of epiphany dancing in his eyes, with his ears like hungry open mouths, Pryer pokes the violin grandly under his chin and draws the bow firmly across the strings. A screech erupts, a scream, a skirl, a thermonuclear bagpipe, like nails being pulled from wood, like a small animal being skinned alive, if there were any of these things anymore in the wide sad world. Pryer holds the violin away from him at arm's length as if it stinks, a look of ineffable pain on his face. Melt and Smudge and Clack and Cookie clap their hands over simhelms, an organic and useless gesture not seen in the wide bland world for ten cubed cycles. Their holos waver.

179

The
Logical
Legend
of
Helio-
pause
and
Cyber-
fiddle

—Effing effers. Pryer is an effing lunatic.
—Pryer is malfunctioning, to subject us to such a thing.
—Pryer is a Bummer.

Pryer stands motionless, and tears, another anachrony, well up in his eyes, and spill down his dustless face from under his simhelm. He has a clear ponder of Pryer the Bummer. He will be the last last. He deecees his lamsuit and fries in the dirty u-vee.

—Break. Melt goes diss.
—Break. Smudge goes diss.
—Break. Clack goes diss.
—Pryer is inadequate. He should have learned how to play that terrible contraption. Anyone with the least familiarity with ancient acoustic instruments knows that. Break. And Cookie goes diss.

Pryer's eyes grow wide. A cartoon lightbulb, of which there are none anymore in the wide dark world, blinks on above his head.

Imagine this.

For tenseeks on end, Pryer saws away at his violin. He has dissed all links, even his simhelm. He ferrets through arc-stuff, dusts off the secrets of tuning and scales, plays around with varying tensions of string and bowhair. He takes to stalking Undergarden, sniffing the green air, admiring the play of light off leaf and tile. He takes to sitting Outside, close by the possibility riffle of Warren Beatty, comfy in lamsuit, watching the red sun sink through yellow air. He builds a violin case from leftover wood with his steel tools.

Therefore: he is all alone, as always no one but himself present to hear, when one day he draws his bow gently across the violin strings, and a pure lovely tone flows forth, and his ears and his heart are filled to brimming with the living wooden voice of his violin. His eyes overspill again with obsolete tears and he sinks to his knees, breathless.

In that moment, Pryer imagines he has a soul, and his soul soars on the sweet sound past Heliopause, to the stars and beyond.

SQ

I think what Dr. Speakie has done is wonderful. He is a wonderful man. I believe that. I believe that people need beliefs. If I didn't have my belief I really don't know what would happen.

And if Dr. Speakie hadn't truly believed in his work he couldn't possibly have done what he did. Where would he have found the courage? What he did proves his genuine sincerity.

There was a time when a lot of people tried to cast doubts on him. They said he was seeking power. That was never true. From the very beginning all he wanted was to help people and make a better world. The people who called him a power-seeker and a dictator were just the same ones who used to say that Hitler was insane and Nixon was insane and all the world leaders were insane and the arms race was insane and our misuse of natural resources was insane and the whole world civilization was insane and suicidal. They were always saying that. And they said it about Dr. Speakie. But he stopped all that insanity, didn't he? So he was right all along, and he was right to believe in his beliefs.

I came to work for him when he was named the Chief of the Psychometric Bureau. I used to work at the U.N., and when the World Government took over the New York U.N. Building they transferred me up to the thirty-fifth floor to be the head secretary in Dr. Speakie's office. I knew already that it was a position of great responsibility, and I was quite excited the whole week before my new job began. I was so curious to meet Dr. Speakie, because of course he was already famous. I was there right at the dot of nine on Monday morning, and when he came in it was so wonderful. He looked so kind. You could tell that the weight of his responsibilities was always on his mind, but he looked so healthy and positive, and there was a bounce in his step—I used to think it was as if he had rubber balls in the toes of his shoes. He smiled and shook my hand and said in such a friendly, confident voice, "And you must be Mrs. Smith! I've heard wonderful things about you. We're going to have a wonderful team here, Mrs. Smith!"

Later on he called me by my first name, of course.

That first year we were mostly busy with Information. The World Government Presidium and all the Member States had to be fully informed about the nature and purpose of the SQ Test, before the actual implementation of its application could be eventualized. That was good for me too, because in preparing all that information I learned all about it myself. Often, taking dictation, I learned about it from Dr. Speakie's very lips. By May I was enough of an "expert" that I was able to prepare the Basic SQ Information Pamphlet for publication just from Dr. Speakie's notes. It was such fascinating work. As soon as I began to understand the SQ Test Plan I began to believe in it. That was true of everybody in the office and in the Bureau. Dr. Speakie's sincerity and scientific enthusiasm were infectious. Right from the beginning we had to take the Test every quarter, of course, and some of the secretaries used to be nervous before they took it, but I never was. It was so obvious that the Test was *right*. If you scored under 50 it was nice to know that you were sane, but even if you scored over 50 that was fine too, because then you could be *helped*. And anyway it is always best to know the truth about yourself.

As soon as the Information service was functioning smoothly Dr. Speakie transferred the main thrust of his attention to the implementation of Evaluator training, and planning for the structurization of the Cure Centers, only he changed the name to SQ Achievement Centers. It seemed a very big job even then. We certainly had no idea how big the job would finally turn out to be!

As he said at the beginning, we were a very good team. We all worked hard, but there were always rewards.

I remember one wonderful day. I had accompanied Dr. Speakie to the Meeting of the Board of the Psychometric Bureau. The emissary from the State of Brazil announced that his State had adopted the Bureau Recommendations for Universal Testing—we had known that that was going to be announced. But then the delegate from Libya and the delegate from China announced that their States had adopted the Test too! Oh, Dr. Speakie's face was just like the sun for a minute, just *shining*. I wish I could remember exactly what he said, especially to the Chinese delegate, because of course China was a very big State and its decision was very influential. Unfortunately I do not have his exact words because I was changing the tape in the recorder. He said something like, "Gentlemen, this is a historic day for humanity." Then he began to talk at once about the effective implementation of the Application Centers, where people would take the Test, and the Achievement Centers, where they would go if they scored over 50, and how to establish the Test Administrations and Evaluations infrastructure on such a large scale, and so on. He was always modest and practical. He would rather talk about doing the job than talk about what an important job it was. He used to say, "Once you know what you're doing, the only thing you need to think about is how to do it." I believe that that is deeply true.

From then on, we could hand over the Information program to a subdepartment and concentrate on How to Do It. Those were exciting times! So many States joined the Plan, one after another. When I think of all we had to do I wonder that we didn't all go crazy! Some of the office staff did fail their quarterly Test, in fact. But most of us working in the Executive Office with Dr. Speakie remained quite stable, even when we were on the job all day and half the night. I think his presence was an inspiration. He was always calm and positive, even when we had to arrange things like training 113,000 Chinese Evaluators in three months. "You can always find out 'how' if you just know the 'why'!" he would say. And we always did.

When you think back over it, it really is quite amazing what a big job it was—so much bigger than anybody, even Dr. Speakie, had realized it would be. It just changed everything. You only realize that when you think back to what things used to be like. Can you imagine when we began planning Universal Testing for the State of China, we only allowed for 1,100 Achievement Centers, with 6,800 Staff? It really seems like a joke! But it is not. I was going through some of the old files yesterday, making sure everything is in order, and I found the first China Implementation Plan, with those figures written down in black and white.

I believe the reason why even Dr. Speakie was slow to realize the magnitude of the operation was that even though he was a great scientist he was also an optimist. He just kept hoping against hope that the average scores would begin to go down, and this prevented him from seeing that universal application of the SQ Test was eventually going to involve everybody either as Inmates or as Staff.

When most of the Russias and all the African States had adopted the Recommendations and were busy implementing them, the debates in the General Assembly of the World Government got very excited. That was the period when so many bad things were said about the Test and about Dr. Speakie. I used to get quite angry, reading the *World Times* reports of debates. When I went as his secretary with Dr. Speakie to General Assembly meetings I had to sit and listen in person to people insulting him personally, casting aspersions on his motives and questioning his scientific integrity and even his sincerity. Many of those people were very disagreeable and obviously unbalanced. But he never lost his temper. He would just stand up and prove to them, again, that the SQ Test did actually literally scientifically show whether the testee was sane or insane, and the results could be proved, and all psychometrists accepted them. So the Test Ban people couldn't do anything but shout about freedom and accuse Dr. Speakie and the Psychometric Bureau of trying to "turn the world into a huge insane asylum." He would always answer quietly and firmly, asking them how they thought a person could be "free" if they lacked mental health. What they called freedom might well be a delusional system with no contact with reality. In order to find out, all they had to do was to become testees. "Mental health *is* freedom," he said. "'Eternal vigilance is the price of liberty,' they say, and now we have an eternally vigilant watchdog: the SQ Test. *Only the testees can be truly free!*"

There really was no answer they could make to that. Sooner or later the delegates even from Member States where the Test Ban movement was strong would volunteer to take the SQ Test to prove that their mental health was adequate to their responsibilities. Then the ones that passed the test and remained in office would begin working for Universal Application in their home State. The riots and demonstrations, and things like the burning of the Houses of Parliament in London in the State of England (where the Nor-Eurp SQ Center was housed), and the Vatican Rebellion, and the Chilean H-Bomb, were the work of insane fanatics appealing to the most unstable elements of the populace. Such fanatics, as Dr. Speakie and Dr. Waltraute pointed out in their Memorandum to the Presidium, deliberately aroused and used the proven instability of the crowd, "mob psychosis." The only response to mass delusion of that kind was immediate implementation of the Testing Program in the disturbed States, and immediate amplification of the Asylum Program.

That was Dr. Speakie's own decision, by the way, to rename the SQ Achievement Centers "Asylums." He took the word right out of his enemies' mouths. He said: "An asylum means a place of *shelter*, a place of *cure*. Let there be no stigma attached to the word 'insane,' to the word 'asylum,' to the words 'insane asylum'! No! For the asylum is the haven of mental health—the place of cure, where the anxious gain peace, where the weak gain strength, where the prisoners of inadequate reality assessment win their way to freedom! Proudly let us use the word 'asylum.' Proudly let us go to the asylum, to work to regain our own God-given mental health, or to work with others less fortunate to help them win back their own inalienable right to mental health. And let one word be written large over the door of every asylum in the world—'WELCOME!'"

Those words are from his great speech at the General Assembly on the day World Universal Application was decreed by the Presidium. Once or twice a year I listen to my tape of that speech. Although I am too busy ever to get really depressed, now and then I feel the need of a tiny "pick-me-up," and so I play that tape. It never fails to send

me back to my duties inspired and refreshed.

Considering all the work there was to do, as the Test scores continued to come in always a little higher than the Psychometric Bureau analysts estimated, the World Government Presidium did a wonderful job for the two years that it administered Universal Testing. There was a long period, six months, when the scores seemed to have stabilized, with just about half of the testees scoring over 50 and half under 50. At that time it was thought that if forty percent of the mentally healthy were assigned to Asylum Staff work, the other sixty percent could keep up routine basic world functions such as farming, power supply, transportation, etc. This proportion had to be reversed when they found that over sixty percent of the mentally healthy were volunteering for Staff work, in order to be with their loved ones in the Asylums. There was some trouble then with the routine basic world functions functioning. However, even then contingency plans were being made for the inclusion of farmlands, factories, power plants, etc., in the Asylum Territories, and the assignment of routine basic world functions work as Rehabilitation Therapy, so that the Asylums could become totally self-supporting if it became advisable. This was President Kim's special care, and he worked for it all through his term of office. Events proved the wisdom of his planning. He seemed such a nice wise little man. I still remember the day when Dr. Speakie came into the office and I knew at once that something was wrong. Not that he ever got really depressed or reacted with inopportune emotion, but it was as if the rubber balls in his shoes had gone just a little bit flat. There was the slightest tremor of true sorrow in his voice when he said, "Mary Ann, we've had a bit of bad news, I'm afraid." Then he smiled to reassure me, because he knew what a strain we were all working under, and certainly didn't want to give anybody a shock that might push their score up higher on the next quarterly Test! "It's President Kim," he said, and I knew at once—I knew he didn't mean the President was ill or dead.

"Over fifty?" I asked, and he just said quietly and sadly. "Fifty-five."

Poor little President Kim, working so efficiently all that three months while mental ill health was growing in him! It was very sad and also a useful warning. High-level consultations were begun at once, as soon as President Kim was committed; and the decision was made to administer the Test monthly, instead of quarterly, to anyone in an executive position.

Even before this decision, the Universal scores had begun rising again. Dr. Speakie was not distressed. He had already predicted that this rise was highly probable during the transition period to World Sanity. As the number of the mentally healthy living outside the Asylums grew fewer, the strain on them kept growing greater, and they became more liable to break down under it—just as poor President Kim had done. Later, he predicted, when the Rehabs began coming out of the Asylums in ever increasing numbers, this stress would decrease. Also the crowding in the Asylums would decrease, so that the Staff would have more time to work on individually orientated therapy, and this would lead to a still more dramatic increase in the number of Rehabs released. Finally, when the therapy process was completely perfected, there would be no Asylums left in the world at all. Everybody would be either mentally healthy or a Rehab, or "neonormal," as Dr. Speakie liked to call it.

It was the trouble in the State of Australia that precipitated the Government crisis. Some Psychometric Bureau officials accused the Australian Evaluators of actually falsifying Test returns, but that is impossible since all the computers are linked to the World Government Central Computer Bank in Keokuk. Dr. Speakie suspected that the Australian Evaluators had been falsifying *the Test itself*, and insisted that they themselves all be tested immediately. Of course he was right. It had been a conspiracy, and the suspiciously low Australian Test scores had resulted from the use of a false Test. Many of the conspirators tested higher than 80 when forced to take the genuine Test! The State Government in Canberra had been unforgiveably lax. If they had just admitted it everything would have been all right. But they got hysterical, and moved the State Government to a sheep station in Queensland, and tried to withdraw from the World Government. (Dr. Speakie said this was a typical mass psychosis: reality evasion, followed by fugue and autistic withdrawal.) Unfortunately the Presidium seemed to be paralyzed. Australia seceded on the day before the President and Presidium were due to take their monthly Test, and probably they were afraid of overstraining their SQ with agonizing decisions. So the Psychometric Bureau volunteered to handle the episode. Dr. Speakie himself flew on the plane with the H-bombs, and helped to drop the information leaflets. He never lacked personal courage.

When the Australian incident was over, it turned out that most of the Presidium, including President Singh, had scored over 50. So the Psychometric Bureau took over their functions temporarily. Even on a long-term basis this made good sense, since all the problems now facing the world Government had to do with administering and evaluating the Test, training the Staff, and providing full self-sufficiency structuration to all Asylums.

What this meant in personal terms was that Dr. Speakie, as Chief of the Psychometric Bureau, was now Interim President of the United States of the World. As his personal secretary I was, I will admit it, just terribly proud of him. But he never let it go to his head.

He was so modest. Sometimes he used to say to peo-

ple, when he introduced me, "This is Mary Ann, my secretary," he'd say with a little twinkle, "and if it wasn't for
her I'd have been scoring over fifty long ago!"

There were times, as the World SQ scores rose and
rose, that I would become a little discouraged. Once the
week's Test figures came in on the readout, and the *average*
score was 71. I said, "Doctor, there are moments I believe
the whole world is going insane!"

But he said, "Look at it this way, Mary Ann. Look at
those people in the Asylums—3.1 billion inmates now, and
1.8 billion staff—but look at them. What are they doing?
They're pursuing their therapy, doing rehabilitation work
on the farms and in the factories, and striving all the time,
too, to *help* each other towards mental health. The prepon-
derant inverse sanity quotient is certainly very high at the
moment; they're mostly insane, yes. But you have to
admire them. They are fighting for mental health. They
will—they *will* win through!" And then he dropped his
voice and said as if to himself, gazing out the window and
bouncing just a little on the balls of his feet, "If I didn't
believe that, I couldn't go on."

And I knew he was thinking of his wife.

Mrs. Speakie had scored 88 on the very first
American Universal Test. She had been in the Greater Los
Angeles Territory Asylum for years now.

Anybody who still thinks Dr. Speakie wasn't sincere
should think about that for a minute! He gave up everything for his belief.

And even when the Asylums were all running quite
well, and the epidemics in South Africa and the famines in
Texas and the Ukraine were under control, still the work-
load on Dr. Speakie never got any lighter, because every
month the personnel of the Psychometric Bureau got
smaller, since some of them always flunked their monthly
Test and were committed to Bethesda. I never could keep
any of my secretarial staff any more for longer than a

month or two. It was harder and harder to find replacements, too, because most sane young people volunteered for Staff work in the Asylums, since life was much easier and more sociable inside the Asylums than outside. Everything so convenient, and lots of friends and acquaintances! I used to positively envy those girls! But I knew where my job was.

At least it was much less hectic here in the U.N. Building, or the Psychometry Tower as it had been renamed long ago. Often there wouldn't be anybody around the whole building all day long but Dr. Speakie and myself, and maybe Bill the janitor (Bill scored 32 regular as clockwork every quarter). All the restaurants were closed, in fact most of Manhattan was closed, but we had fun picnicking in the old General Assembly Hall. And there was always the odd call from Buenos Aires or Reykjavik, asking Dr. Speakie's advice as Interim President about some problem, to break the silence.

But last November 8, I will never forget the date, when Dr. Speakie was dictating the Referendum for World Economic Growth for the next five-year period, he suddenly interrupted himself. "By the way, Mary Ann," he said, "how was your last score?"

We had taken the Test two days before, on the sixth. We always took the Test every first Monday. Dr. Speakie never would have dreamed of excepting himself from Universal Testing regulations.

"I scored twelve," I said, before I thought how strange it was of him to ask. Or, not just to ask, because we often mentioned our scores to each other; but to ask *then*, in the middle of executing important world government business.

"Wonderful," he said, shaking his head. "You're wonderful, Mary Ann! Down two from last month's Test, aren't you?"

"I'm always between ten and fourteen," I said. "Nothing new about that, Doctor."

"Some day," he said, and his face took on the expression it had when he gave his great speech about the Asylums, "some day, this world of ours will be governed by men fit to govern it. Men whose SQ score is zero. Zero, Mary Ann!"

"Well, my goodness, Doctor," I said jokingly—his intensity almost alarmed me a little—"even *you* never scored lower than three, and you haven't done that for a year or more now!"

He stared at me almost as if he didn't see me. It was quite uncanny. "Some day," he said in just the same way, "nobody in the world will have a Quotient higher than fifty. Some day, nobody in the world will have a Quotient higher than thirty! Higher than ten! The Therapy will be perfected. I was only the diagnostician. But the Therapy will be perfected! The cure will be found! Some day!" And he went on staring at me, and then he said, "Do you know what my score was on Monday?"

"Seven," I guessed promptly. The last time he had told me his score it had been seven.

"Ninety-two," he said.

I laughed, because he seemed to be laughing. He had always had a puckish sense of humor. But I thought we really should get back to the World Economic Growth Plan, so I said laughingly, "That really is a very bad joke, Doctor!"

"Ninety-two," he said, "and you don't believe me, Mary Ann, but that's because of the cantaloupe."

I said, "What cantaloupe, Doctor?" and that was when he jumped across his desk and began to try to bite through my jugular vein.

I used a judo hold and shouted to Bill the janitor, and when he came I called a robo-ambulance to take Dr. Speakie to Bethesda Asylum.

That was six months ago. I visit Dr. Speakie every Saturday. It is very sad. He is in the McLean Area, which is the Violent Ward, and every time he sees me he screams and foams. But I do not take it personally. One should never take mental ill health personally. When the Therapy is perfected he will be completely rehabilitated. Meanwhile, I just hold on here. Bill keeps the floors clean, and I run the World Government. It really isn't as difficult as you might think.

DORIS LESSING

FROM

Shikasta

History of Shikasta, VOL. 3012, *The Century of Destruction*
EXCERPT FROM SUMMARY CHAPTER

During the previous two centuries, the narrow fringes on the northwest of the main landmass of Shikasta achieved technical superiority over the rest of the globe, and, because of this, conquered physically or dominated by other means large numbers of cultures and civilizations. The Northwest fringe people were characterized by a peculiar insensitivity to the merits of other cultures, an insensitivity quite unparalleled in previous history. An unfortunate combination of circumstances was responsible. (1) These fringe peoples had only recently themselves emerged from barbarism. (2) The upper classes enjoyed wealth, but had never developed any degree of responsibility for the lower classes, so the whole area, while immeasurably more wealthy than most of the rest of the globe, was distinguished by contrasts between extremes of wealth and poverty. This was not true for a brief period between Phases II and III of the Twentieth Century War. [SEE VOL. 3009, *Economies of Affluence.*] (3) The local religion was materialistic. This was again due to an unfortunate combination of circumstances: one was geographical, another the fact that it had been a tool of the wealthy classes for most of its history, another that it retained even less than most religions of what its founder had been teaching. [SEE VOLS. 998 and 2041, *Religions as Tools of Ruling Castes.*] For these and other causes, its practitioners did little to mitigate the cruelties, the ignorance, the stupidity, of the Northwest fringers. On the contrary, they were often the worst offenders. For a couple of centuries at least, then, a dominant feature of the Shikastan scene was that a particularly arrogant and self-satisfied breed, a minority of the minority white race, dominated most of Shikasta, a multitude of different races, cultures, and religions which, on the whole, were superior to that of the oppressors. These white Northwest fringers were like most conquerors of history in denuding what they had overrun but they were better able than any other in their ability to persuade themselves that what they did was "for the good" of the conquered: and it is here that the above-mentioned religion is mostly answerable.

World War I—to use Shikastan nomenclature (otherwise the First Intensive Phase of the Twentieth Century War)—began as a quarrel between the Northwest fringers over colonial spoils. It was distinguished by a savagery that could not be matched by the most backward of barbarians. Also by stupidity: the waste of human life and of the earth's products was, to us onlookers, simply unbelievable, even judged by Shikastan standards. Also by the total inability of the population masses to understand what was going on: propaganda on this scale was tried for the first time, using methods of indoctrination based on the new technologies, and was successful. What the unfortunates were told who had to give up life and property—or at the best, health—for this war, bore no relation at any time to the real facts of the matter; and while of course any local group or culture engaged in war persuades itself according to the exigencies of self-interest, never in Shikastan history, or for that matter on any planet— except for the planets of the Puttioran group—has deception been used on this scale.

This war lasted for nearly five of their years. It ended in a disease that carried off six times as many people as those killed in the actual fighting. This war slaughtered, particularly in the Northwest fringes, a generation of their best young males. But—potentially the worst result—it strengthened the position of the armament industries (mechanical, chemical, and psychological) to a point where from now on it had to be said that these industries dominated the economies and therefore the governments of all the participating nations. Above all, this war barbarized and lowered the already very low level of accepted conduct in what they referred to as "the civilized world"—by which they meant, mostly, the Northwest fringes.

This war, or phase of the Twentieth Century War, laid the bases for the next.

Several areas, because of the suffering caused by the war, exploded into revolution, including a very large area, stretching from the Northwest fringes thousands of miles to the eastern ocean. This period saw the beginning of a way of looking at governments, judged "good" and "bad" not by performance, but by label, by name. The main reason was the deterioration caused by war: one cannot spend years sunk inside false and lying propaganda without one's mental faculties becoming impaired. (This is a fact that is attested to by every one of our emissaries to Shikasta!)

Their mental processes, for reasons not their fault never very impressive, were being rapidly perverted by their own usages of them.

The period between the end of World War I and the beginning of the Second Intensive Phase contained many small wars, some of them for the purpose of testing out the

weapons shortly to be employed on a massive scale. As a
result of the punitive suffering inflicted on one of the
defeated contestants of World War I by the victors, a
Dictatorship arose there—a result that might easily have
been foreseen. The Isolated Northern Continent, conquered only recently by emigrants from the Northwest
fringes, and conquered with the usual disgusting brutality,
was on its way to becoming a major power, while the various national areas of the Northwest fringes, weakened by
war, fell behind. Frenzied exploitation of the colonized
areas, chiefly of Southern Continent I, was intensified to
make up for the damages sustained because of the war. As
a result, native populations, exploited and oppressed
beyond endurance, formed resistance movements of all
kinds.

The two great Dictatorships established themselves
with total ruthlessness. Both spread ideologies based on
the suppression and oppression of whole populations of
differing sects, opinions, religions, local cultures. Both
used torture on a mass scale. Both had followings all over
the world, and these Dictatorships, and their followers,
saw each other as enemies, as totally different, as wicked
and contemptible—while they behaved in exactly the same
way.

The time gap between the end of World War I and
the beginning of World War II was twenty years.

Here we must emphasize that most of the inhabitants
of Shikasta were not aware that they were living through
what would be seen as a hundred years' war, the century
that would bring their planet to almost total destruction.
We make a point of this, because it is nearly impossible for
people with whole minds—those who have had the good
fortune to live (and we must never forget that it is a question of our good fortune) within the full benefits of the
substance-of-we-feeling—it is nearly impossible, we
stress, to understand the mentation of Shikastans. With

the world's cultures being ravaged and destroyed, from end to end, by viciously inappropriate technologies, with wars raging everywhere, with whole populations being wiped out, and deliberately, for the benefit of ruling castes, with the wealth of every nation being used almost entirely for war, for preparations for war, propaganda for war, research for war; with the general levels of decency and honesty visibly vanishing, with corruption everywhere— with all this, living in a nightmare of dissolution, was it really possible, it may be asked, for these poor creatures to believe that "on the whole" all was well?

The reply is—yes. Particularly, of course, for those already possessed of wealth or comfort—a minority; but even those millions, those billions, the ever-increasing hungry and cold and unbefriended, for these, too, it was possible to live from meal to scant meal, from one moment of warmth to the next.

Those who were stirred to "do something about it" were nearly all in the toils of one of the ideologies which were the same in performance, but so different in self-description. These, the active, scurried about like my unfortunate friend Taufiq, making speeches, talking, engaged in interminable processes that involved groups sitting around exchanging information and making statements of good intent, and always in the name of the masses, those desperate, frightened, bemused populations who knew that everything was wrong but believed that somehow, somewhere, things would come right.

It is not too much to say that in a country devastated by war, lying in ruins, poisoned, in a landscape blackened and charred under skies low with smoke, a Shikastan was capable of making a shelter out of broken bricks and fragments of metal, cooking himself a rat and drinking water from a puddle that of course tasted of oil and thinking, "Well, this isn't too bad after all. . . ."

World War II lasted five years, and was incompara-

bly worse in every way than the first. All the features of
the first were present in the second, developed. The waste
of human life now extended to mass extermination of civilian populations. Cities were totally destroyed. Agriculture
was ruined over enormous areas. Again the armament
industries flourished, and this finally established them as
the real rulers of every geographical area. Above all, the
worst wounds were inflicted in the very substance, the
deepest minds, of the people themselves. Propaganda in
every area, by every group, was totally unscrupulous,
vicious, lying—and self-defeating—because in the long
run, people could not believe the truth when it came their
way. Under the Dictatorships, lies and propaganda *were*
the government. The maintenance of the dominance of the
colonized parts was by lies and propaganda—these more
effective and important than physical force; and the retal-
iation of the subjugated took the form, first of all and most
importantly in influence, of lies and propaganda: this is
what they had been taught by their conquerors. This war
covered and involved the whole globe—the first war, or
phase of the war, involved only part of it: there was no part
of Shikasta by the end of World War II left unsubjected to
untruth, lies, propaganda.

This war saw, too, the use of weapons that could
cause total global destruction: it should go without saying,
to the accompaniment of words like democracy, freedom,
economic progress.

The degeneration of the already degenerate was
accelerated.

By the end of World War II, one of the great
Dictatorships was defeated—the same land area as saw
the worst defeat in the first war. The Dictatorship which
covered so much of the central landmass had been weakened, almost to the point of defeat, but survived, and made
a slow, staggering recovery. Another vast area of the central landmass, to the east of this Dictatorship, ended half a

century of local wars, civil wars, suffering, and over a century of exploitation and invasion by the Northwest fringes by turning to Dictatorship. The Isolated Northern Continent had been strengthened by the war and was now the major world power. The Northwest fringes on the whole had been severely weakened. They had to let go their grip of their colonies. Impoverished, brutalized — while being, formally, victors — they were no longer world powers. Retreating from these colonies they left behind technology, an idea of society based entirely on physical well-being, physical satisfaction, material accumulation — to cultures who, before encounter with these all-ravaging Northwest fringers, had been infinitely more closely attuned with Canopus than the fringers had ever been.

This period can be — is by some of our scholars — designed *The Age of Ideology*. [For this viewpoint SEE VOL. 3011, SUMMARY CHAPTER.]

The political groupings were all entrenched in bitterly defended ideologies.

The local religions continued, infinitely divided and subdivided, each entrenched in their ideologies.

Science was the most recent ideology. War had immeasurably strenghtened it. Its ways of thought, in its beginnings flexible and open, had hardened, as everything must on Shikasta, and scientists, as a whole — we exclude individuals in this area as in all others — were as impervious to real experience as the religionists had ever been. Science, its basic sets of mind, its prejudices, gripped the whole globe and there was no appeal. Just as individuals of our tendencies of mind, our inclinations towards the truth, our "citizens" had had to live under the power and the threat of religions who would use any brutalities to defend their dogmas, so now individuals, with differing inclinations and needs from those tolerated by science had to lead silent or prudent lives, careful of offending the bigotries of the scientific global governing class: in the service of national governments and therefore of war—an invisible global ruling caste, obedient to the warmakers. The industries that made weapons, the armies, the scientists who served them—these could not be easily attacked, since the formal picture of how the globe was run did not include this, the real picture. Never has there been such a totalitarian, all-pervasive, all-powerful governing caste anywhere: and yet the citizens of Shikasta were hardly aware of it, as they mouthed slogans and waited for the deaths by holocaust. They remained unaware of what "their" governments were doing, right up to the end. Each national grouping developed industries, weapons, horrors of all kinds, that the people knew nothing about. If glimpses were caught of these weapons, then government would deny they existed. [SEE *History of Shikasta,* VOLS. 3013, 3014, and CHAPTER 9 this volume, "Use of Moon as Military Base."] There were space probes, space weapons, explorations of planets, use of planets, rivalries over their moon, about which the populations were not told.

And here is the place to say that the mass of the populations, the average individual, were, was, infinitely better, more sane, than those who ruled them: most would have been appalled at what was being done by "their" representatives. It is safe to say that if even a part of what was being kept from them had come to their notice, there would have been mass risings across the globe, massacres of the rulers, riots . . . unfortunately, when peoples are helpless, betrayed, lied to, they possess no weapons but the (useless) ones of rioting, looting, mass murder, invective.

During the years following the end of World War II, there were many "small" wars, some as vicious and extensive as wars in the recent past described as major. The needs of the armament industries, as much as ideology, dictated the form and intensities of these wars. During this period savage exterminations of previously autonomous "primitive" peoples took place, mostly in the Isolated

Southern Continent (otherwise known as Southern Continent II). During this period colonial risings were used by all the major powers for their own purposes. During this period psychological methods of warfare and control of civilian populations developed to an extent previously undreamed of.

Here we must attempt to underline another point which it is almost impossible for those with our set of mind to appreciate.

When a war was over, or a phase of war, with its submersion in the barbarous, the savage, the degrading, Shikastans were nearly all able to perform some sort of mental realignment that caused them to "forget." This did not mean that wars were not idols, subjects for pious mental exercises of all sorts. Heroisms and escapes and braveries of local and limited kinds were raised into national preoccupations, which were in fact forms of religion. But this not only did not assist, but prevented, an understanding of how the fabric of cultures had been attacked and destroyed. After each war, a renewed descent into barbarism was sharply visible—but apparently cause and effect were not connected, in the minds of Shikastans.

After World War II, in the Northwest fringes and in the Isolated Northern Continent, corruption, the low level of public life, was obvious. The two "minor" wars conducted by the Isolated Northern Continent reduced its governmental agencies, even those visible and presented to the public inspection, to public scandal. Leaders of the nation were murdered. Bribery, looting, theft, from the top of the pyramids of power to the bottom, were the norm. People were taught to live for their own advancement and the acquisition of goods. Consumption of food, drink, every possible commodity was built into the economic structure of every society. [VOL. 3009, *Economies of Affluence.*] And yet these repulsive symptoms of decay were not seen as direct consequences of the wars that ruled their lives.

During the whole of the Century of Destruction, there were sudden reversals: treaties between nations which had been at war, so that these turned their hostilities on nations only recently allies; secret treaties between nations actually at war; enemies and allies constantly changing positions, proving that the governing factor was in the need for war, as such. During this period every major city in the northern hemisphere lived inside a ring of terror: each had anything up to thirty weapons aimed at it, every one of which could reduce it and its inhabitants to ash in seconds—pointed from artificial satellites in the skies, directed from underwater ships that ceaselessly patrolled the seas, directed from land bases perhaps halfway across the globe. These were controlled by machines which everyone knew were not infallible—and everybody knew that more than once the destruction of cities and areas had been avoided by a "miracle." But the populations were never told how often these "miracles" had taken place—near-lethal accidents between machines in the skies, collisions between machines under the oceans, weapons only *just* not unleashed from the power bases. Looking from outside at this planet it was as if at a totally crazed species.

In large parts of the northern hemisphere was a standard of living that had recently belonged only to emperors and their courts. Particularly in the Isolated Northern Continent, the wealth was a scandal, even to many of their own citizens. Poor people lived there as the rich have done in previous epochs. The continent was heaped with waste, with wreckage, with the spoils of the rest of the world. Around every city, town, even a minor settlement in a desert, rose middens full of discarded goods and food that in other less favored parts of the globe would mean the difference between life and death to millions. Visitors to this continent marveled—but at what people could be taught to believe was their due, and their right.

This dominant culture set the tone and standard for most of Shikasta. For regardless of the ideological label attaching to each national area, they all had in common that technology was the key to all good, and that good was always material increase, gain, comfort, pleasure. The real purposes of life—so long ago perverted, kept alive with such difficulty by us, maintained at such a cost—had been forgotten, were ridiculed by those who had ever heard of them, for distorted inklings of the truth remained in the religions. And all this time the earth was being despoiled. The minerals were being ripped out, the fuels wasted, the soils depleted by an improvident and shortsighted agriculture, the animals and plants slaughtered and destroyed, the seas being filled with filth and poison, the atmosphere was corrupted—and always, all the time, the propaganda machines thumped out: more, more, more, drink more, eat more, consume more, discard more—in a frenzy, a mania. These were maddened creatures, and the small voices that rose in protest were not enough to halt the processes that had been set in motion and were sustained by greed. By the lack of substance-of-we-feeling.

But the extreme riches of the northern hemisphere were not distributed evenly among their own populations, and the less favored classes were increasingly in rebellion. The Isolated Northern Continent and the Northwest fringe areas also included large numbers of dark-skinned people brought in originally as cheap labor to do jobs disdained by the whites—and while these did gain, to an extent, some of the general affluence, it could be said that looking at Shikasta as a whole, it was the white-skinned that did well, the dark-skinned poorly.

And this *was* said, of course, more and more loudly by the dark-skinned, who hated the white-skinned exploiters as perhaps conquerors have never before been hated.

Inside each national area everywhere, north and south, east and west, discontent grew. This was not only because of the gap between the well-off and the poor, but because their way of life, where augmenting consumption was the only criterion, increasingly saddened and depressed their real selves, their hidden selves, which were unfed, were ignored, were starved, were lied to, by almost every agency around them, by every authority they had been taught to, but could not, respect.

Increasingly the two main southern continents were torn by wars and disorders of every kind — sometimes civil wars between blacks, sometimes between blacks and remnants of the old white oppression, and between rival sects and juntas and power groups. Local dictators abounded. Vast territories were denuded of forests, species of animals destroyed, tribes murdered or dispersed. . . .

War. Civil War. Murder. Torture. Exploitation. Oppression and suppression. And always lies, lies, lies. Always in the name of progress, and equality and development and democracy.

The main ideology all over Shikasta was now variations on this theme of economic development, justice, equality, democracy.

Not for the first time in the miserable story of this terrible century, this particular ideology — economic justice, equality, democracy, and the rest — took power at a time when the economy of an area was at its most disrupted: the Northwest fringes became dominated by governments "of the left," which presided over a descent into chaos and misery.

The formerly exploited areas of the world delighted in this fall of their former persecutors, their tormentors — the race that had enslaved them, enserfed them, stolen from them, above all, despised them because of their skin color and destroyed their indigenous cultures now at last beginning to be understood and valued . . . but too late, for they had been destroyed by the white race and its technologies.

There was no one to rescue the Northwest fringes, in the grip of grindingly repetitive, dogmatic Dictatorships, all unable to solve the problems they had inherited—the worst and chief one being that the empires that had brought wealth had not only collapsed, leaving them in a vacuum, but had left behind false and unreal ideas of what they were, their importance in the global scale. Revenge played its part, not an inconsiderable part, in what was happening.

Chaos ruled. Chaos economic, mental, spiritual—I use this word in its exact, Canopean sense—ruled while the propaganda roared and blared from loudspeaker, radio, television.

The time of the epidemics and diseases, the time of famine and mass deaths had come.

On the main landmass two great Powers were in mortal combat. The Dictatorship that had come into being at the end of World War I, in the center, and the Dictatorship that had taken hold of the eastern areas now drew into their conflict most of Shikasta, directly or indirectly. The younger Dictatorship was stronger. The older one was already in decline, its empire fraying away, its populations more and more in revolt or sullen, its ruling class increasingly remote from its people—processes of growth and decay that had in the past taken a couple of centuries now were accomplished in a few decades. This Dictatorship was not able to withstand the advance of the eastern Dictatorship whose populations were bursting its boundaries. These masses overran a good part of the older Dictatorship, and then overran, too, the Northwest fringes, in the name of a superior ideology—though in fact this was but a version of the predominating ideology of the Northwest fringes. The new masters were clever, adroit, intelligent; they foresaw for themselves the dominance of all the main landmass of Shikasta, and the continuance of that dominance.

But meanwhile the armaments piled up, up, up. . . .

The war began in error. A mechanism went wrong, and major cities were blasted into death-giving dusts. That something of this kind was bound to happen had been plentifully forecast by technicians of all countries . . . but the Shammat influences were too strong.

In a short time, nearly the whole of the northern hemisphere was in ruins. Very different, these, from the ruins of the second war, cities which were rapidly rebuilt. No, these ruins were uninhabitable, the earth around them poisoned.

Weapons that had been kept secret now filled the skies, and the dying survivors, staggering and weeping and vomiting in their ruins, lifted their eyes to watch titanic battles being fought, and with their last breaths muttered of "Gods" and "Devils" and "Angels" and "Hell."

Underground were shelters, sealed against radiation, poisons, chemical influences, deadly sound impulses, death rays. They had been built for the ruling classes. In these a few did survive.

In remote areas, islands, places sheltered by chance, a few people survived.

The populations of all the southern continents and islands were also affected by pestilence, by radiations, by soil and water contamination, and were much reduced.

Within a couple of decades, of the billions upon billions of Shikasta perhaps one percent remained. The substance-of-we-feeling, previously shared among these multitudes, was now enough to sustain, and keep them all sweet, and whole, and healthy.

The inhabitants of Shikasta, restored to themselves, looked about, could not believe what they saw — and wondered *why* they had been mad.

RALPH LOMBREGLIA

Somebody
Up
There
Likes
Me

I logged on and got a Network fortune cookie, followed by
e-mail from my distant wife.

Afternoon favorable for romance. Try a single person for a change.

Date: Mon, 12 Apr 99 14:27 GMT
From: Snookie Lee Ludlow <snooks@women.tex.edu>
To: Dante Allegro Annunziata <dante@media.sjcm.edu>
Subject: RE: For your delectation

Dante,
Your last missive was so cold, I thought somebody sent me an
Alaskan sockeye salmon. Then I saw on TV where the sockeye's
extinct, so now I don't know what your problem is.

Stop hurting people, you monster.

Snooks

I was on the old mainframe terminal in my office at
school, surrounded by cinder-block walls and shelves
stuffed chaotically with tapes and disks. I hadn't seen a
friendly face in a week. Sometimes when I was down, the

random-sentence generator cheered me up, so I knocked off a few new ones.

The president's unlikely urchin is tripping.
The awful dogs are howling.
Couldn't robots dine on jurisprudence?
And why shouldn't buildings puzzle over people?

You could feed the generator your own personal glossary of terms.

Vengeful Snookie bubbles San Antone into flames while academic watchmen practice celestial sloth in bed.

In my last mail to Snookie Lee, I had sent some morsels like these — affectionately, to make her smile — and she'd taken them all wrong: the whole story of Snooks and me. She was in San Antonio and I was in San Jose, and some people say that when a woman moves 1,500 miles from her mate to get a Ph.D. in women's studies, it's the beginning of the end, if not the end of the end, and refuting those prophets of woe is not easy. Yes, we had taken some bad falls, Snookie Lee and I. We were edging into the Humpty Dumpty zone. But I thought we could put it together again, and I was doing my best to convince Snookie of that.

<flame on>
MY letter was cold! Ha! You've been like ice! Maybe *my* feelings are hurt! I'm the loyal and true one! I'm the one who acts like he cares! You're the one who's trying to dump the whole thing down the sewer!
<flame off>

I made my computer do anagrams of your sweet name, Snooks— about 100,000 before I pulled the plug. Then I spent a whole day picking my favorites when I was supposed to be grading papers. Do men do this if they're not in love?

Like, elude solo now. Loud, sleek loin woe. Look, we use old line. Woo skill elude one. I use lone lewd look. Look, Lee, we sin loud. Oil noose well, Duke. Look, Lee, widen soul. Would Snook Lee lie? Look, slow Lee due in.

Do lie low, keen soul,

Dante

Besides Snookie's letter I had four from Mary Beth—
three from last week, which I had not read, and a new one
posted early this morning, all bearing the subject line
"Your position here"—and I could have gone on to read
them now, but I wasn't in the mood. Mary Beth was the
chair of language and media studies at San Jose College of
the Mind, where I was a junior professor. She was also out
to get me. Indeed, Mary Beth's machinations were part of
the reason that Snookie was gone. Snooks had wanted to
teach too, to chisel those young minds, and she deserved
her chance. Not only did she have sufficient credentials,
but she had more heart than the whole College of the
Mind put together. But Mary Beth wouldn't give her even
a section of Mastering Capitalistic Prose. I volunteered to
give her a section of mine, and Mary Beth said no. When
they offered me the position, they said I'd come up for
tenure in three or four years; after Snooks applied to
teach, Mary Beth took me off the tenure track.

I met Snooks at a poetry slam in 1995, when I was finishing my graduate media degree at MIT. She was up from
Alabama to show them a thing or two at Harvard, where
she had made it all the way to her senior year. Somehow
we never crossed paths in Cambridge, though she was all
over town and hard to miss. We slammed, finally, in the
bowels of Boston, in a basement bookstore on Newbury
Street, where Snookie Lee declaimed verses of outrage
and indignation while shaking her spiky hair and waving
Simone Weil at the audience. They loved her. I had to follow her on with my sheaf of technological rhapsodies.
They hated me. But the opinion I cared about was Snookie
Lee's. I sidled up to her after the gig and asked what she
thought of my stuff. She hated it, but she loved my name.

On the strength of that, I asked her out. "I've got a date with Dante!" she said, laughing, to one of her girlfriends.

She was all bluff and flying feathers, and then she was my everything. We graduated and I got the offer from College of the Mind, and since my fellow Ph.D.'s seemed ready to slit my throat for the job, I took it. Snookie said she would follow me if I promised it was nice. My best childhood friend, Boyce Hoodington, had lived twenty miles north, in Palo Alto, for years, and he loved it out there. He was a project leader for a company trying to simulate human consciousness with a computer. Many California outfits were trying to do that, without much luck, but Boyce's firm had achieved a few small, sexy triumphs that kept the investors turned on. The firm's computer now recognized specific people when they walked into the room, greeted them, and commented on the clothes they were wearing. It could do other things, Boyce had told me—things he wasn't allowed to talk about.

So I promised Snookie she'd like California, and we lived there for three incredibly crummy years—crummy for me, the indentured professor in the house, thermonuclear for Snooks. Our problems went beyond Mary Beth. We experienced other disillusionments, too, such as the discovery that certain faculty couples masquerading as our friends were doing us dirty behind the scenes. Looking back on it, trying to fix the damage by getting married was not the best idea. Snookie said so at the time. I won't say that in those dark days when she didn't get out of bed till 4:00 P.M., and never took off her robe, and College of the Mind was leaking its acid into my brain, I was Jovian about it. But I still think that in the disappointing run of men I'm a prize.

I told all this to Snookie Lee as we stood on the dead lawn of our rented bungalow, her ancient, eggplant-colored Le Car parked halfway up on the sidewalk, stuffed full of her things. She was going to San Antonio to get her own Ph.D. In the last year of our three Snooks ended up as a night-shift checkout girl at a discount drug superstore, and the worst thing was, she liked it. She stopped blaming me for ruining her life. She now said that I'd inadvertently brought about her rebirth. She'd made a lot of new girlfriends at the store, muscular young women who weren't ever going to College of the Mind or college of the anything, and Snooks would go aerobic dancing and skating with them. She decided that the best thing in life was sisterhood. I hardly ever saw her anymore. On our separation day her friends spun over on their blades to bid Snookie Lee goodbye. They stood wobbling on the brown grass in their colorful tights and kneepads, saying supportive things to Snooks and giving bad looks to me.

I said, "Sisterhood means a lot to me, too, you know." The women had a good guffaw over that. I told Snooks she was breaking my heart.

She said, "You know those plastic ant-farm things? How you buy one, and then later decide you don't really want ants after all, and you empty the whole thing out on the ground? That's heartbreak, Dante. For the ants, I mean. You're not heartbroken. You don't even look sad."

"I'm very goddamn heartbroken," I said. "Don't tell me how heartbroken I am." The girlfriends rolled closer to Snookie Lee. I *was* heartbroken, but Snookie and I had beaten each other down so badly that our parting scene was playing like dinner theater. "And that analogy's no good," I told her. "Those ant-farm ants are an exotic breed that can't live in the wild. Otherwise they wouldn't *be* heartbroken. They'd be happy. They'd be free."

"You're free," Snookie Lee said.

"I never asked to be free! I'm exotic!" I exclaimed, but I got nowhere. Snookie Lee drove away.

I was about to log off when my terminal chirped and said, in its silly voice, *"You have new mail."* I hoped the message

was from her. If she was online, maybe I could ping her for
a real-time chat. But the letter turned out to be from
Boyce. I punched it up.

Date: Mon, 12 Apr 99 20:53 GMT
From: Boyce P. Hoodington <boyce@softbrain.com>
To: Dante Allegro Annunziata <dante@media.sjcm.edu>
Subject: Death and pasta

Would have got back to you sooner, but I died. Have not logged on
in days, and now speak to you from the beyond. My #*^!%!* computer went down like the Hindenburg—cellular port hosed, mother-
board toasted. I'm on the dusty laptop now, shades of Orville Wright.
It periodically stalls out and drops through the clouds of our thrilling
but turbulent present-day network. If I suddenly disappear, that's why.

I must have a new box, Dante! Let's shop for it together! Tonight, after
partaking of a momentous baked ziti. Mounds of baby peas, asparagus, and musky salad greens from the garden have turned our
kitchen into a Tuscan stone cottage. I may videodisk it, it's so beautiful. But Janet regards me strangely when I videodisk food. And wait
till you taste this fresh-faced fumé with overtones of apple and pear.
Spanking beverage. Bought a case. Snatched a spicy zinfandel, too.
Come on up!—BPH

P.S. I'll tell my sad corporate story. Slithering beast of commerce, it's
a snakepit out here. Be thankful you chose the cloistered life.

P.P.S. We must talk about Snookie. You don't sound good, my brother. Janet has thoughts for you. Never mind free enterprise, Dante;
women are the great challenge of our lives, the parabolic arena
where we Rollerblade like angels at the speed of light, and where, I
fear, we are destined to wipe out grotesquely. Yet we skate on blindly into the night. Why? Because of love, that hot transistor smoking
within us.

My office hours at College of the Mind had another hour
to run, but not a single student had come to see me so far.
True, my door was closed and locked, and I was being
very quiet. My lights were off. If I left now, I could go
home and take a shower, change into my jeans (Mary
Beth forbade teaching in jeans), and still make it to
Boyce's for happy hour. I blowgunned my answer into the
bitstream—

I Brake for Baked Ziti

—and was yet again on the cusp of logging off when I remembered the text-dissociation software they had on the server. It could sometimes ease the misery inflicted upon people by words. I gave it Snookie's letter to eat.

St. Dante,

I, thou monster. I saw on Sockeye TV where the salmon is cold. Cold, cold, cold. I thought somebody sent me an Alaskan Salmonster, but now I don't know what your last missive was. Your problem's extinct, you hurting salmon.

You, monstero, the Sockeye Salmolast.

Salmonstop,

Snooksego

It didn't kill much pain, but I sent it to her anyway.

I drove my Fuji Chroma up 280 from San Jose to Palo Alto amid contorted oaks on hilltops, like bonsai trees in amber waves of grain, except the waves weren't grain, they were dead meadow grass, two or three feet high and browned-out from drought, emblem of our republic. Also a fire hazard that should have been mowed down. A red-tailed hawk sailed from a knobby tree, plunged to the undulating grass, and flapped back to its branch with mythic pumps of the wings, taking a field mouse on a commuter hop to God.

The foothills reminded me of Hobbit-land, furry café-au-lait knolls where Frodo, Gandalf, et al., would have felt at home. Zipping up the artery in my tiny car, I succumbed to a conviction that Hobbits were living there now, in burrows beneath the gnomish topography. The old Tolkien books—the interactive laser-disk versions—had lately made a great comeback with students, and I'd been using them in my classes at College of the Mind. For doing that and certain other groovy things, I was considered a cool professor, and my sections never failed to fill up. I got glowing reviews in the campus electronic magazine, to the profound irritation of Mary Beth, whose classes the students routinely panned. And yet educating endless waves of the young had begun to unnerve me. The act of teaching unnerved everyone eventually, but usually because your students were always nineteen while you withered into your grave before their eyes. My problem was different—I remained the same while they mutated into a different species. My students implanted digital watches in the skin of their wrists, tattooed and barbered themselves so as not to appear human, took personalized drugs made from their own DNA, and danced epileptically to industrial noise. I fantasized about taking them on a field trip to the foothills for the semester-wrap picnic and then, in the thick of the Hobbit hunt, vanishing—never to be seen again. Perhaps they'd start a religion based on the mystery of my disappearance. Perhaps spirituality would flower on earth once more.

When I pulled up to Boyce's, his front lawn was preternaturally thick and green, like a gigantic flattop haircut for St. Patrick's Day. He and Janet loved landscaping and were always ministering to their lawn. I wished I had a nice house and yard like theirs. Actually, I wished I had anything. It hit me that I should enter the private sector, like Boyce, where your bosses didn't punish you for doing your job. I found him in his modern, shiny kitchen at the back of the house, assembling a fine baked ziti in a big casserole dish. He was a North Carolina Methodist, supposedly, but some Mediterranean blood had got in there somehow. The man could cook. "Romano!" he said in greeting, pointing to a quarter wheel of the stuff.

"I got e-mail from Snookie today," I said, grating the cheese.

"Excellent!" Boyce said. "You're talking! What did she say?"

"That I was a monster."

"All women say that about men, Dante. It's a figure of speech."

"What does it mean?"

"It means we're monsters."

We built the ziti and slid it into the oven. Boyce poured us big goblets of fumé. "To a new life for us all."

We clinked and sipped. "What do you want a new life for?" I asked.

"I meant the new one we're all getting, want it or not."

"What happened?"

"Tell you outside. Where nature can absorb the toxins."

We took our glasses to the verdant back yard. Boyce and Janet had a triple-depth lot—150 feet of Palo Alto crust in which Boyce had laid drip-irrigation lines, so that now it looked like the Garden of Eden back there. Lemons and limes and oranges hung over our heads at the round terrace table. Zippy the hummingbird was doing his air-and-space show, flashing in from nowhere to sip at his feeder, and then buzzing our heads before zinging back to the treetop where he lived. The little nugget of his beelike body stood in relief against the sky, microscopic stud on a eucalyptus branch.

"You can't see the knife?" Boyce said, twisting to show me his back.

I looked around him. "You've got it hidden pretty well."

"I'm out."

"Of what?"

"SoftBrain Technologies."

"What? You were in charge of the whole project. It was your division."

"The division they lopped off in the corporate downsizing."

"They lop off whole divisions?"

"That was the normal part. The stinky part was trick-
ing me into lopping it for them."

And then Boyce told his tale. Nearly a year before,
without telling him, his bosses had cut a deal to sell the
consciousness-emulation division. The buyers thought
they were paying too much and wanted something extra
thrown in, something big and sweet. Boyce was assigned a
strange and urgent top-secret task, on which he worked
his heart out until just the week before—working, though
he didn't know it, for his own extinction. I demanded that
he tell me this top-secret thing.

"Oh, it was so typical. So depressingly superficial.
Nothing. They wanted to see the computer hold a credible
conversation."

"But it's been doing that for years."

"Not with its lips."

"*Lips!* It has *lips?* I didn't know it had lips!"

"I just violated my nondisclosure agreement. Don't
spread that around."

"Lips!"

Monday of the previous week, at 9:00 A.M., Boyce
had demoed the lips for the company brass and some invited guests with English accents. The lips were gorgeous.
Everybody loved the lips. The brass congratulated Boyce
in a way that implied a promotion and a load of stock. He
returned to his office to pop corks with the team, though it
was only coffee-break time. He felt the burgeoning glory
of his division, soon to be the company jewel. At 3:00 P.M.
he got the call to close it down. The British guests were the
buyers. They were taking the sucker to England, lips and
all.

It took me a minute to absorb this slimy information.
"But they *liked* you," I said at last.

"Oh, they still do," Boyce said. "They love me. I'm a
great guy."

In the week since his severance he'd been home in

seclusion, drinking boutique wine and having his spine realigned by a private masseuse. Only this morning had Boyce awakened with a craving to re-enter the world.

"How's Janet taking it?"

"Overjoyed. She thinks I've been miraculously spared from my own worst tendencies. She thinks I was going corporate—me, of all people."

"Were you?"

"Of course I wasn't! I thought the lips were stupid. Here we were on the trail of consciousness itself, and all the managers cared about was lips."

"Humanity's signal-to-noise ratio isn't so hot, is it?"

"Worst in the animal kingdom. By a mile."

"But we've put out some pretty clean signal, too," I said reflectively. "Over the years. Down through the centuries. It adds up."

Boyce slapped my arm. "That's what I woke up this morning thinking!" he exclaimed. "That's what I've learned from all this!"

"What?"

"That everything we've done with computers until now is totally trivial and wrong! Why have we not yet created a fantastic, free, self-reflective knowledge base of every good thing humanity has ever thought or dreamed? Not just consciousness, Dante. *Cosmic* consciousness! That's what I want to build now. The computerized mind of the world!"

"And you say Janet's not worried about you?"

"She doesn't know yet. She'll love it when I explain it. I kind of got the idea from her, in fact. But since you mention it, it's you she's worried about."

Fumé went up my nose and fizzed my sinuses. *"Me?"*

"She wants me to watch you very closely. She thinks you may do some harm to yourself."

One is rarely prepared to meet the shabby figure one actually cuts in the world, even if one already has a pretty clear mental image of the wretch. "You don't think that, do you, Boyce?"

"Would it make you feel better or worse if I did?"

"Worse. Definitely worse."

"Then I don't."

My harming myself was a silly idea, but it was nice to have friends who considered me a walking pipe bomb and yet continued to care. True, that was practically Janet's job: she was a Jungian therapist, not to mention a splendid woman at whose sagacious feet I should probably throw myself for guidance. She was certainly the best thing that ever happened to Boyce, and her wonderfulness made me wish that I had a wife too. Then I remembered— I did.

"Can I use your Chokecherry to check my mail?" I asked Boyce.

"Be my guest, but it might not even get you on. I had a hell of a time with it today. A few keys are falling off, too."

"I'll nurse it along."

"Try slapping it."

I ducked the pendulous oranges and crossed the back yard beneath fantastical shapes in the California clouds, smiling at the idea of Boyce's still using the old Chokecherry 100. The kitchen was like a lung filled with baked ziti's life-affirming breath. I walked through it and on into the darkened living and dining rooms, where the recently restuccoed walls were already cracked again from tremors. In Boyce's study the big computer lay dead on its table, the little Chokecherry sleeping beside it and waking up reluctantly when I touched its wobbly keys. Once, people had thrilled to own this little appliance of the brain. True to its name, it choked when I logged on, but I lashed it forward with repeated jabs of the Escape key. It tried to read me the fortune cookie that appeared on the screen, but the loudspeaker was broken and the latest assessment of my destiny sounded like a faltering Bronx cheer.

It may be that your whole purpose in life is simply to serve as a warning to others.

And then my one new letter flashed onto the gray wafer of screen. It was from Snookie Lee.

Date: Mon, 12 Apr 99 21:09 GMT
From: Snookie Lee Ludlow <snooks@women.tex.edu>
To: Dante Allegro Annunziata <dante@media.sjcm.edu>
Subject: RE: Dissociated Love

Dante,
I'm going nuts and you're helping me do it. You're helping quite nicely.

What was that stuff you sent? "Salmonstop" and all that. "Snooksego." What was that supposed to be? I don't understand your problem anymore. I used to think I did. I'm not studying to be a shrink. I'm studying to be a scholar, which I now realize means I need a shrink myself. Maybe yours would take me on; she's used to people with bullet holes in their feet AND their heads.

Would Snook Lee lie? No, she wouldn't. I'm taking my orals an hour from now. You'll claim you didn't know, though I've told you numerous times. You don't listen when I talk. I'm not nervous. Nerves are not why I feel like barfing. I feel like Polly, the girl who wanted a cracker. They've stuffed me full of their theories, and now they want me to spit them back. But I don't even believe in half that stuff. More than half. My professors aren't bad people, they just turn their students into apes. No, they don't do it, this system does it! This rotten system! I hate it!

But why am I telling you this? You're an ape yourself!

This is what I've been living with. I would've told you before, but I, for one, don't believe in throwing up on people. I gotta go.

Snooks

P.S. Get help.

From the time-stamp on Snookie's letter, I figured her orals were over by now. I clacked out my answer on Boyce's broken keys.

I'm up at Boyce's for dinner. I'm sorry you're not getting this before your exams. I would have wished you luck. You never told me they were today! You didn't! This is something you're always doing, telling me you told me things when you didn't tell me.

You were having pre-exam hysteria, Snooks—all that stuff about spitting back theories and whatnot. Classic symptoms. Just calm down and be yourself and you'll do fine. God, what saccharine advice. Fortunately, you didn't get it. If you're reading this, it's all over, and you did just fine, didn't you? Academia does this to people, Snooks. I, for one, am getting out.

What you have your Ph.D., I'll work in the drugstore and you can teach college! I can't wait!

I am not an ape and you know it.

Love, love, love,

Dante

P.S. Remember Boyce's incredible baked ziti? It's in the oven right now. And then we're going computer shopping for him. I'm gonna call you later.

I shot my letter into the colossal web of the Net. When I looked up, Janet was standing in the door. "Fixing Boyce's computer?" she said.

"Hi. No, I was just saying something to Snookie Lee."

Janet looked around. "Snookie's here?"

"I meant I was e-mailing her."

"Oh, e-mail. Not talking on the videophone?" We giggled over that for a second. Janet famously loathed all technology after the fountain pen. "Boyce thought the little computer was broken too," she said.

"It is, Janet. Just because you can answer your mail doesn't mean a computer works. See?" I picked up the Chokecherry and turned it upside down. Five or six keys fell off and a guitar pick dropped out. "He needs a new computer."

"I've heard. Well, you're communicating, at least."

"Of course we're communicating," I said, skeptical that Janet really considered Boyce's layoff a great development. "I'm here, aren't I? But it would be a hell of a lot easier with a better computer."

"Oh, I'm sure a better computer would help immensely. When was the last time you told her you loved her?"

"I thought we were talking about Boyce."

"We were clearly talking about Snookie Lee."

"We were talking about Boyce and computers! You shrinks always do that."

"What?"

"That! Ambush people."

"Have you told Snookie you loved her any time in the past two years?"

"Of course I have."

"She says you haven't"

"Goddamn gossip!" I cried, and threw the Chokecherry onto Boyce's desk. It broke in two pieces. "When did she tell you that? You two have been talking? What else did she say?"

"Plenty."

In Boyce's ziti the asparagus had given itself to the pasta like a submissive lover. The food was so ambrosial that we didn't even need the spicy zin, though we drank it anyway. My own baked ziti never came out nearly this good, and I was the Italian one. In my present frame of mind I could take a thing like that hard, as a comment on my general integrity.

"Did you know that Janet has serious misgivings about us, Dante?" Boyce asked. "About our relentless fascination with technological goods, the way machines work, what's the latest thing." We were having dinner outside, at the round redwood table, where I sat between Boyce and Janet, opposite the empty fourth chair. "Something about it is fishy, she thinks."

"I didn't know that," I said.

"Yes, I may start studying you two," Janet said. "I may write a book on this phenomenon."

Janet had her own private practice full of wealthy clients. She wasn't jumping through flaming tenure hoops under the stony gaze of some Mary Beth, and yet she still had thoughts of writing books. What pluck!

"Why do you know so much about computers?" she asked me. "Him I can understand. But you're supposed to be a humanities guy."

"Fear of death," I said. "Sexual terror."

"Nice try."

"Because he knew I'd need a new one someday," Boyce said, "and he wanted to help me pick it out."

"Good, Boyce," I said. "Right. But follow through. What kind of computer would you like? You haven't told us."

"A Revelation 2000."

This magical product name buzzed past my ear with such an unreal twang that I looked around to see if little Zippy had just gone by again. The Revelation 2000 was the first microcomputer with a halographic screen, 1,000–bit audio/video, three billion instructions per second, and direct wireless uplink to geosynchronous satellites. It was the sexiest hardware you could put on a desk. And though I personally subscribed to the old chestnut about buying computers—get the most iron they'll let you charge on your card, and if you can't use all that power, you're doing something wrong—I couldn't believe Boyce was talking about a Rev 2K. "Revelations cost a fortune," I said.

"I've got one lined up for three thousand bucks."

"Bull, Boyce! They're twenty times that."

"My man has one for three."

"What man?"

"This guy Mickey. I've never met him. He's a friend of Brubaker's."

"Oh, no, Boyce. No."

"Honey," Janet said, "I don't think 'Brubaker' was the correct magic word."

"You said you were never dealing with Brubaker again."

"It's a *friend* of his, Dante. Plus, I'm a big boy now."

"He's saying I'm being too protective," I said to Janet.
"That seems to be it," she said.

Brubaker was an avatar of free enterprise who'd been
in bed at one time or another with almost every breathing
being doing business in the Valley. Like countless others,
Boyce had worked for the mythical Bru. Unlike most, he
remained on friendly terms with Brubaker after the experience, but then, Boyce was friends with everybody.
Brubaker had seen the high times, and now he was
researching the lows. He'd been charged with various
white-collar crimes in recent years, wriggling off every time
except the last, when they popped him for soliciting capital
investment without a prospectus. He got a hefty fine and
sixty days of community service—which he discharged by
teaching street youths to set up their own "S" corporations.

"Stolen goods," I said to Boyce. "Hijacked tractor-
trailer."

"You know I wouldn't do that."

"How does Brubaker meet these people?"

"I don't ask."

"That's the understanding you have?"

"No, I don't ask because he'd tell me."

"Since when is three thousand dollars cheap?" Janet
said.

"Last computer I'll ever buy, honey," Boyce told her.
"Cross my heart."

"Are you going to use it to change the world?"

"You're reading my mind."

"All right, then, you can have it," she said, sipping her
zinfandel and staring into the reddening California sky. "I
think I'll call my book *Modern Man in Search of a Dumpster
for His Soul.*"

Boyce turned to me. "And you were upset about
being called a monster."

■

I was halfway to the street when I realized that Boyce wasn't behind me. He was standing on his Crayola-green lawn, under the lady's-slipper-colored dome of California sky, staring at my cerulean vehicle parked at the curb in the striated shadow of a mimosa tree. "Do I look like I can ride in a Chroma?" he said. I was forgetting that Boyce, six foot four, couldn't even get into the freeway bubble I drove. I joined him on the lawn leading to his car. The sprinklers popped up and sprayed our legs like mechanical cats. "The downside of homeownership," Boyce called out, as we dashed off his effervescing grass.

"You finally get a pot to pee in, and it pees on you." We made it back to the sidewalk and shook our ankles. "Still, I wouldn't mind. A little pot to pee in with Snookie Lee. But I guess SoftBrain Technologies won't have a gig for me now."

"I guess not, cowboy. You wanted one?"

"I was thinking maybe technical writer."

"Impeccable sense of timing, Dante."

His silver Kodak Image hulked in the transcendental evening light. The automobile was so large it seemed designed to lure Japan into the quicksand with us once and for all—the two rivals going down in a cruise-controlled death embrace. When we approached it, the driver's door slid open, but not mine. "Look at that," I said. "It didn't do my side. A snoutful of microchips and it can't even open the door."

"You have to stand where it can see you, dude."

I walked to the passenger side, and the door retracted with an overdesigned hermetic suck. "My Chroma sees me no matter where I am," I said. When we were gliding through the peaceful streets, pastel homes clicking by like Necco wafers, I said, "So. Mickey."

"Brubaker says the overall impression is of an alienated vet. But in fact Mickey is not a vet. Not of any actual war."

"He's in a private militia?"

"No, just the opposite. Mickey wouldn't join any organized anything. He's a loner. He's the guy who came out the other side of the Valley dream."

"He went in the front?"

"Wrote system code in the glory days, burned out on that, went independent, specialized in lockout software. He's into hardware now."

"Designing it?"

"Testing it, more like."

Offices and malls and taco stands swept by on El Camino. We arrived at the outskirts of Palo Alto, where start-ups roiled in every dingy industrial park, in the bedrooms of brick apartment buildings, at the whittled wooden tables of the old hamburger bars. Nothing could kill the entrepreneurial spirit, not even the nineties in California. Everybody had an angle, everybody had a scheme. It was endless, and now Boyce was one of them. He parked in front of a run-down hacienda with silver Quonset huts on either side. Night had nearly fallen. The air was acrid with the resin of burning electronics.

"You guys seen Mickey?" somebody asked when we got out of the car. A tall black man in rags had stepped out of the bushes.

"No, we haven't," Boyce said.

The guy took a step into the light, and I saw that his clothes weren't rags. They were expensive designer things with all kinds of shapes and flaps cut into them.

"We just got here," Boyce said. "Where is he?"

"Didn't I clearly imply that I do not know where Mickey is?" the guy said, and went back into the shadows.

Then a white guy dressed in rags approached us from the opposite direction. "You guys seen Mickey?" he said.

"Would you mind stepping into the light?" I said, leading him underneath the lamp at the curb. This guy was really in rags, actual rags.

Boyce said, "What's with all you cats asking if we've seen Mickey?"

"All us cats?" the guy said. "Do I know you guys? Have I ever, like, *seen* you guys?"

"I just told the other dude. No, we have not seen Mickey."

"What other dude?"

I pointed at the bushes. "Over there somewhere. Wearing real fancy clothes. He's looking for Mickey too."

"He didn't actually say he was looking for Mickey," Boyce said. "He wanted to know if *we'd* seen Mickey. Just like you."

"That's true," I said. "Maybe you guys don't want to see Mickey at all."

"I see Mickey all the time," the guy said, and walked off into the darkness.

A small Filipino woman answered the door when we rang the bell. She seemed surprised to see us. "Isn't Mickey expecting us?" Boyce said.

"You're different," the woman said, and led us into her dwelling, where furniture and clothing and plastic media trash tumbled together indistinguishably in every room. We wound up in a wood-paneled den where two children played on shag carpeting in the blue glow of a sexual-hygiene program on the big TV. They looked a lot like their mother—for that was who she had to be. The kids were no more interested in us than in the blurry sex on the tube. I thought of my students, aliens whose human parents paid my bills, and I understood them better now. This was where they'd grown up. The house was from the sixties, when people put wet bars in their recreation rooms. On the dusty surface of a side table lay two handguns and a rifle—not toys, not dusty.

Mrs. Mickey walked us along a breezeway to one of the Quonset huts we'd seen from the street. At the entrance, midway along the metal pod's fuselage, she left us staring inside from the threshold. The shape and corrugation made it feel like an aircraft hanger—one in which had taken place, for some reason, the Battle of Silicon Valley. Mutilated corpses of computers from the past ten years lay in heaps around the cylindrical room, most horribly crushed or burned or melted. At a workbench in the midst of this wreckage, surrounded by banks of test equipment, a large bearded man in sleeveless fatigues was blowing a heat gun at a computer in a plain black box and laughing. Text and a picture were bending like taffy on the screen. A high-pitched squeal was emerging from the thing. An oscilloscope portrayed the computer's demise in ghostly green wiggles—lots of waves, lines with some waves, nothing but lines. Finally the screen crackled violently and then went blank. Blue-black smoke twirled from the computer's vents into an exhaust hood above the bench.

"He's an *abuse tester*," I whispered to Boyce. "You didn't tell me that. He kills computers for a living."

"Don't say 'kills,'" Boyce said. *"Stresses."*

"Piece of crap!" the man barked at the melting computer, and then he looked up and saw us standing there. He stood very still, staring at us, breathing deeply, with the heat gun still in his hand.

"Mickey?" Boyce said. "Are you Mickey? Hi, I'm Boyce. You were expecting us, right? Brubaker said we were coming?"

The man said nothing. Boyce looked worried, and worry was not a Boycean trait. It made me worried myself. But then, staring into this situation, I realized something about Mickey. He had just completed a kill and he wouldn't want to fight. He'd feel unthreatened and kingly. Unless overtly attacked, he'd be docile. He might even let smaller creatures pick at the edge of his prey. I pointed to the smoking prototype in his bench. "Did you drop it on the floor yet? I hear that's the first thing you're supposed to do. Drop it on the floor."

These words revived his inner animal. "You hear that 'cause that's what I do! *I* developed the protocol! *Me!*" He slapped himself on the chest. "Damn right I dropped it on the floor. I dropped it on the floor several times!" And then he laughed uproariously.

We were all right. He was verbalizing. Brubaker had told Boyce to expect a bearlike creature who communicated mainly by snuffling in his sinus passages, scratching himself, and emitting inexplicable giggles or guffaws.

Suddenly Mickey stopped laughing. "Brubaker told me one guy."

"That's me. Boyce. I just brought my friend along. Dante."

"Dante?" Mickey said, his face clouding over as he pronounced my name. He stared across the hut at old Fillmore West posters taped to the rippling metal walls. "The tomato family? Don't tell me this is the ketchup heir, the little tomato-paste trust-fund boy."

"Not *Del Monte,*" Boyce said. "Dante. He's not from ketchup money."

"They're all related," Mickey said.

"The Del Montes maybe, but he's not a Del Monte."

Mickey cackled again, but he put his heat gun down, and though he didn't explicitly invite us in, he didn't not invite us either, so we picked our way through the technological waste. "The Revelation brothers," Mickey said.

"That's us," Boyce said.

A color TV in Mickey's lair was tuned to a news story about the thousands of people living at Moffett Air Field now that NASA's demise had left the old base free to become a homeless shelter. It was an election year, and a local politician came on to gas a few bites about the looting of taxpayer coffers.

"Bring out the old rockets," Mickey said. "Ship 'em to Mars!"

"What are you saying that for?" I said. "You have

homeless friends yourself. We saw a homeless guy right here in front of your house."

Mickey peeped out a small window. "Where?"

"Right out front, man. He was asking for you too. 'You guys seen Mickey?' he said."

"That's no homeless guy!"

"He looked homeless," Boyce said.

"They just dress up like that."

Our deal seemed on the verge of going bad, so I said, "Hey, let's see this great computer."

"Hey, let's see this great computer," Mickey said.

"Well, if you don't mind."

He opened a door in an unpainted plasterboard wall and rolled the Revelation in on a cart. It wasn't burned or smashed or even dented. It maybe had a few scratches on it. He plugged it into the wall and flipped the switch. "Come on, sport," he said to me. "Let's see you do your stuff."

I'd never actually seen a 2000 in person before. Holographic software objects floated in the space between the computer and me, one of them announcing the machine's readiness for telephony in any form. I sat down and logged onto my account, bracing myself for power and speed. Even so I wasn't ready. The thing whomped me onto the Network like a jujitsu flip.

Hanlon's Razor:
Never attribute to malice that which is adequately explained by stupidity.

You have new mail.

from: marybeth@media.sjcm.edu
"Your position here"

from: marybeth@media.sjcm.edu
Re(1) "Your position here"

from: marybeth@media.sjcm.edu
Re(2) "Your position here"

from: marybeth@media.sjcm.edu
Re(3) "Your position here"

231

■

Some-
body
Up
There
Likes
Me

from: marybeth@media.sjcm.edu
Re(4) "Your position here"

"You got mail, dude," Mickey said.

"I see that, Mickey."

"Who's marybeth?"

"My boss."

"How come she's writing you so much? You two into something? You got something going with the boss lady, Don?"

"Dante, Mickey. Don Tay." The thought of having something going with Mary Beth was so ludicrous I forgot what I was doing. I sat there like an idiot who didn't know what a computer was for.

"Don't know how to read mail?" Mickey said. "No problem on a Revelation. Just tell it what you want it to do."

"I don't want to read that mail right now. I'll read it some other time."

"But then how are you gonna know how blazing the Revelation is at your daily tasks? *Read the mail,*" he barked at the box.

My first letter from Mary Beth joined us in the room as though we were reading the woman's mind. You couldn't describe the 2000 as "fast" — reality and the Revelation were basically indistinguishable. Everything just *was,* and in 3–D it all seemed almost edible besides. It was an amazing hardware experience. The message content was kind of a downer, though.

Date: Mon, 5 Apr 99 20:23 GMT
From: Mary Beth Hinckley<marybeth@media.sjcm.edu>
To: Dante Allegro Annunziata <dante@media.sjcm.edu>
Subject: Your position here

My dear Dante,
I assume some awareness on your part, however dim, of your con-

tract's impending expiration, and of your ongoing evaluation for renewal in this department.

"What's this 'my dear' crap?" Mickey said.
"Scorn."
"Is she like this in person?" Boyce asked.
"No, she's more relaxed in the mail."

I—all of us, actually—have been reading your student evaluations. They make a most striking collection of documents. Indeed, we've never seen anything quite like it. The students are deliriously uncritical of you, Dante. It seems you can do no wrong. Are you, perhaps, being uncritical of them? There is no learning without criticism, mon cher. We're not here to have the children like us. We're here to teach, to mold, to impart.

More than being peculiar—nay, unprecedented—I'm afraid such student reaction to a professor raises serious questions. We must talk.

MBH

"You poor bastard," Boyce said. "Why didn't you share it with us? You didn't have to bear it alone."
"I've always told you I hated the place."
"That's true, you have."
"You put some major mojo on this chick," Mickey said. "She wants you, Don. She wants you bad."
"I don't think so, Mickey. For one thing, she's not a chick."
"Listen to me, dude. I know. *Next*," he said, and Mary Beth's next letter materialized in our midst, followed by the others in succession as Mickey said "*Next*" again and again, each letter more aggrieved than its predecessor, until finally her last message bodied forth from the screen, dated this afternoon.

Signor Annunziata:

Your silence is rude and mystifying, but I'll say no more about it here. Indeed, I'll say no more here at all, since this is the last mail you'll receive from me.

The formal hearing into your future will be held tomorrow, Tuesday, 13

April, at 9 AM, in the Provost's office. Feel free to join us, in the flesh or via video, though the proceedings will be conducted in absentia in any event. If you're feeling pressed for time, I expect a very brief session.

What happened, Dante? You seemed so promising at first. And with that lovely name. I hoped you'd join our little family. But not as the Prodigal Son.

MBH

"I like how they're doing it in absentia whether you're there or not," Boyce said.

"That captures it, doesn't it? But I'll hack on your Revelation till dawn, shave and shower, drag myself in there, plead for my job. It's all I have. I'll say I've been sick. I'll get some students to claim they don't like me."

"*Reply*," Mickey said, causing an empty text-window to appear, at which he recited an incantation that scrolled obediently up the screen as he spoke. Mickey was one of those holdovers from the early days of computers, people who type everything with Caps Lock on, and he must have trained the Revelation to do the same whenever it heard his voice.

STUCK UP BITCH

DON'T MESS WITH DONNY

HE COULD OF BEEN YOURS

BUT YOU WERE HOTTY

NOW SUFFER

"Hotty?" Boyce said.

"Yeah. Stuck up. Superior. *Hotty*."

"Oh. I see."

"That's great, Mickey," I said. "Thank you for coming to my defense. I'm touched, really I am. Now erase it, please."

"*Send*," he said, and his voodoo poem-curse to Mary Beth vanished from the screen, sucked away by the Network's solar wind.

Sometimes you don't know how close you are to flaming out till it happens, and this was the case with me. I sat down on a deformed plastic chair in this computer criminal's Quonset hut, and I began to cry. Not big out-and-out boohooing, but there's crying and there's not crying, and I was crying.

"What's he doing?" Mickey asked Boyce, backing away from me.

"He seems to be crying," Boyce said. "You okay, pal?"

"Well, make him stop," Mickey said.

"How am I gonna do that? You just got him fired from his job, man."

"She was messing with his mind. What does he wanna work there for anyway?"

"What does anybody want to work anywhere for, Mickey? Plus, things aren't going real well with his wife right now."

"What's the problem?"

"She left."

My weeping did become out-and-out boohooing at this point.

"He's a total loss, isn't he?" Mickey said, gazing down at me. "But he likes computers, right? Computers make him happy, it seems like."

"They always do seem to cheer him up," Boyce said.

Mickey went into his secret room and wheeled out another cat.

"What's that?" I said, sniffling. "That looks like another Revelation."

"I was gonna keep it for parts, but you seem so sad, dude. I don't like people feeling sad. It makes me feel weird. You want it?"

"How much?"

"Same as for him."

"Three thousand bucks? Where are you getting these?"

"Don't ask questions like that, Don. You want it, I take cash. You don't want it, you never saw it."

I had thirty-five hundred bucks in my savings account, and after that it was the graveyard shift at Drugs 'n' Such. "I'll take it." I turned to Boyce. "Get me to a bank machine."

Mickey put his huge, heavy arm on my shoulder. "Then you're feelin' better about things?"

"Yeah, I am, Mickey, thanks. Can I ask you a question, though? I'm just curious. What's in the other Quonset hut? The one on the other side of the house?"

"What's in it? My in-laws. You want one of them, too? We could work something out. Can't do better than a nice Filipino girl."

We drove out onto the strip to look for an ATM. As the owner of a Revelation 2000, I could network with Boyce's machine and be part of his new venture, the construction of humanity's electronic mind. He offered me a job. I accepted. Then he revealed the identity of his major investor. I worked for Brubaker now.

Alongside a taco stand we found a riotously bright bank machine, its colored panels burning like gas in the California night. It sucked my card and started beeping at me.

Greetings, valued customer Dante Allegro Annunziata!
You have new Network mail! Read it now at your Mitsubishi ATM
(Small service charge applies.)
(Reminder: your credit account is past due.)

I pushed the button and they dropped me right into my mail, no list of letters received, no fortune cookie, no nothing. They literally didn't give me the time of day. What did I expect? It was a bank. I had only one new letter anyway, from Snookie Lee.

Date: Tue, 13 Apr 99 02:03 GMT
From: Snookie Lee Ludlow <snooks@women.tex.edu>
To: Dante Allegro Annunziata <dante@media.sjcm.edu>
Subject: I did a wild thing

Dante,
I went kind of crazy. I did a wild thing.

They asked me their parrot questions, like I knew they would. No big surprise. But when I actually heard it happen, something inside me plopped. I refused to answer. I refused to say anything at all. I just sat there doing a Bartleby in my oral exams. It was so weird. I couldn't believe it. They couldn't believe it either. Surely you're going to say something, they said. I'd prefer not to, I said. This can't be happening, said my adviser. It's happening, I said. I can't believe you're not finishing this degree, she said. I'd prefer not to, I said.

There's a blank place after that. Somebody drove me home. I called Janet. She's picking me up at the airport in San Jose. I'm flying in at 10 PM. I sold my Le Car about a month ago. I guess I never told you that. Got five hundred bucks for it. We have to talk. This does not mean I'm staying. I'm on my way home to Alabama. Well, the long way. If I did stay, it would be because I had seen a goddamn miracle walking around in your pants, I'll tell you that

Oil noose well, you said. Oil well indeed. I slipped out. But how did you know that? You are one spooky cat.

Snooks

P.S. Lie low, keen soul, you said. Slow Lee due in. How did you *know* that? I've been having some bourbon. It reminds me of my lost home in the South. Been looking at your pictures too. You were always so cute, you Italian thing.

P.P.S. That doesn't necessarily mean anything.

"This is incredible," Boyce said. He'd been reading over my shoulder. "She wouldn't speak in her oral exams? She sat there in silence?"

"Yes, and what a woman she is!" I exclaimed, dropping into savings for my three thousand bucks, full of hope and dreams beyond reckoning, even by a Revelation 2000. A gigantic flashing jet was crossing the sky, coming in for a landing at San Jose. I checked my watch. It was tomorrow morning, Greenwich Mean

Time. "Snookie's on that plane!" I cried, and with my life's liquid assets wadded up in my hand, I dashed for Boyce's Kodak Image and the golden future of knowledge and love.

SIMON ORTIZ

Men
on
the
Moon

I.

Joselita brought her father, Faustin, the TV on Father's Day. She brought it over after Sunday mass and she had her son hook up the antenna. She plugged the TV into the wall socket.

Faustin sat on a worn couch. He was covered with an old coat. He had worn that coat for twenty years.

It's ready. Turn it on and I'll adjust the antenna, Amarosho told his mother. The TV warmed up and then it flickered into dull light. It was snowing. Amarosho tuned it a bit. It snowed less and then a picture formed.

Look, Naishtiya, Joselita said. She touched her father's hand and pointed at the TV.

I'll turn the antenna a bit and you tell me when the picture is clear, Amarosho said. He climbed on the roof again.

After a while the picture turned clearer. It's better, his mother shouted. There was only the tiniest bit of snow falling.

That's about the best it can get, I guess, Amarosho said. Maybe it'll clear up on the other channels. He turned the selector. It was clearer on another.

There were two men struggling with each other. Wrestling, Amarosho said. Do you want to watch wrestling? Two men are fighting, Nana. One of them is Apache Red. Chiseh tsah, he told his grandfather.

The old man stirred. He had been staring intently into the TV. He wondered why there was so much snow at first. Now there were two men fighting. One of them was Chiseh, an Apache, and the other was a Mericano. There were people shouting excitedly and clapping hands within the TV.

The two men backed away from each other once in a while and then they clenched. They wheeled mightily and suddenly one threw the other. The old man smiled. He wondered why they were fighting.

Something else showed on the TV screen. A bottle of wine was being poured. The old man liked the pouring sound and he moved his mouth. Someone was selling wine.

The two fighting men came back on the TV. They struggled with each other and after a while one of them didn't get up and then another person came and held up the hand of the Apache who was dancing around in a feathered headdress.

It's over, Amarosho announced. Apache Red won the fight, Nana.

The Chiseh won. Faustin watched the other one, a light-haired man who looked totally exhausted and angry with himself. He didn't like the Apache too much. He wanted them to fight again.

After a few moments something else appeared on the TV.

What is that? Faustin asked. There was an object with smoke coming from it. It was standing upright.

Men are going to the moon, Nana, his grandson said. It's Apollo. It's going to fly three men to the moon.

That thing is going to fly to the moon?

Yes, Nana.

What is it called again?

Apollo, a spaceship rocket, Joselita told her father.

The Apollo spaceship stood on the ground emitting clouds of something that looked like smoke.

A man was talking, telling about the plans for the flight, what would happen, that it was almost time. Faustin could not understand the man very well because he didn't know many words in Mericano.

He must be talking about that thing flying in the air? he said.

Yes. It's about ready to fly away to the moon.

Faustin remembered that the evening before he had looked at the sky and seen that the moon was almost in the middle phase. He wondered if it was important that the men get to the moon.

Are those men looking for something on the moon? he asked his grandson.

They're trying to find out what's on the moon, Nana, what kind of dirt and rocks there are, to see if there's any life on the moon. The men are looking for knowledge, Amarosho told him.

Faustin wondered if the men had run out of places to look for knowledge on the Earth. Do they know if they'll find knowledge? he asked.

They have some information already. They've gone before and come back. They're going again.

Did they bring any back?

They brought back some rocks.

Rocks. Faustin laughed quietly. The scientist men went to search for knowledge on the moon and they brought back rocks. He thought that perhaps Amarosho was joking with him. The grandson had gone to Indian

School for a number of years and sometimes he would tell his grandfather some strange and funny things.

The old man was suspicious. They joked around a lot. Rocks—you sure that's all they brought back?

That's right, Nana, only rocks and some dirt and pictures they made of what it looks like on the moon.

The TV picture was filled with the rocket, close up now. Men were sitting and moving around by some machinery and the voice had become more urgent. The old man watched the activity in the picture intently but with a slight smile on his face.

Suddenly it became very quiet, and the voice was firm and commanding and curiously pleading. Ten, nine, eight, seven, six, five, four, three, two, liftoff. The white smoke became furious and a muted rumble shook through the TV. The rocket was trembling and the voice was trembling.

It was really happening, the old man marvelled. Somewhere inside of that cylinder with a point at its top and long slender wings were three men who were flying to the moon.

The rocket rose from the ground. There were enormous clouds of smoke and the picture shook. Even the old man became tense and he grasped the edge of the couch. The rocket spaceship rose and rose.

There's fire coming out of the rocket, Amarosho explained. That's what makes it go.

Fire. Faustin had wondered what made it fly. He'd seen pictures of other flying machines. They had long wings and someone had explained to him that there was machinery inside which spun metal blades which made them fly. He had wondered what made this thing fly. He hoped his grandson wasn't joking him.

After a while there was nothing but the sky. The rocket Apollo had disappeared. It hadn't taken very long and the voice from the TV wasn't excited anymore. In fact the voice was very calm and almost bored.

I have to go now, Naishtiya, Joselita told her father.
I have things to do.

Me, too, Amarosho said.

Wait, the old man said, wait. What shall I do with this
thing? What is it you call it?

TV, his daughter said. You watch it. You turn it on
and you watch it.

I mean how do you stop it. Does it stop like the radio,
like the mahkina? It stops?

This way, Nana, Amarosho said and showed his
grandfather. He turned the dial and the picture went away.
He turned the dial again and the picture flickered on
again. Were you afraid this one-eye would be looking at
you all the time? Amarosho laughed and gently patted the
old man's shoulder.

Faustin was relieved. Joselita and her son left. He
watched the TV for a while. A lot of activity was going
on, a lot of men were moving among machinery, and a
couple of men were talking. And then it showed the rocket again.

He watched it rise and fly away again. It disappeared
again. There was nothing but the sky. He turned the dial
and the picture died away. He turned it on and the picture
came on again. He turned it off. He went outside and to a
fence a distance from his home. When he finished he studied the sky for a while.

II.

That night, he dreamed.

Flintwing Boy was watching a Skquuyuh mahkina
come down a hill. The mahkina made a humming noise. It
was walking. It shone in the sunlight. Flintwing Boy
moved to a better position to see. The mahkina kept on
moving. It was moving towards him.

The Skquuyuh mahkina drew closer. Its metal legs
stepped upon trees and crushed growing flowers and

grass. A deer bounded away frightened. Tshushki came
running to Flintwing Boy.

Anaweh, he cried, trying to catch his breath.

The coyote was staring at the thing which was coming towards them. There was wild fear in his eyes.

What is that, Anaweh? What is that thing? he
gasped.

It looks like a mahkina, but I've never seen one like it
before. It must be some kind of Skquuyuh mahkina.

Where did it come from?

I'm not sure yet, Anaweh, Flintwing Boy said. When
he saw that Tshushki was trembling with fear, he said gently, Sit down, Anaweh. Rest yourself. We'll find out soon
enough.

The Skquuyuh mahkina was undeterred. It walked
over and through everything. It splashed through a stream
of clear water. The water boiled and streaks of oil flowed
downstream. It split a juniper tree in half with a terrible
crash. It crashed a boulder into dust with a sound of heavy
metal. Nothing stopped the Skquuyuh mahkina. It hummed.

Anaweh, Tshushki cried, what shall we do? What can
we do?

Flintwing Boy reached into the bag at his side. He
took out an object. It was a flint arrowhead. He took out
some cornfood.

Come over here, Anaweh. Come over here. Be calm,
he motioned to the frightened coyote. He touched the coyote in several places of his body with the arrowhead and
put cornfood in the palm of his hand.

This way, Flintwing Boy said, and closed Tshushki's
fingers over the cornfood gently. And they faced east.
Flintwing Boy said, We humble ourselves again. We look
in your direction for guidance. We ask for your protection.
We humble our poor bodies and spirits because only you
are the power and the source and the knowledge. Help us
then—that is all we ask.

They breathed on the cornfood and took in the breath of all directions and gave the cornfood unto the ground.

Now the ground trembled with the awesome power of the Skquuyuh mahkina. Its humming vibrated against everything. Flintwing Boy reached behind him and took several arrows from his quiver. He inspected them carefully and without any rush he fit one to his bowstring.

And now, Anaweh, you must go and tell everyone. Describe what you have seen. The people must talk among themselves and decide what it is about and what they will do. You must hurry but you must not alarm the people. Tell them I am here to meet it. I will give them my report when I find out.

Coyote turned and began to run. He stopped several yards away. Hahtrudzaimeh, he called. Like a man of courage, Anaweh, like a man.

The old man stirred in his sleep. A dog was barking. He awoke and got out of his bed and went outside. The moon was past the midpoint and it would be morning light in a few hours.

III.

Later, the spaceship reached the moon.

Amarosho was with his grandfather. They watched a replay of two men walking on the moon.

So that's the men on the moon, Faustin said.

Yes, Nana, that's it.

There were two men inside of heavy clothing and equipment. The TV picture showed a closeup of one of them and indeed there was a man's face inside of glass. The face moved its mouth and smiled and spoke but the voice seemed to be separate from the face.

It must be cold. They have heavy clothing on, Faustin said.

It's supposed to be very cold and very hot. They wear the clothes and other things for protection from the cold and heat, Amarosho said.

The men on the moon were moving slowly. One of them skipped and he floated alongside the other.

The old man wondered if they were underwater. They seem to be able to float, he said.

The information I have heard is that a man weighs less than he does on earth, much less, and he floats. There is no air easier to breathe. Those boxes on their backs contain air for them to breathe, Amarosho told his grandfather.

He weighs less, the old man wondered, and there is no air except for the boxes on their backs. He looked at Amarosho but his grandson didn't seem to be joking with him.

The land on the moon looked very dry. It looked like it had not rained for a long, long time. There were no trees, no plants, no grass. Nothing but dirt and rocks, a desert.

Amarosho had told him that men on earth—the scientists—believed there was no life on the moon. Yet those men were trying to find knowledge on the moon. He wondered if perhaps they had special tools with which they could find knowledge even if they believed there was no life on the moon desert.

The mahkina sat on the desert. It didn't make a sound. Its metal feet were planted flat on the ground. It looked somewhat awkward. Faustin searched vainly around the mahkina but there didn't seem to be anything except the dry land on the TV. He couldn't figure out the mahkina. He wasn't sure whether it could move and could cause fear. He didn't want to ask his grandson that question.

After a while, one of the bulky men was digging in the ground. He carried a long thin hoe with which he scooped dirt and put it into a container. He did this for a while.

Is he going to bring the dirt back to earth too? Faustin asked.

I think he is, Nana, Amarosho said. Maybe he'll get some rocks too. Watch.

Indeed several minutes later the man lumbered over

to a pile of rocks and gathered several handsize ones. He held them out proudly. They looked just like rocks from around anyplace. The voice from the TV seemed to be excited about the rocks.

They will study the rocks too for knowledge?

Yes, Nana.

What will they use the knowledge for, Nana?

They say they will use it to better mankind, Nana. I've heard that. And to learn more about the universe we live in. Also some of them say that the knowledge will be useful in finding out where everything began and how everything was made.

Faustin smiled at his grandson. He said, You are telling me the true facts, aren't you?

Why yes, Nana. That's what they say. I'm not just making it up, Amarosho said.

Well then—do they say why they need to know where everything began? Hasn't anyone ever told them?

I think other people have tried to tell them but they want to find out for themselves and also I think they claim they don't know enough and need to know more and for certain, Amarosho said.

The man in the bulky suit had a small pickaxe in his hand. He was striking at a boulder. The breathing of the man could clearly be heard. He seemed to be working very hard and was very tried.

Faustin had once watched a crew of Mericano drilling for water. They had brought a tall mahkina with a loud motor. The mahkina would raise a limb at its center to its very top and then drop it with a heavy and loud metal clang. The mahkina and its men sat at one spot for several days and finally they found water.

The water had bubbled out weakly, gray-looking and didn't look drinkable at all. And then they lowered the mahkina, put their equipment away and drove away. The water stopped flowing.

After a couple of days he went and checked out the place. There was nothing there except a pile of gray dirt and an indentation in the ground. The ground was already dry and there were dark spots of oil-soaked dirt.

He decided to tell Amarosho about the dream he had.

After the old man finished, Amarosho said, Old man, you're telling me the truth now? You know that you have become somewhat of a liar. He was testing his grandfather.

Yes, Nana. I have told you the truth as it occurred to me that night. Everything happened like that except that I might not have recalled everything about it.

That's some story, Nana, but it's a dream.

It's a dream but it's the truth, Faustin said.

I believe you, Nana, his grandson said.

Biographical Notes

MARGARET ATWOOD is a poet, essayist, novelist, and short-story writer whose books include *The Handmaid's Tale, Cat's Eye, Wilderness Tips,* and *The Robber Bride.* She lives in Toronto.

O. Henry Award winner THOMAS FOX AVERILL is Associate Professor of English and Writer-in-Residence at Washburn University of Topeka, Kansas, and the author of two story collections, *Passes at the Moon* and *Seeing Mona Naked.*

ALISON BAKER is the author of two books of fiction, *How I Came West, and Why I Stayed* and *Loving Wanda Beaver.* Her story "Better Be Ready 'Bout Half Past Eight," included here, won a 1994 O. Henry Award.

MICHAEL BISHOP lives in Pine Mountain, Georgia. His most recent books include *Apartheid, Superstrings, and Mordecai Thubana; Count Geiger's Blues; Brittle Innings,* the 1995 winner of the Locus Award for Best Fantasy Novel; and a story collection, *At the City Limits of Fate.*

TERRY BISSON's books include *Wyrldmaker, Talking Man, Fire on the Mountain,* and *Voyage to the Red Planet.* He has won many prizes, including a Nebula, a Hugo, and a Theodore Sturgeon Memorial Award.

MICHAEL BLUMLEIN is a writer as well as a physician whose stories have been collected in *The Brains of Rats* and whose first novel is *The Movement of Mountains.* "Tissue Ablation and Variant Regeneration: A Case Report" was his first published story. It appeared in *Interzone* in 1984.

OCTAVIA E. BUTLER has won a Hugo Award for "Speech Sounds," included here, as well as a Nebula Award. Among her numerous books are *Bloodchild* and the *Xenogenesis* trilogy. In 1995, she received a grant from the John D. and Catherine T. MacArthur Foundation.

STEPHEN DIXON is the author of seventeen books, including the novels *Frog* and *Interstate,* both of which were nominated for the National Book Award. He is a professor in The Writing Seminars at Johns Hopkins University.

AUDREY FERBER has published fiction in the *Santa Clara Review,* the anthology *Eating Our Hearts Out,* and in the forthcoming *An Intricate Weave: Women Write About Girls and Girlhood.* Her essays have appeared in the *San Francisco Chronicle.* Ferber lives in San Francisco.

KAREN JOY FOWLER's books include the novel, *Sarah Canary,* and the story collection, *Artificial Things.* She lives in Davis, California.

RICHARD GOLDSTEIN's stories have been published in *The Sun, Belletrist, Gorezone, Thema, Jewish Currents,* and elsewhere. He works in a hospital emergency room in Los Alamos, New Mexico, and writes a monthly humor-fiction column for the *Santa Fe Sun.*

National Book Award winner URSULA K. LE GUIN has published poetry, essays, short fiction, and novels, including *The Left Hand of Darkness* and *The Dispossessed*. She lives in Oregon.

DORIS LESSING is the author of more than thirty books — novels, stories, reportage, poems, and plays, including *The Golden Notebook* and the futuristic quartet, *Canopus in Argos: Archives*. She was born in Persia in 1919, grew up in Southern Rhodesia, and has lived in England for nearly five decades.

RALPH LOMBREGLIA is the author of two collections of stories, *Men Under Water* and *Make Me Work*. His fiction has twice been chosen for the *Best American Short Stories* series, and "Somebody Up There Likes Me," included here, received an O. Henry Award in 1996.

SIMON ORTIZ has published four books of poetry and two collections of stories, *The Howbah Indians* and *Fightin'*. He has taught literature and writing at San Diego State University, Navajo Community College (Tsaile, Arizona), and the University of New Mexico.

Acknowledgments

Grateful acknowledgment is made to the following authors, editors, publishers, and literary agents for permission to reprint the stories in this collection.

"Homelanding" from *Good Bones and Simple Murders* by Margaret Atwood. Copyright © 1983, 1992, 1994 by O.W. Toad, Ltd. A Nan A. Talese Book. Used by permission of Doubleday, a division of Bantam Doubleday Dell Publishing Group, Inc.

"The Onion and I" by Thomas Fox Averill, copyright © 1996 by Thomas Fox Averill. First published in *Virtually Now: Stories of Science, Technology, and the Future,* by permission of the author.

"Better Be Ready 'Bout Half Past Eight," from *How I Came West, and Why I Stayed* by Alison Baker, copyright © 1993 by Alison Baker, published by Chronicle Books, San Francisco. Reprinted by permission of Chronicle Books.